Saturday
of Glory

DAVID SERAFÍN

Saturday
of Glory

ST. MARTIN'S PRESS
NEW YORK

Copyright © 1981 by David Serafin
For information, write: St. Martin's Press,
175 Fifth Avenue, New York, N.Y. 10010
Manufactured in the United States of America

Library of Congress Cataloging in Publication Data

Serafin, David.
   Saturday of glory.

   I. Title.
PR6069.E6S2   1982   823'.914   81-16711
ISBN 0-312-69975-1   AACR2

For D.B.R.
cicerone sin par

Author's Note

While the characters who appear in this novel are figures of fiction and their activities entirely imaginary, every attempt has been made to set them within real national events and in exact location.

D.S.

Madrid, St James's Day,
25 July 1977

PALM SUNDAY, 3 APRIL

7.10 p.m.

Strangely, there was no scream. Just a brushing noise as the body passed through the branches of the trees, and then a dull squelch as it hit the ground. The two elderly ladies who were chatting with the porter on the pavement instinctively drew back into the doorway before turning to see what had happened. When finally one of them looked, she dropped the green palm-branch she had carried all day at the church services, and gave a strangled cry.

The dead man's neck was twisted in a frightful way, and the blood was gushing out of a main artery and running down the camber of the roadway into the gutter; there, grotesquely, the red stream carried a dead leaf along to the nearby drain.

The aged porter tried in vain to get the ladies to go inside to his lodge. He walked over to the corpse and looked at the contused face.

'My God, it's Señor Santos, from the attic apartment. Come inside, Señoras, please. I'll have to make an 091 call.'

Inside the glass-panelled lodge he got out glasses and a bottle of brandy and offered some to the shocked lady churchgoers.

There was very little traffic along the Calle de Alfonso XII at that hour on a Sunday evening, especially since most of the inhabitants of Madrid seemed to have departed for Benidorm or Palma to spend Holy Week in a less than religious frame of mind.

The porter looked anxiously up and down the street for signs of the arrival of the police. Two passing motorists had stopped, and he asked them to keep clear of the corpse.

'Was he knocked down by a hit-and-run driver?' asked one of them, a respectable-looking professional man.

'I don't think so,' answered the porter, trembling slightly. 'I think he fell from the eighth floor.'

'Odd that he should have landed so far out in the road-way,' said the motorist, looking up at the windows above. 'Have you called the police?'

'Oh yes, immediately it happened,' said the porter.

At that moment they could hear the siren of a police vehicle which was turning around the Plaza de la Independencia. Then they saw the blue jeep with wire-covered windows of the Policía Armada approaching at high speed. It slewed to a halt just short of the body and the pool of blood, and four grey-uniformed policemen jumped out.

'Is it a road accident?' one of them demanded of the porter.

'No, sir. I think he fell from the top floor.'

'H'm, we'd better call in to the Comisaría. They'll send an inspector out.'

7.30 p.m.

Inspector Martín from the Comisaría del Retiro arrived in an official, chauffeur-driven Seat. He made a brief visual inspection of the corpse, then asked the porter some swift but searching questions.

Who had witnessed the fall? What time had it occurred? Could he identify the deceased? Had anyone gone up to the dead man's apartment after the fall? Had he seen anyone enter or leave the building during the past hour?

On hearing the porter's nervously-uttered answers, he decided to call the Juzgado de Guardia without delay, and ask for the judge who was on duty to come and superintend the lifting of the body. On second thoughts, he decided to call the Central, and ask for a representative of the Brigada Criminal to examine the scene first. His instinct told him there was more in this than a straightforward suicide, though he couldn't analyse the reasons for his suspicions. There was nothing to lose in calling in the Dirección General de Seguridad at once.

MONDAY, 4 APRIL

7.30 a.m.
As he shaved carefully with the new Wilkinson razor his
younger son had brought him from London, Superintendent Luis Bernal felt his stomach churn at the acrid smoke
which seeped into the bathroom from the *tostadas* his wife
was frying in the kitchen next door. Eugenia Carrero's
upbringing on a farm near Ciudad Rodrigo had marked
her for good, despite the forty-one years of her married
life in Madrid. Every morning at 7.30 she would heat up
an ancient iron pan, bought from a passing tinker during
one of her frequent visits to Salamanca province, where
she would collect the rents in the shape of hams, large
black sausages and *chorizos* or small blood sausages, which
she extracted from the poverty-stricken tenants of the
lands she had inherited from her father. Then, slicing up
the iron-hard bread left over from lunch the day before,
she would plunge the pieces into the overheated and much
re-used olive oil, itself a product of her own olive-groves
and pressed by her own hand in the yard of her ancient
farmhouse the previous January.

To accompany this typical but unpalatable breakfast,
she was making what passed for coffee out of a mixture of
roasted chicory-root and ilex acorns, with a few genuine
coffee-beans thrown in for appearances' sake. Bernal
hoped that the telephone would ring, demanding his
presence in the Dirección General de Seguridad, before he
would have to put up a show of dipping the ghastly
tostadas into the undrinkable coffee; on most days it didn't
ring, so ensuring that they would start the morning with
a *disgusto* – as much an emotional displeasure for Eugenia
as it was a gastronomic one for him. Only three years
before he had been operated on for a gastric ulcer, and

although he had lost weight, he could now stomach almost anything except his wife's country cooking.

He looked at himself critically in the glass as he trimmed his small moustache: not bad for fifty-eight; hair receding but still not showing signs of grey (he helped it along with a little surreptitious pomade); sharp, dark eyes in a strong, broad face; thick-set body with hairy chest and a slight paunch, on short legs. He knew his colleagues called him El Caudillo behind his back, from his slight resemblance to General Franco, and he had learned to cultivate this likeness and a general air of benign paternalism because of their usefulness in interrogations. With a final splatter of Men's Club 52 cologne, he escaped from the bathroom just as the ancient sewerage system went into one of its periodic convulsions, emitting a powerful draught of foul air through the lavatory pan and the bidet outlet pipe as the neighbour on the floor below began his ablutions. How often Luis had plagued Eugenia to move to one of the new apartment blocks that had sprung up along the Avenida de Menéndez y Pelayo, across the Retiro Park from their ancient flat off the Calle de Alcalá.

Not only would she not countenance moving from the apartment that had been her home throughout her married life; she also refused to agree to the slightest improvement, apart from the butane-gas cooker (which stood like an unwelcome intruder alongside the ancient coke stove), the small refrigerator which rested uneasily under the fifty-year-old gas geyser, and the rackety hired television set in the lounge. When he was promoted from Inspector de primera to Comisario or Superintendent in the Criminal Brigade in the 'sixties, Bernal's greatly increased salary and his wife's constant parsimony meant that he had begun to build up a considerable bank balance, out of which he had paid the deposit on a flat for his elder son Santiago when he had married in 1970, and, four years later, the purchase price of a small but elegant studio apartment for himself in the Calle de Barceló. He had never revealed the existence of this bolt-hole to Eugenia, and as the years passed he found increasing pleasure in leading this double existence: a bachelor life in the late afternoons and on the occasional Sundays, when she thought him hard at work, and on most nights the pretence of a marital existence in the ancient apartment off the Calle de Alcalá.

Adjusting his silk tie, bought at Celso García, he put his head into the rancid blue smoke which enveloped the severe, bombazine-black shape of his wife, and said, 'Look, Geñita, I've got to rush this morning, to investigate that suspected suicide case we had on Alfonso XII yesterday evening. The forensic team will be waiting for me at the office.'

Dropping her fork and crossing herself at the mention of suicide, she said grimly, 'Well, get some of these *tostadas* inside you first. It's cold this morning. There's snow on the sierra.'

She had already been out on the terrace, which faced northward towards the Sierra de Guadarrama, to tie firmly to the rail of the balcony the palm-branch she had carried in church the previous day; it would remain there, as a symbol of her iron faith, for a year until it had withered and become battered by the weather. She would also have inspected her roof-garden, consisting of over a hundred plants and shrubs, a number of them leaning unhappily out of old paint-tins and oil-cans, since she wouldn't dream of wasting money on buying earthenware pots.

He made a gesture of breaking one of the *tostadas* into the nauseous coffee, and when she went off to wake up their younger son Diego, who would be leaving with his university friends today to go on a skiing holiday in Candanchú in upper Aragon, Bernal grasped the opportunity to empty the contents of the mug into the lavatory pan in the bathroom and went back hastily to the kitchen just as Eugenia returned. Looking suspiciously at the empty cup – she always assumed, not without reason, that he was guilty of something, for she tended to regard husband, sons, her new grandson and indeed all menfolk as secret or potential malefactors – she began to pour him more of the evil-smelling brew.

'I really have to run now, Geñita. *Hasta luego,*' and making a quick dash into the bathroom, ostensibly to brush his teeth but in reality to pull the lavatory chain – it would be a nice *quid pro quo* for the stout insurance agent who lived on the floor below – he scurried along the long tiled passage, pulling on his camel-hair overcoat. He paused momentarily to check that his service revolver was in place and to leave an envelope containing 10,000 pesetas on the bed of the still sleeping Diego – he knew his younger son would need that much just for his nocturnal escapades; like father, like son, he thought, though his elder son Santiago had always proved a depressing model of piety, taking after his mother.

On the landing he peered down the six floors of the lift-shaft, trying to judge the position of the ancient mahogany cabinet with its polished brass handles and decorated mirrors. It was hydraulically operated and one of the few such lifts remaining in service in Madrid; it had been condemned four years before by the Ayuntamiento of the City as unsafe, but the various meetings of the flat-owners had still not been able to agree on spending money on its replacement. He decided it would be better for his safety and health to run down the stairs, thus avoiding possible contact with the chatty neighbours and having only to acknowledge the mournful greeting of the *portera*, who, when she was not pretending to dust the plastic rubber-plant which adorned the ancient hallway, sat in her dark lodge counting her rosary and spying on the tenants.

'*Buenos días, don Luis.* A chilly morning for the criminals, eh? It's going to rain again later on, for sure.'

'*Muy buenos, Señora.* Let's hope we have a quiet Semana

Santa, with everyone away on holiday.'

'If God wishes it, Don Luis.' As usual, she did not seem too convinced of the Deity's good offices in the matter.

8 a.m.

Emerging into the Calle de Alcalá, Bernal saw that the city still lay under its thin matitudinal cape of polluted air, which today the sun might not manage to clear away. He stopped at the news-kiosk to buy the *Hoja del Lunes*, the only newspaper published in Madrid on Monday mornings, and greeted the *quiosquero*, whose stand was embrazened by *Playlady*, *Lib*, *Convivencia* and many other mildly pornographic magazines which had not ceased to pour off the presses since Franco's death, heralding the new *destape* or 'uncovering'.

A few steps further on, he turned into Félix Pérez's bar and treated himself to a proper breakfast of a large glass of hot coffee and a freshly baked croissant. He glanced at the headlines: the cause of the terrible collision of the two jumbo jets in Tenerife airport was still being raked over; the minor incidents and street clashes between the political extremists were given some space; the most staggering headline, however, concerned the Government's abolition of the Movimiento Nacional, the only political party permitted by the Franco Régime during thirty-eight years.

Bernal was glad he had kept out of politics as far as possible. Although his father had been an assault guard during the Republic, who had been killed during the riots of 1936, and he himself had been a Civil Guard cadet just before the outbreak of the War in Ciudad Rodrigo, where he had met Eugenia at a village fair, during his years with the General Directorate of Security he had been strictly an investigator of crime. That was what had always fascinated him: the multiple and complex motives that drove people over the edge, or just made them careless enough to get caught. For he believed that everyone was a criminal in greater or lesser degree, and had something to hide from his neighbours and colleagues, though it might only be his innermost desires.

Slapping down a five-duro and a one-duro piece on the counter to cover the twenty-eight-peseta breakfast, he called out to the barman, '¡Cobra aquí, Pepe! Hasta luego.'

Bernal turned up his coat-collar as he emerged from the bar, and glanced briefly beyond the beds of tidy red and yellow tulips set in the lawns underneath the Alcalá arch. He looked down towards the Calle de Alfonso XII, remembering the scene there at 7.40 the previous evening.

When he had answered the call of the Retiro District Comisaría, the duty judge was in attendance and the police photographer had already done his work; the attendants were about to lift the body of the young man into the ambulance to remove it to the Laboratorio Anatómico Forense. But he had had time to see the strange angle of the deceased's neck, and – what had surprised him most – the extreme amount of blood on the roadway: very fresh and light red, as though from a main artery; and oddest of all, the pair of worn brown shoes, with the laces still tied, lying askew in the blood. Was it possible that they could have been knocked off the man's feet as he fell from the eighth floor, and could the angle of descent have brought him so far out into the roadway?

After the fingerprint team had finished in the man's flat, the district inspector, Martín, and the duty judge had placed the official seal on the dead man's door for the night. Later, when the forensic and fingerprint reports were in, Bernal would take his team back there to try and establish the facts.

Glancing at his watch, he decided to join the crush of commuters on Line 2, which carried the office- and shop-workers from Ventas to Sol. He must try to be in by 8.30 to set a good example to his group, which still had the best reputation in the Criminal Brigade. Not least because he was expecting a new junior inspector this morning: he remembered the official notification from Personnel,

'Fernández Ruiz, E., 28, Inspector de segunda'. He wished he could pick his own men, as in the past, but nowadays Personnel sent along whomsoever took their fancy among the new breed of college-trained detectives from the Escuela General de Policía. Still, if Fernández proved incompetent or difficult to work with, he would try to arrange to get him transferred to one of the other groups.

8.30 a.m.

Somewhat out of breath as he emerged from the stairs of Sol Metro station and turned into the narrow Calle de Carretas alongside the old Gobernación building, which still housed the Ministry of the Interior and much of the General Directorate of Security – unpopularly known as *la degeese* – Bernal saw Dr Peláez, the police pathologist, entering the doorway, no doubt to bring him the report on the dead man in Alfonso XII. Peláez wore thick spectacles and was short, stout and as bald as an egg. He was famous for his amazing physical stamina: Bernal had known him do six or seven autopsies in a day, and he guessed that he had been up until 1 or 2 a.m. on this job, and had later typed up the report himself at home. Years ago, Peláez had tried to cure Bernal of his squeamishness about corpses, urging him to think of a human body in the same way that an engineer thought of a machine, the only difference being that the oil happened to be red. This concept had not really removed Bernal's distaste for gore and putrefaction, but it always came to mind on those gruesome occasions.

'*Hola, Peláez, ¿qué hay?*'

'A simple suicide, they told me, eh? Possibly even an accidental fall! But you've got a tough one here, Bernal. Wait till you see this report. Call me later at the lab, if you need more help.' He threw him the large buff envelope and marched off down to Sol, no doubt to fortify himself with a coffee and a *sol y sombra*, an explosive mixture of brandy and anisette.

As Bernal entered the outer waiting-room, he noticed a long-legged girl with a good figure and appealing brown eyes sitting nervously on the edge of one of the armchairs. Greeting her coolly, he supposed she might be a relative or friend of the deceased wanting information and permission to arrange the funeral. He didn't feel able to tackle her until he had had time to read Peláez's report. In the large outer office he shook hands with Paco Navarro, the inspector who had served more than twenty years with him; stolid, taciturn and reliable, he had probably been in since eight o'clock checking the night reports for him.

Bernal hung up his coat in his small glass-panelled office and opened Peláez's envelope. Skimming through the lengthy technical jargon, he extracted the essential points:

SANTOS LÓPEZ, Raúl. 34 years. Unmarried. Son of Esteban Santos Alonso and Pilar López Montero. Journalist. No police antecedents, either social, political or criminal.

Bernal assumed that Peláez's assistant had extracted much of this from the deceased's *carnet* of identification, and the local inspector had checked the colour photograph and print of the right index finger thereon with the central records at the Centro de Identificación Nacional. He often wondered how the police in other countries where there was no system of identity cards managed to operate; of course, the criminal classes in Spain could buy forged or illicit *carnets*, and the foreign residents and tourists could be a nuisance, but when it came to identifying corpses the Spanish system meant that all the people over sixteen out of thirty-five million inhabitants could be tracked down, assuming the cadaver had a right index finger, of course.

He skipped through the descriptive part, noting that the deceased had been in good health without organic disease, with a tanned complexion and torso, an athletic physique (yet he had been a heavy smoker of Virginia cigarettes), had eaten a good lunch, apparently of *paella* (a very common dish at Sunday lunch), and had only a small alcohol content in the bloodstream. Bernal glanced at the accompanying photographs: masculine good looks in life, sure to have been attractive to women (perhaps to the girl waiting outside), yet he had never married; in death a look of horror, of fright, rather, in the still-open eyes on the mortuary slab, with the neck stiffened in the twisted position as rigor mortis had begun to set in, hiding the deep wound on the right side.

Cause of death: rupture of the right carotid artery by a sharp metallic edge or instrument measuring not more than 0.2 mm. wide; other major injuries consistent with fall from considerable height: broken neck, fractured skull, damage to left hip, femur and tibia; all of which would have proved fatal in any case, but death appears to have occurred from aforesaid arterial rupture before contact with roadway.

He now saw what Peláez had meant. Could it have been murder, and not an accident or suicide? As soon as the technical laboratory sent in the report on the fingerprints in the dead man's apartment, he would have to go over there and examine everything more thoroughly.

Bernal lit his second cigarette of the day and glanced through the glass panel; Ángel had still not turned up. The youngest of his inspectors, Ángel Gallardo had for five years been the toast of the office, indeed the whole Criminal Brigade. Only just turned thirty, he was lithe, athletic, vivaciously birdlike and darkly handsome, bubbling with wit and the latest street gossip. A product of a working-class home in Vallecas suburb, he was a *madrileño* to the core: there was hardly a fashionable bar, night-club or discothèque in the city where he wasn't well known – not as a policeman, but as a *bon viveur*, surrounded by adoring females of all ages, many of whom he exploited to do his ironing, clean his small studio flat off the Gran Vía, wash his football kit, and, Bernal knew, help him to while away the small hours in his large double bed. All they knew about him was that he had some kind of well-paid job in the Gobernación. Erratic and unreliable, he

was yet an essential ingredient in the team, a ready source
of information about the night-time activities of the rich
and the famous, the rapidly changing vice scene of the
city, and the various rackets which sprang up in the red-
light districts. Bernal resisted all the requests for his transfer
to the anti-vice group or to the Brigada Especial de
Investigación de Estupefacientes: his excellent cover
would be blown in vice or drugs as soon as he made an
arrest. It was infinitely preferable to have him freebooting
around the city, pouring in scribbled notes for the
dossiers each morning, despite his sudden late arrivals and
equally sudden departures, and his exorbitant claims on
the expense account, which easily covered all his social
activities. Well, he would need him later to look into
Santos's social circle, and sniff out what he could about
the dead journalist.

He called Navarro in. 'Anything in the night reports?'

'Usual political stuff. The Warriors of Christ the King
kicked up a bit of a row in two bars off Goya, and made
the customers give the extended arm salute and sing the
Cara al Sol. A few minor attempts to hold a demonstration
of the young communists in Callao and the Plaza de
España; easily dealt with by the Antidisturbios. Of
possible interest to us: a young man stabbed to death in
the Calle de Recoletos, near those discothèques and night-
clubs, but Group Four were on night duty and are
investigating.'

'We'll check with Inspector Zurdo later to see if there's
any possible connection. Have you seen Ángel yet?'

'No, but he rang in to say two young ladies are helping
him sober up and he'll be here soon.'

'Typical. I'm surprised it wasn't he who was knifed in
Recoletos.'

'He says to ask you why you don't send the Public
Health analyst round the night-clubs from time to time.
He's sure he's got methyl alcohol poisoning from the
falsified Gordon's gin they serve up in some of them.'

'Tell him to stick to San Franciscos. The fruit juice would be cheaper for our expense account. By the way, who's the young lady in the waiting-room?'

'A Señorita Fernández. She said she had to wait for you.'

'Perhaps she's a relative of this chap Santos. You know, we've got a tough case here. Have a look at Peláez's report while I talk to the girl. Has the fingerprint report come in yet?'

'Not yet. I expect they're typing it up now.'

'All right. Bring it in when it comes. Perhaps you'd better call her in now, and send for some coffee in case she breaks down.'

9 a.m.

Señorita Fernández seemed even more elegantly appealing and nervous in the pale light coming in from the window behind Bernal's chair, and she exuded a faint scent which he recognized as expensive and Parisian, possibly Worth's *Vol de Nuit.* Somewhat tentatively she approached the desk and shook hands. 'Comisario Bernal? I am your new Inspector, Elena Fernández. Here are my credentials.'

Bernal was shaken to the core. He had heard, of course, that the Police School in the Calle de Miguel Ángel was beginning to admit one or two women graduates to the training programme, but in all his years with the Brigade he had never seen any female personnel other than the lady doctor and the wardresses in the cells in the basement of the DGS building and the mini-skirted municipal policewomen who for the past two years and more had graced the main streets, blowing their whistles furiously at offending motorists. What could the Personnel Director be thinking of? Or was it one of his practical jokes?

'Well, well, er, please sit down, Inspectora.' He supposed that was how one should address a female inspector, but the official notification had clearly stated 'Inspector.' He felt resentful at this piece of trickery, as he was sure it was, from Personnel. What could they do with her? How would she ever fit in, especially considering Ángel's lewd comments on Madrid life? Well, he for one would have to draw in his horns a bit. Or would he bowl this girl over, with a *coup de foudre* effect? 'Welcome to our little group. Señorita. Please tell me about yourself. Then later I'll introduce you to the rest of our team, or at least to those of us who aren't on holiday.'

Elena regarded Bernal with admiration. She at once spotted the resemblance to General Franco, and this warmed her to him. After all, she was a granddaughter of the Régime and her family owed everything to it. Her father was the seventh son of a poor family from Cáceres, and had come to Madrid in the 'forties to look for work. From a job as a builder's labourer he had risen to become the owner of a construction company, and had made millions of pesetas from the building boom of the 'sixties. He had been instrumental in getting his favourite daughter into the Social Anthropology course in the Complutensian University of Madrid, despite her disappointing grades in the pre-university exams, and there she had flowered, becoming an important element in the SEU, the government-controlled students' union; after her graduation, her father was horrified when she announced her desire to become a detective. A woman detective! Impossible! Unheard of! But she had got the details from the Police School and applied for admission. Her security clearance was impeccable: her father's contacts with various ministers, her record in the Feminine Section of the Movement at college and university, her social cachet, all this had made her an eminently suitable candidate for the new experiment. The School's Director had especially asked Personnel to allot her to this particular group. Not only was it the only one headed by a fully-fledged Comisario, rather than just a chief inspector, but she knew that Bernal was admired as a textbook detective and was placed in the international class. With him she would witness no browbeating or beating up of suspects, or hear tortured cries from the cells. He belonged to the camp of the *profesionalistas* in the DGS, who wanted to be professional policemen, not to the *militaristas*, the Franco diehards whose model was still Hitler's SS and Gestapo.

'Well, Superintendent, I did Social Anthropology at the Central, the Complutense, you know, and I've just passed the exams at the Police School. I never thought in my wildest dreams I'd have the good luck to be seconded to your group.'

Bernal tried to suppress a wince as he listened to her account. He had always had a chip on his shoulder about university graduates, until his own sons had gone to the Central and he had come to realize that a university education, at least in Franco's Spain, meant next to nothing in academic terms: three or four lectures a week in huge lecture-halls, with almost no personal tutorials. The students learnt more at home or in the reading-room of the Biblioteca Nacional. What they did was to educate one another as a class: they acquired the same lingo, the same air of self-confidence and omniscience, just by mixing socially. When this realization came to him, Bernal felt almost superior to them: he was virtually an auto-didact from the immense amount of wide reading he had done during the years when he felt inferior to these sons and grandsons of the Régime.

'Perhaps you know my younger son, Diego Bernal Carrero, who is still trying to get his physics degree at the Central, though with so many students there . . .'

'Yes, I met him once at a party. He's a keen skier, isn't he?'

Among his other multifarious activities, thought Bernal; perhaps after all she would prove a useful contact in a different social circle from that frequented by Ángel. 'That's right, though it might be best if you don't meet him too often from now on. Do your friends know that you've been studying at the Police School?'

'No. We were advised to keep it to ourselves and to say

that we had a job in the civilian section of the Gobernación.'

'Quite right, because I think I can use you best in an undercover way. Of course there will be plenty of paper work in the office, but from time to time you'll have the chance to elicit information from within your social set.'

Elena thought that this sounded quite interesting, though she was disappointed at the prospect of not being able to rush about in the official cars and examine the scenes of crimes with magnifying-glasses.

'The case we've got for this morning concerns the suspected suicide on Alfonso XII last night. You won't have read anything of it in this morning's newspaper, because we asked for a press ban for the time being so that we can see what its ramifications are, considering that the dead man was an agency reporter. Perhaps you'd like to look through this forensic report and give me your ideas on what we should look for when we go over the man's flat later. Ah, here's Paco with the coffee.'

He waved at Navarro to enter and waited for him to put the coffee on the desk before making the introductions, in case he dropped the tray from astonishment at having a new female colleague. Navarro had always seemed extremely shy with women, particularly with young and good-looking women, yet he had a vivacious and well-preserved wife who had borne him ten children.

'Inspectora Fernández, may I present Inspector Navarro?' He noticed Paco's unsuccessful attempt to conceal his disbelief as he nervously shook hands. 'The Inspectora has been seconded to us from the Police School and we must see that she is made as comfortable as possible.'

'Delighted to know you, Inspector. I have heard so much about you and the excellence of Superintendent Bernal's group.'

Bernal hoped the courtesies would not be too prolonged. 'Perhaps you would like to take your coffee to the desk

Navarro will clear for you and then see what you will need from Stationery and Supplies. I'll get on with checking last week's report on that blackmail case so that we can send it off to the magistrate at the Juzgado no. 20.'

9.30 a.m.
Rather like the ten groups of detectives in the Brigada Criminal, the thirty-two Juzgados de Instrucción or magistrates' courts in Madrid were arranged on a rota system, and the one that happened to be on duty on a particular day took charge of any offences then reported. The only exception had been Juzgado no. 1, the Public Order Court, which used to have supreme authority over political offences until the Government had recently discontinued this system at the same time as it had ostensibly abolished the Socio-political Brigade of the police.

Of course, the Ley de Peligrosidad y Rehabilitación Social, innocuously numbered Law 16 of 1970, had its own special courts. It was an eminently useful piece of legislation, Bernal considered, though it was denounced by the liberals, socialists and reds as an outrageous infringement of personal liberty, since it enabled the arrest of people who hadn't done anything wrong but who fell into one of the categories of 'social danger'. So sweeping was this law that it was very nearly a replacement of much of the older Penal Code, and it meant that almost anyone could be arrested under its pretext and sent to a 'rehabilitation centre' for a period of between six months and five years, and any establishment could be closed for between one month and a year. There was no appeal. It could have been drafted by his wife, Bernal mused. Just to mention its possible application in an interrogation was usually sufficient to bring about the eager co-operation or even total submission of the witness or suspect. Bernal had never seen the need to beat up people or drag them across the room by the hair. If one did that, one couldn't be sure if they were telling the truth

or simply saying what one wanted to hear. A brief explanation of the scope of the Law of Social Danger normally
sufficed, he found. He supposed that Inspectora Fernández
would have all the articles of this law and all those contained in the Código Penal at her fingertips, whereas he
and Navarro sometimes had to look up the supplements
and amendments before preparing the reports for the
examining magistrates.

He read carefully through the report on the blackmail
case, with his pen at the ready to correct errors of punctua-
tion and spelling. He thought it extraordinary how
uneducated the new breed of typist was. From the small
red splashes on the edge of the pages he guessed that the
one who had prepared this report had spent much of the
time repainting her fingernails. He gave it a final check
and signed in a neat hand; his was probably the only
legible signature in the whole brigade, since the rest were
either victims of the national fetish of signing in scrawls
and flourishes or were afraid to sign at all, in case of later
repercussions. He affixed the official seal and called
Navarro.

'Could you ring Prieto and demand that report on the
fingerprints?'

'OK, chief. I think the Señorita would like a word.'

'Come in, Inspectora. What is your preliminary view of
this apparent suicide?'

'May I enquire about the door of Santos's apartment?
Was it unbolted, but firmly shut on the automatic latch?'

'You have seen the important point. Yes, your supposition is basically correct. When the porter hunted for
his spare key, which he said he never used except to enter
to water the plants on the terrace when Santos was away
on holiday, he took me up in the lift and I unlocked the
door, but I had to turn the key twice clockwise, indicating
that Santos had shut the door, put in the key on the
inside to apply the double lock and then removed it. His
key was found in his trousers' pocket.'

'I take it that the inside handle and lock were finger-printed?'

'Yes, and we are waiting for the report. All the more obvious surfaces of the apartment were also fingerprinted, at my request.'

'A very wise precaution, in view of what we now know from the forensic report.'

Bernal noticed that she was already saying 'we', and far from thinking it proprietorial, he was faintly pleased that she was already thinking of herself as part of the group.

'Do we know who else possessed a key?' she asked.

'According to the porter, only the cleaning woman, who came in twice a week on Tuesdays and Fridays. We'll question her later today. What do you make of the position of the body, so far out in the roadway?'

Elena pondered for a moment. 'I take it no one saw him fall from the balcony of the flat?'

'No. As you probably know, there are no buildings opposite, just the railings of the Retiro, and there is a high bank at that point, which would virtually prevent any strollers in the park from seeing the houses opposite, unless they happened to climb the bank; but it's not likely they would want to look down on the traffic. There appear to have been no passers-by on the pavement on the park side, but the porter was chatting to two female neighbours in the doorway as the body landed. It was fortunate that no cyclist or car-driver happened to be pulling in to the kerb at that moment. There was only light traffic at that time on a Sunday.'

'I take it that the porter saw no one leave the building immediately afterwards?'

'He could not be sure because of the confusion, with other people running up to see what had happened, not to mention the shocked cries of the two ladies he was talking to, who were on their way back from church.' The same church as his wife had attended that evening most probably, thought Bernal.

'Has the building got iron-railed balconies on each floor?'

'It has a wide stone *marquesina* or cornice at the first-floor level, wide balconies with wrought-iron rails on the first two floors above that and narrower ones from there up to the seventh.'

'Could not the wound in the deceased's neck and the strange position of the body be explained by a ricochet effect from his striking one of the lower balconies as he fell?'

'Very good, Inspectora. That occurred to me at the time, and I had the benefit of seeing the body *in situ*. I managed to examine the two wide lower balconies and the cornice, but found nothing. Of the narrower ones above, I could only look at two, because the residents were out and the porter has the keys of only a few of the flats, where the owners have a special arrangement with him. He's an ex-combatant, and quite intelligent and observant.'

'Well, surely the fingerprint report will clinch it, since we should be able to find out if any strange prints are superimposed over the deceased's.'

'That's what I hope, but you'll find that these cases don't usually come out as in the textbooks.' He realized from her sudden discomposure that he had unintentionally got at her inexperience. 'We should get the report at any moment if Prieto's team would get a move on.'

10 a.m.

There was a sudden explosion of laughter and joking in the outer office as Ángel breezed in and began to give Navarro an account of the previous night's perambulations. Bernal could see Paco making warning gestures as Inspectora Fernández turned to look with curiosity at the newcomer through the glass panel. Bernal moved to the door and called Ángel in. 'I'd like you to meet Inspector Gallardo, Señorita. Ángel, this is Inspectora Fernández Ruiz, who has been seconded to us from the Police School.'

Bernal noticed Ángel's immediate reaction of delight and he hoped he wouldn't go so far as to kiss her hand.

'*¡Hombre!* What a charming surprise! The old place will never be the same again! It will be great to have a smashing young lady in the office!'

Elena did not entirely manage to control her blushes, but brought out a sharpish reply: 'Delighted to meet the group's playboy.'

'What have they been telling you about me? Don't believe a word of it! It's all in the line of business.'

'Well, let's keep it that way here too,' she said sweetly, 'and then there won't be any problems.'

Admiring her coolness, Bernal wondered whether the School gave the lady inspectors special tuition in how to handle amorously inclined male colleagues. 'Ángel, you'd best read this forensic report and then see what you can find out among the journalistic circles about this man Santos. You can do last night's reports for the dossiers later.'

'OK, *jefe*. Will do. We'll take *tapas* together before lunch, Señorita. I know all the best bars where they serve them around here.' He breezed out to his desk and began reading the forensic dossier and the night reports with his legs dangling across the chair in a very nonchalant manner.

Navarro came in with the report from the fingerprint team and handed it to Bernal, who said: 'Take Miss Fernández to get her official security pass for the building, Paco, so that she can use the facilities of the restaurant, poor as they are. Then you can see about stationery and so on for her desk at the same time. I'll let you see this report for your first reactions when you get back, Señorita.'

'Please call me Elena, Superintendent; I think it would be nicer than using titles all the time.'

'Very well, Elena, but don't let Ángel get too familiar, unless you want him to, of course.'

'Don't worry, *jefe*, I've had plenty of experience at

handling his type at the University.'

Bernal found himself warming to her already; she was beginning to awaken the remnants of his paternal instincts, almost as though she were the daughter he had never had.

He began reading Prieto's report with close attention. For the purposes of comparison they had taken the fingerprints of the deceased journalist Santos and of the porter who had let them into the apartment, which was on the top floor of the building. The report explained that the apartment was really an attic studio, consisting of a small entrance hall, one large room with a row of small windows facing east on to the Retiro park, a small bathroom, and a storage room cum kitchen with a door leading out to a roof terrace at the back. They had found good partial sets of latent prints on the brass inner door handle and lock, which they had identified as the porter's, superimposed over those of the deceased. The back of the door had shown a few older latent prints, all of the same person, as yet unidentified, but which might well belong to the cleaning woman. This would be verified later when she was interviewed. In the studio they had checked the most likely surfaces, and had found direct prints on a bottle of Chivas Regal whisky, on a whisky glass and on the glass-topped table, and all these prints belonged to the deceased. On other suitable surfaces, there and in the bathroom, they had found many old and faded prints belonging to upwards of seven people, which would prove very difficult to identify; they thought it possible that they had been deposited during a party, or on various social occasions. The window that had been found open had been given special attention: the only fresh prints on the sill and frame were those of the deceased, some of which were smeared and partially obscured, possibly by his clothing, since he would have had to squeeze himself through the narrow frame to reach the sloping tiled roof which fell away to the eaves of the building.

As Bernal pondered on the implications of the report,

Ángel ambled in holding the photograph of Santos: 'I've seen this chap about in the theatres and clubs from time to time, *jefe*, but I didn't know who he was. I saw him a month or so ago in the theatre, in the Valle Inclán it was, when I took Dolores to see *Nacha de noche*. You saw that, chief? She's the tops, that Argentinian actress, Nacha Guevara, and her cabaret turns are terrific, especially when she sings "Te Quiero".' Noticing Bernal's growing impatience, he hurried on. 'The last time I saw him was in the Boccaccio discothèque, a couple of weeks ago; he had a good-looking brunette in tow. No, come to think of it, I've seen him since then.' He shut his eyes and concentrated hard; Bernal knew that he had a phenomenal memory for faces and places; once a face registered, Ángel could usually recall where and approximately when he had seen it, sometimes months or even years before. 'That's it! When I took Mari Carmen to the JJ Club in Callao, ten days ago, to see El Gran Pavlovsky.' Bernal wondered whether Ángel took a different girl out with him every night. 'He's the great transvestite artist from Buenos Aires. You'll have noticed that the town is packed out with exiles from Argentina. Pavlovsky's show is very well dressed and undressed, if you know what I mean. There are two chorus girls with the sharpest tits you're ever likely to see in Madrid, with little stars stuck on and a bit of silver paint sprayed from an aerosol-can like icing on the cake, as it were. You must go and see it one night, *jefe*.'

'Isn't the place full of gays?'

'Oh no, *jefe*, it's a very chic place, especially since *El País* gave the show such a write-up. A lot of bankers and businessmen with their wives and girl-friends go there, as well as wedding parties from time to time. There's dancing until one-thirty a.m., then there's the cabaret for an hour and a half. As I say, the chorus line has its attractions, and Ángel Pavlovsky is the greatest, with a marvellous patter and six or seven routines. You've never seen such a lot of ostrich feathers! I've seen plenty of *travestís* in the

Madrid clubs, in the line of duty, you understand, and some of them are even supposed to have had the operation and flash their newly installed doodahs at the audience, but Pavlovsky's quite different. The only transvestite artist who has hair on his chest and who doesn't try to walk like a woman. That's why it's so funny. It would be quite natural for a journalist coming out of the Palacio de la Prensa next door to take his girl-friend out for a fling there. It's expensive too, at six hundred pesetas a knob on a Saturday night, with the right to just one drink.'

Bernal hated the noise and smoke in night-clubs and discothèques and never went to them, but Ángel usually gave such vivid accounts he scarcely needed to. 'If you've seen this girl with him twice, the chances are she was his steady girl-friend. We'll probably be able to track her down when Paco and I go over his things. Have a look at this fingerprint report.'

Paco and Elena now returned and Bernal called Navarro in: 'Get on to the press agency Santos worked for and ask to speak to the chief. It might be best if you went round there now, to find out what kind of stuff he was working on. It might have some bearing on the suicide, because that's what it looks like. I'll go round to the Retiro district Comisaría and get that local inspector, Martín, to take me to Santos's apartment. Elena, you could come round there under your own steam and act as my secretary. Don't come in an official car; I don't want you to use one at all for the time being, or be seen in public with Paco or me. You can go out with Ángel, of course, since you've both got the same cover of being civil servants in the Gobernación. You'll have to show your pass to the police-man at the door of the apartment, naturally, but use the one from the Ministry. There's time for you to read the fingerprint report before you set out, because I'll have to go via the Calle de Fernanflor, and I'd better take one of the large Seat one-three-one's, so as to impress them in the local station. Ángel, I want you to sniff round the journalists' bars and find out who Santos's friends were. You can liaise with Paco, but I expect you know a good few journalists off your own bat.'

'Lots of them, *jefe*.'

'All right, then; we'll all meet back here between twelve-thirty and one. Call down for a driver for me, Paco.'

10.30 a.m.

As he was driven sedately down the Carrera de San Jerónimo, Bernal rehearsed what he would have to say later to Santos's parents, who had been sent for from Santander where the father owned a small optician's shop, though he was now semi-retired. They had been informed of their son's death by the local police and had been asked to travel to Madrid to make the formal identification. They would be as anxious as Bernal to find out the reasons for his death, but it would be a difficult meeting. He hated conducting these family interviews when a tragedy had occurred, and would try to find out all he could first from the man's papers and possessions, so that it would be little more than a formality. In any case, in his experience, parents rarely knew what their children got up to, and next to nothing about their emotional lives, especially not when they lived away from home.

The Seat limousine drew up outside the Retiro Comisaría and Bernal went in to look for Inspector Martín. He was always careful to leave the local man, under his own discreet supervision, in charge of all the detailed work of the investigation, which was why, he supposed, he was well liked in the district *comisarías*.

He knew that many of his colleagues of equal rank, which was officially equivalent to that of a lieutenant-general in the Spanish army, stormed into these cases and rode rough-shod over the district men, treating them like country bumpkins. Bernal thought Martín had done well to call in the DGS at once, without touching anything or even entering the apartment, because his quick chat with

the porter had made him realize that there might be
important ramifications in the sudden death of a reporter,
which might go beyond the merely personal. He had hoped
to have someone like Martín to fill the vacant post in his
group, but Personnel in its wisdom had sent him Señorita
Fernández. Ah well, she might become useful in a few
months, and if she proved capable of drafting and typing
reports, as was likely once she learned the jargon, then she
might save him a lot of office work; but as for using her
much in the field . . . it wasn't really on.

Martín greeted him respectfully and asked him whom
he should bring. 'Just one uniformed man, I think, Martín,
to stand at the door. We don't want to make the neighbours too curious.'

They set out in the Seat to cross the Paseo del Prado at
Neptuno and drive up Felipe IV past the Royal Spanish
Academy. Bernal told the driver to drop them at the
corner and then to park in a side street nearby and wait
for Inspector Martín's orders. 'I think it best to keep this
case under tabs until we are surer of our ground, Martín.'

'Yes, chief. It might have political overtones.'

Bernal knew that Martín was a *profesionalista* like himself, not a *militarista*, and passed all political cases quickly
over to the old Brigada Social, with its present ambiguous
status and even more doubtful future. As they walked the
last few yards along Alfonso XII, Bernal told the uniformed *gris* who accompanied them to go on ahead and
alert the porter. At the door, this ex-combatant met them
courteously, obviously anxious to be helpful, and took
them up in the lift, the cabin of which had been electrified
and modernized, but the shaft and the doors on each
landing still showed signs of Isabelline opulence. The whole
building, indeed, belonged to the upper bourgeoisie from
the time of its construction to the present: elegant apartments for doctors, company directors and top-class civil
servants. No smells of stale food or sewerage here, thought
Bernal, only the well-kept hall and stairways paved in

white marble, with tiny brass lamps on the walls and the
shiny mahogany solidity of massive doors. At the seventh
floor they emerged to walk up the last flight to the attic
level. These old *buhardillas* under the roofs had probably
housed the servants or coachmen in the old days and they
had been expected to manage without lifts.

Martín inspected the official seals on the door: they
were still intact and he cut the wires with a pair of small
pocket scissors. The porter provided the key and they
entered the studio. Bernal was surprised to see the tapestries and oil-paintings in the morning light; they were of
good quality and antique. The three smallest tapestries
reminded him of the larger ones he had seen in the Prado,
which had been woven in the Tapicería Real from
cartoons drawn by Goya; the original designs could still
be seen, in mirror image of the tapestries, in the Escorial.
The large oil-painting of a lady holding a blue flower,
seated alongside a table that bore a bowl of fruit, looked to
be a family portrait, perhaps executed in the 'thirties.
There were a number of canvases stacked against the wall,
mainly still-lifes, and on an easel there leant the unfinished
portrait of a brown-haired girl. The table near the window
from which Santos had exited was covered with tubes of
oil-paints and brushes. Bernal glanced at the rest of the
room: a studio couch covered with crimson silk cushions in
an alcove, a small glass-topped coffee table, a sideboard
with a collection of antique plates from Talavera, Toledo
and Manises, some well-chosen reproduction gilt chairs, a
round dining table, an old chest with its front side opening
downwards, revealing fitted polychromed drawers, a large
gilt writing desk. Altogether, the *pied-à-terre* of someone
with money, taste, and a sense of style.

Bernal looked hard at the writing desk. 'Do you notice
anything different from when you left last night, Martín?'

Martín's gaze carefully swept the room. Having
observed the direction of Bernal's glance he approached
the writing desk without touching it. He spotted a piece of

paper protruding from one of the lower drawers, and underneath, an envelope just visible on the Chinese silk rug. 'I don't remember seeing the desk disturbed like this, Superintendent. Perhaps Prieto's fingerprint boys?'

'It's not like them to open drawers unless we specifically request it. You can see where they have been brushing the dusting powder, and there's none to be seen on that drawer. Without touching anything, have a look at the windows and doors.'

Martín came back looking crestfallen. 'Someone's been in during the night, *jefe*. No doubt about it. The door from that storeroom to the terrace has been forced with a jemmy. I inspected the inner bolt myself before I left last night.'

'Don't touch the phone but go down to the porter's lodge and call Prieto to come back at once, and get the team from the technical lab here as well. We'll get to the bottom of this.'

11 a.m.

As he waited for Martín to return, Bernal examined the writing desk more closely. On it was an expensive IBM electric typewriter of the latest self-correcting type, obviously a professional indulgence on Santos's part. Around it were scattered drafts of articles and reference books in some confusion: with a journalist or writer it would be impossible to tell if these things had been disturbed by an intruder or whether the user had left them in disorder. There was no paper in the typewriter, and it was unplugged from the electric point in the wall. Without approaching too closely, he examined the floor. He remembered Edmond Locard's dictum: an intruder would probably leave some sign of his presence at the scene (a hair from his head, perhaps, or a piece of his clothing caught on some object), while he would be likely to take away something unwittingly (dust on his shoes, a tiny trace of paint from the wall – the latter was particularly likely in

France or Spain, where wall paints were formerly water-based). But Bernal did not have great hopes of this room; perhaps Varga's technical team would find something on the forced door leading to the terrace.

He moved lightly through the bathroom, glancing at the state of the towels and the array of toilet preparations on the shelf. Santos had not deprived himself of much: an aerosol spray of *Pour Homme* eau de toilette by Yves St Laurent, with aftershave lotion from the same Parisian house; a large Remington electric razor; a Wilkinson safety razor of the swan-necked type; Fabergé Crème Shave; ZP 11 anti-dandruff shampoo; a Philips hairdryer; Badedas bath gelée and talc; Nivea Sunfilta Crème; in short, almost everything the modern man needed. The bathroom led to a storeroom cum kitchen: an odd arrangement, but the only practical one given the lay-out of the attic. Here there was only a roof-light, but the door at the end was ajar and gave on to an oddly-shaped terrace, tucked between the jutting tiled roofs of the house. From here there was a fine view of the church of Los Jerónimos and the slope of the Carrera de San Jerónimo as it ran past Las Cortes or parliament building, with the Hotel Palace visible below on the corner of the Plaza de Cánovas del Castillo, or Neptuno as everyone called it because of the elegant Carlos III fountain of the sea-god in its centre.

Like Martín before him, Bernal could see the marks of the jemmy that had been used to force the roof-door, and it seemed to him to be a professional job. Little damage had been done to the frame or to the main woodwork of the door, and no other marks were to be seen. Being careful not to touch anything, he moved out on to the terrace, where there were three reclining chairs covered in a floral plastic material, a white metal table and a small orange sunshade fitted to the eaves of the roof. He saw at once that any intruder would have had to climb over the dividing wall from the terrace of the next house; he couldn't have climbed from below because of the over-hanging eaves. Returning slowly to the studio, Bernal called the policeman from the door.

'Any sign of Inspector Martín?'

'I believe he's on his way up, Superintendent. I can hear him talking to the porter in the hallway.'

The lift began its lumbering ascent and Martín emerged.

'Prieto and Varga are both on their way, *jefe*. I've asked Prieto to come immediately, and Varga in half an hour.'

'Good man. While we're waiting we must go next door to see how the intruder got over to the adjoining terrace.'

'I thought of that, and I've phoned for another uni-formed man to come in case we need him next door. I went to talk to the porter there, and he says that the people who live in the attic studio are on holiday in the Canaries. They are a retired bank manager and his wife, and they don't spend much time in Madrid. They go to stay with their children a lot. I hope I did the right thing?'

'Of course. Let's go round there now. Has the porter got a key?'

'Yes, here it is. I've told him not to leave the hallway till we get there.'

Before they went down in the lift, Bernal told the police-man that a Señorita Fernández, his 'secretary', would arrive shortly; 'Ask her to wait on the landing until I return.'

'Understood, *jefe*,' said the burly middle-aged *gris*.

Bernal hoped that Elena would remember her cover and not try to pull rank with the policeman.

The house next door was very similar to the one they had just left, also built in the latter part of the nineteenth century. The porter turned out to be a pleasant young man with a limp, who hastened to open the lift door for them and to accompany them to the top floor. As they ascended, Bernal questioned him about the security of the building at night.

'Well, look, sir, I see everyone who goes in or out until ten-thirty p.m., when I lock the street door. All the residents have their own keys for it and are supposed to lock it on their way in or out. Some of the older people have been complaining about how stiff the lock is, so last week I called in a locksmith to ease it. Even so, I often find it left unlocked when I take the dog out for a stroll.'

'So some stranger may have been able to get in last night if one of the residents left the door unlocked?'

'Well, it's possible, but they shouldn't have any problem locking it now. Naturally we want to stop courting couples and tramps from coming in and doing their business on the stairs.'

Bernal had another thought. 'Were you in your lodge all the time between say nine o'clock and half past ten last night?'

'Yes, I had my supper on the table just inside the door and I saw no stranger go in or out.'

'And this morning, what time did you open up?'

'At half past seven. That's when I wash the tiles in the hall and the steps. Then I slipped round the corner to the bakery to buy some buns for our breakfast, but my wife keeps an eye on the hallway. She didn't mention seeing anything out of the ordinary.'

'Inspector Martín will check with her later.'

The lift arrived at the seventh floor and they walked up the last flight to the attic floor. The door seemed to be firmly locked, but Bernal took the key from Martín and wrapped his handkerchief around it before inserting it into the lock. He pointed out a number of faint scratch marks around the lock to Martín, as well as noting some tiny traces of carbon, indicating use of a skeleton-key, then he unlocked the door carefully. It was double locked. He told the porter to stay at the doorway without touching anything, and the officers entered the gloomy apartment. The chairs were covered with white dust-sheets and the window blinds were drawn. Again using the handkerchief,

Bernal put the main light on. They could see that the studio was almost identical in lay-out to the one next door, and nothing seemed to have been disturbed. They advanced through the bathroom to the storeroom, and again found everything normal: the two bolts on the door leading to the terrace were properly drawn shut.

'We can't open these, Martín, until Prieto gets here and dusts for prints. Let's go back there now and wait for him. If that extra uniformed man has arrived, we can send him up to guard this door. It doesn't look as if anything has been stolen here, but we'd better inform the owners so that they can come back and check if they wish.'

11.30 a.m.

Back in Santos's apartment, they found Prieto and his assistant already unpacking their dusting-kit and fixed-distance camera, with Señorita Fernández waiting inside the small hallway. The *gris* at the door said, 'Superintendent, your secretary is here.'

Bernal noticed with satisfaction that the Inspectora had played her part to a tee, and he said: 'There's no need to take notes for the moment, Señorita, but you can stay with us and memorize our comments.'

'Of course, Superintendent.'

Martín wondered if this was a new method of working in the central DGS; he had never heard of an investigating officer taking his secretary around with him. He looked hard at Señorita Fernández and Bernal; perhaps they were having an affair? The old Caudillo looked as though he still had plenty of go in him. He refrained, however, from making any comment.

Prieto asked, 'What else needs to be dusted, *jefe*?'

Bernal said, 'There's been a break-in since you left last night, Prieto. I want you to examine the writing-desk drawers and the bolt on the terrace door. But the intruders probably wore gloves. At least we'll find out where they searched.'

'Better than that, *jefe*. We've got the technique of checking glove-prints now, by the fibre impressions they leave, but you'd have to find the pair of gloves they used, of course. We've opened a file on unidentified glove-prints from various break-ins for comparative purposes, so we can tell if they use the same pair on two different jobs.'

Prieto started blowing his grey powder over the edges and faces of the desk drawers. Bernal knew that they used an all-purpose powder nowadays for direct and latent prints, and that later Prieto would want the lights out in order to examine the suspect areas under his ultraviolet lamp.

'There are new smudges here, I think, *jefe*. But we'll compare the photographs later. Can I open the drawers?'

'Yes, you'll have to check some of the papers in there as well. They were possibly searching for a particular document this journalist was preparing or holding. Does anything seem to be missing?'

'It's hard to tell in such a jumble. You'd better look at the position of the papers before I dust them, but I'll take some photographs for you. It's Varga's job really, but to save time . . .'

'Thank you, Prieto. Martín and I will look at the book-case while you get on with the desk. We won't touch the books until you get around to them. After that, I'm afraid you'll have to go to the flat next door and dust the entrance door and the door to the terrace. We think they got in that way.'

The glass-fronted bookcase contained a wide variety of reading-matter: paperback translations of English and American thrillers, some volumes of modern poetry by Cernuda, Alberti and Miguel Hernández, a lot of political and sociological stuff, some of it in French and English, and a number of reference books: proverbs, quotations, a copy of *Who's Who in Spain*.

'A lot of it for his work, Martín.'

'Yes, *jefe*. And a bit of light reading.' Martín pointed to some mildly pornographic books published in Paris.

'We'll get Prieto to see if anyone has gone through this cupboard. People sometimes hide papers in or behind books.'

Señorita Fernández followed them in silence, but Bernal noticed that her eyes were everywhere. He hoped she wouldn't try to be brilliant on her first case.

The technical team now arrived and Varga greeted Bernal warmly. He was one of the few superintendents the chief technician liked working for – a professional's regard for a professional. Varga looked like the typical Spanish artisan: short, squat, with powerful shoulders, black curly hair with a broad forehead, thick, useful-looking hands. He too had a young assistant with him, as well as a photographer, who began unpacking his equipment.

'You'll have to wait until Prieto has taken his ultra-violet photos in here, Varga, then I want you to look particularly at the desk, the bookcase and the open window. But you could make a visual inspection of the door leading to the terrace. Remember that Prieto hasn't dusted it yet.'

'OK, *jefe*. You think it was a professional job?'

'I'm sure of it. Perhaps someone looking for papers or documents of a compromising kind. Nothing of value seems to have been stolen. It's too much of a coincidence for a burglary to occur independently on the night of the owner's apparent suicide.'

'I'm with you, *jefe*. We'll see if we can find some tiny traces for you. Always ready to oblige.'

Prieto now asked for the room to be darkened and took his photographs of the desk drawers and the papers in them. The uncanny blue-grey glow of the lamp showed up a number of strong fingerprints on the desk in sharp blue outline. Prieto said: 'We got prints like these last night, chief. But I'm concentrating on these smudges which I don't remember seeing yesterday.'

When they had finished transferring the latent prints

by 'Lift-Print', Varga took over. 'Perhaps you'd like to wait on the landing. We're going to take some dust samples with our vacuum cleaner from various parts of the room, but you'll have ruined it all by now, tramping in and out and blowing fingerprint dust everywhere.' He glared at Prieto, his life's enemy on every investigation.

Bernal said he would wait on the terrace with Martín and Miss Fernández, and they went out through the forced door and examined the top of the whitewashed wall.

'There are foot scuff-marks there, Superintendent!' exclaimed Elena, 'and the geranium in this pot is broken and some of the earth has been spilled.'

'Varga may be able to get something from it, but last night's light rain has blurred it,' said Bernal gloomily. 'He obviously got over here quite easily, and then used a jemmy on the door. But why? What did Santos possess or what was he working on that made someone take such a risk? What do you think, Martín?'

'Well, it could be commercial, political or criminal, something connected with his job. Or personal, such as blackmail, or a financial or sexual misdemeanour, of which something incriminating was kept here. We don't know whether they found what they were looking for, do we?'

Bernal thought for a moment, then said, 'I don't think we'll get any further on the track of it here, except to look for a list of his friends and to take away with us his private papers and correspondence. We'll probably have to tackle it from the other end, from his job and his contacts. Unless we come up with something unexpected, of course.'

As they went back in, Varga was examining the jemmy-marks on the door. 'I can take a Plasticine-cast of these, Superintendent, and compare them with our little collection of tool-marks. If he's done any other job in the last four years with the same instrument, we'll have it on file.'

'That may give us an idea of the line he works in,' said

Bernal. 'It doesn't seem to be valuables.'

Varga's assistant, an earnest bespectacled young man, rushed out to them and said, 'I've found a couple of bloodstains, *jefe!*'

They accompanied him to the window of the studio, and he leant out and pointed to two tiny splashes, shaped like exclamation-marks, on the red tiles of the sloping roof. Varga took out a glass and examined them. 'H'm. The points are outermost,' he said, 'indicating that they fell with some speed from a body or object moving in the outward direction. But, as you know, Superintendent, they don't necessarily indicate the direction the bleeding person was moving in, since he may have flailed his arms or legs in the opposite direction to the one he was taking. But it looks obvious here that he was bleeding as he hurtled out of the window.'

Bernal racked his memory for the chapter on blood-stains in the official handbook. 'These fine splashes indicate a distance of a metre or more from where the blood fell?'

'Or very rapid movement,' said Varga. 'From a fairly immobile injured person's head or neck, let us say, they would form round blobs, and the amount of serration or indentation around the edges of the blobs would then indicate the distance, unless it was of two and a half or three metres, in which case they would fall as tiny splatters. These long, thin exclamation-marks show rapid movement, and it's hard to tell the exact distance of fall, really. There should have been more stains further out on the tiles, but last night's shower of rain has washed them away. These two found by my bright young lad here were protected by the overhang of the window ledge. They wouldn't have been seen last evening, when it was nearly dusk.'

This discovery changed Bernal's plans. 'I'll leave you to take photographs and the samples to check the blood group against the deceased's. I want to talk to Peláez again. We need a pathologist's view of the whole thing.'

12 noon
Back in his office, Bernal decided to hear what Navarro had found out at the press agency where Santos had worked and to see what Ángel had managed to pick up. He had told Elena to go on in a taxi while he dropped Martín off at the district station. They had left a uniformed man in each apartment; they didn't want any more unwelcome intruders – it was complicated enough as it was. Martín would arrange a thorough search of the flat during the afternoon, after Varga's team had finished the technical examination. He called Elena in and asked her to order coffee for six, since he was expecting Peláez, who would grumble no doubt at being torn away from his latest corpse.

On his desk Bernal noticed an official envelope which looked as though it originated from the Minister's Secretariat. He slit it open and found a scribbled note from one of the under-secretaries: *Would you be so good as to call in before 1.30 and inform us as to the state of your investigation on the dead journalist Raúl Santos?* Naturally he would, but he wondered to whom the 'us' referred. Or was it an example of the royal 'we'? It was amazing how these minor politicians succumbed to a *folie de grandeur*. And why this sudden interest in the Santos case? Of course they saw the routine incident reports up there in the elegant offices overlooking the Puerta del Sol, and perhaps they smelled a possible political scent in this case, just when the Government was in the middle of legalizing the political parties and dismantling the Francoist National Movement, but did they know something he didn't? It was urgent to have a council of war with his team.

Elena strode elegantly in. 'The coffee's on its way, *jefe*. What a fascinating case this is. I read in the handbooks that with a fall from a height it is always very difficult to decide between accident, suicide and murder. But those blood-stains! And the break-in! Don't they suggest murder?'

'That's why we need to talk to Peláez the pathologist again, Señorita.' He suddenly remembered that he must try to call her Elena. 'If someone had slit open the right side of Santos's neck at the window and then pushed him out, wouldn't there have been many more bloodstains in the apartment?'

Elena pondered seriously on this. 'Not if they had him pinned forward with the upper part of his body out of the window.'

'Very good, Elena! Well reasoned, but you said "they". Would it have needed more than one assailant?'

'Possibly not, if the single assailant was holding Santos's right arm twisted behind him in a half-nelson, for example, with his left hand and then used the knife or razor held in his right. But the window frame is very narrow.'

'And when he had cut the artery in Santos's neck, how would he have pushed him out, without either dropping the weapon or making bloodstains on the inside of the window frame and on the floor?'

'I see what you mean. A second assailant might have been holding Santos's legs, for example, and lifted them and pushed him out after the first assailant had cut his throat.'

Bernal admired her sang-froid as she discussed these gruesome possibilities. 'But Elena, one of them at least would have borne bloodstains on his hands, possibly on his face and clothing as well, not to mention those on the weapon. How did he get out without anyone noticing anything, or leaving any other tracks? There was no sign that the bathroom or the small sink in the storeroom had been used to wash off stains. And we are assuming that this assailant left by the entrance door and went down the main stairs, or even in the lift.'

'What if he left by the terrace through the apartment next door? The rain would have washed the marks away.'

'And he was able to bolt the terrace door in Santos's apartment after him, on the inside? To help us think this out, perhaps you would ring the Meteorological Station in the Retiro and see if they know at what time it rained during the night.'

'Righto, *jefe*.' Her eyes gleamed with excitement at the first real task she had been given in the whole case.

Bernal decided he wouldn't say anything about the subsecretarial enquiry to his team at this stage. He would wait and see what they made of the facts so far. Navarro now arrived and hung up his overcoat in the outer office. 'I've got some information, *jefe*. Santos's boss says that he was a cheerful sort. He was shocked to hear of his jump and swore that Raúl Santos was the last person who would do away with himself. He worked mainly on feature articles about showbiz and cinema artists, occasional profiles of politicians, that sort of thing. The agency then sold the articles to various national and provincial newspapers and magazines. He says he didn't think Santos was investigating anything very scandalous, though he was a lone wolf and tended to hand in things in addition to the pieces he had been assigned. He gave me all the drafts Santos had recently turned in, and I had a look at his office desk and brought over the correspondence and the few reference books that were there.' He carried in a large attaché-case and opened it on Bernal's desk. 'You'll see that some of the pages of these reference books have paper markers in them. We'd better look at the entries on those pages carefully. I told the agency boss not to mention Santos's death to anyone for the moment, though it's going to be difficult to keep it quiet for long.'

'As long as we can, Paco. It now looks much more like murder.' He filled Navarro in on the blood traces Varga's assistant had found and on the details of the break-in. 'It seems to be either a political affair, or a piece of private vengeance or blackmail or the like. Do you think Santos could have been a blackmailer? He appears to have lived very well. What was his salary?'

'Thirty-five thousand a month, plus the fees for additional articles.'

'He lived above his means, then, if that's all he earned. We'll have to look first at all the documentary evidence. In the meantime, ask the Duty Officer not to put any other cases on to us until we've got further with this one. There are plenty of other groups sitting on their backsides or propping up the bars down there.' Bernal looked gloomily out of the window.

Elena hurried in importantly. 'Superintendent, the met. station says there was light rain only, between one-twenty and two-forty-three this morning; a total of –' she glanced at her notes – 'o-point-six-three litres per square metre.'

'That shows us that the break-in occurred before one-twenty, because the rain partly obliterated the footmarks on the terrace wall. But we don't know how long before. We'll have to talk to the lame young porter again. After all, the intruders could have got into the next-door apartment at any time yesterday, even if they didn't break into Santos's flat until after Martín had sealed it at nine-fifteen p.m. Perhaps they even waited to watch us leave, expecting that we would treat it at first as a suspected suicide and not investigate as thoroughly as in a homicide. But were those intruders, whether one or more, distinct from the murderer or murderers? That is the complication. The whole forensic search is obscured if there were two separate lots, first the assailants, then the burglars.'

Navarro chipped in, 'Isn't it likely that they were one and the same? If the burglars were a different set of people, how would they have found out about the earlier murder?'

Bernal hesitated a moment before replying, 'Only by witnessing the scene of the apparent suicide or by finding the house crawling with our agents later. That would have been a perfect distraction for the young porter next door while they got into the attic flat there.' Bernal thought of a third possibility, but did not voice it: they could have seen the police report in the incidents room at the DGS, or listened in to the police radio communications.

Navarro went on, 'The first assailants did not break into Santos's apartment. Therefore, either they had a key or he invited them in. Now most people in Madrid will not open the door to strangers without inspecting them and enquiring their business through the door-grille first. Either he recognized them, or was satisfied with their explanation. And how did they leave without touching the inside of the door, even with gloves? Prieto's first report said that only the porter's prints overlay Santos's on the door, and he touched it presumably when he let you and Martín into the flat soon after Santos's fall.'

Bernal thought hard, and then asked Paco and Elena, 'Have you asked yourselves about the door being double locked? Why should the owner or tenant of an apartment enter by the only door from the stairs, close it on the automatic lock and then re-insert his key and turn it once more, when he had a strong bolt on the inside which he could have drawn, but did not?'

'Lots of people double lock their doors, Superintendent,' said Elena, 'to prevent a thief from opening it with a strip of plastic or a credit card, which is so common these days. My father insists on our double locking ours.'

'But when you go in or when you go out?' asked Bernal.

'Well, always when we go out leaving the house empty, of course. And late at night, but in that case the last one in bolts the door as well.'

'Exactly,' said Bernal, 'and if you lived alone and double locked the door from the inside, you would most likely leave the key on the inside – this was a solid mahogany door, remember – or you would simply run the bolt home.'

'But he may have needed his key-ring to open something else, such as his desk,' Paco said.

'Yes, of course, but you have both forgotten that Santos's key-ring was found in the pocket of the trousers he was wearing when he fell. Now, unless the assailants had earlier searched for a spare key, which seems improbable with Santos still alive, how could they have double locked the door as they left? We know they didn't leave through the storeroom and the door to the roof-terrace, because we found that door bolted on the inside. They must have had another key to the flat-door, which they inserted into the inside lock, thus leaving Santos's fingerprints untouched on that side. Then they simply had to turn the key to open the door to make their getaway after the murder. Once on the landing they only had to re-insert the key carefully, pull the door shut by pulling on the key, then they turned it once anti-clockwise to double lock the door. By this means they hoped to make us think that Santos had locked himself in before he jumped. What worries me is the next part. One of the assailants, and I think there must have been at least two, would have had some bloodstains on his right hand and arm, assuming he was right-handed – and the gash on Santos's neck suggests that – and he would have been carrying a blood-covered blade or dagger. How did he get out of the building without leaving any traces or being noticed? Of course, the people milling about on the pavement before the arrival of the police would have helped, but they took a terrible risk.'

Elena chipped in, 'Could they not have entered another apartment in the same building and cleaned up before leaving?'

'That has occurred to me, and we'll have to ask Martín to examine all the other fifteen apartments. Though it will be a slow business, with so many of the residents away on holiday for Semana Santa. We can't force their locks and they may not be back until Easter Sunday or Monday at the earliest.'

12.30 p.m.
Peláez and Ángel now arrived together, the latter obvi-

ously bursting to tell Bernal something. But Peláez got in first and said, 'Since your call, I went back to the morgue and looked at this chappie again. I know what you're going to ask, Bernal. The incision in the neck could have been caused by a blade, possibly an open razor, since there are signs that it began below and to the right of the chin and followed rapidly around the neck piercing the carotid. There is bruising on each side of it, though, which first suggested impact with a narrow sharp object during the fall; perhaps the sharp edge of a balcony rail, but there are no signs of rust or paint in the wound. Remember it is hard to judge in an incision the direction of the cut if the cutting-edge is clean.'

'Could the bruising have been caused by manual pressure prior to the incision?' asked Bernal.

'Ah, I see exactly what you're getting at. Unfortunately the fall occurred almost contemporaneously with the incision and bruising. There are no finger-impressions in the bruising, nor any marks of a ligature. I'd say your supposition could be correct. That an assailant pushed him forward through the window, squeezing his neck with the edge of his gloved left hand, as in a karate chop, then produced a razor or long flick-knife in the right hand and began to apply it from below and to the front of the squeezing hand. It's certainly possible. Hasn't Varga found any bloodstains? There would have been quite a spout of blood unless a second assailant secured Santos's legs and arms and pushed his body out almost simultaneously.'

'One of Varga's men found two small splashes just outside the window-sill. Unfortunately the rain during the night washed the sloping tiled roof and the balcony rails below. The street was blood-splattered, of course, mainly in the gutter and part of the roadway. When I arrived on the scene, I thought it odd that the stains were so far out, but I assumed the body had ricocheted off a balcony edge or off the lower cornice and had been launched through the trees lining the pavement on the roadway. It was nearly dusk by the time we got up to the flat and we looked at all the balcony rails we could.'

'What about the trees? The rain wasn't heavy, was it? You might find something there.'

Bernal thought that Varga wouldn't be too delighted at the prospect of having to climb up the grimy bark of two plane-trees and examine the branches for bloodstains, but he said, 'Yes. It will have to be done. We might be able to judge the height at which the body was hurled so far out into the road and clinch the matter of a later ricochet or not during the fall. Paco, ring Varga and tell him about the trees.'

Ángel could contain himself no longer. '*Jefe*, I've been in the journalists' bars around Callao, and in the Taberna del Alabardero near the Ópera – that bar that was done up as a *mesón* by two bullfighters, where you can get marvellous *tapas* to take with an apéritif. It seems that Santos was known as a friendly type, a bit of a womanizer, but recently he'd settled down with this brunette I told you about, who's called Marisol. No one appears to have known her surname. They say she hadn't lived in Madrid for long. She's from Extremadura, and is a bit of a *paleta* or unsophisticated type, just in from the sticks. She speaks with a strong *extremeño* accent. They say she worked as an "artiste" in various dubious night-clubs before Santos met her, but they think he keeps her now, in a rented flat in the Calle de Lavapiés. Apparently they had a tiff recently, one night in the Morrison Bar on the Gran Vía, possibly over money.'

'It'll be like looking for a needle in a haystack if we can't find her surname,' said Bernal. 'There must be a couple of thousand girls called María Soledad, and the Lavapiés quarter is full of girls in from the country living in small flats. Perhaps she'll come forward of her own accord. She's bound to try to telephone Santos sooner or later, and we're intercepting all calls to his number. But when Prieto has finished dusting Santos's papers for possible prints, we'll be able to go through them carefully. And Paco has just brought in the stuff from Santos's desk at the press agency. You and Elena can look through them in the outer office, Ángel.'

'OK, *jefe*, we'll get cracking on it.'

'Peláez, I've got one more question,' said Bernal. 'Were there any scratches or bruises on Santos's palms or forearms, suggesting he put up a struggle?'

'None, Bernal. Only some scratches on the face and the backs of the hands which were probably the result of the fall through the branches of the trees. But I think you must treat it as murder. Otherwise none of Santos's blood could have been spilled just outside the window, not before he hit something as he fell. Those two spots of blood Varga's man found will clinch it if they belong to the same blood group, of course.'

'Righto, Peláez. That's how we'll report it provisionally. We'll need confirmation of the blood traces, naturally. Varga may find something on the clothing once he has time to do a microscopic examination in the lab. The assailants may have left some tell-tale mark.' Bernal was struck with a sudden thought. 'What about the deceased's shoes, Peláez? I was surprised to see them lying in the pool of blood on the roadway, with the laces still tied. Do you think the effects of the fall from the eighth floor or the impact would have caused them to fall off his feet?'

'Extremely unlikely, I'd say. That detail helps to confirm the idea of a second assailant, who lifted Santos by the feet and tipped him out. He either loosened the shoes in the attempt so that they fell off and rolled down the roof, or they came off in his hands and he threw them out quickly as an afterthought. The people on the pavement probably wouldn't have noticed a very slight delay, especially as they would have been shocked by seeing all that blood.'

'Many thanks, Peláez. You've been most helpful. Let's

hope we don't have many more like this one.'

'I never lose hope of seeing an interesting case of this sort, Bernal.' The gleam in Peláez's eyes enhanced by the pebble lenses suggested more than a mere professional interest, rather an enthusiasm for these macabre autopsies, which Bernal hated so much. 'I'll send you the final report, allowing for the likelihood of homicide, as we've just outlined. Varga's report should clinch it. Now you've got to find the perpetrators, eh?'

Bernal shook hands with him gloomily. 'I think we are dealing with pros, not amateurs, though it's curious that they double locked the door. They also panicked a bit in using a blade and leaving bloodstains; they couldn't have known it was going to rain. Without those details, and the break-in, of course, we might not have suspected murder at all. Since they may not have had anything to do with the burglary, they've only made a couple of mistakes so far.'

'And the shoes, Bernal, don't forget the shoes,' Peláez said at the door.

'Ah, yes, but I wouldn't have thought twice about them, or the door, for that matter, if it hadn't been for the burglary. That upset their apple-cart. *Adiós, Peláez, hasta la próxima*, but let's hope the next one won't be too soon.'

'*Adiós, Bernal. Hasta pronto.*'

Paco now came back from the telephone. 'Varga's tearing his hair with all he's got to do in the two apartments and later in the lab. He's sent the first lot of stuff back for his technicians to get started on. He says the trees are the last straw, but he's going to ring the Parks Department of the Ayuntamiento and try to borrow one of their lorries with a hydraulic lift that they use for pruning trees. He wasn't impressed with your idea of shinning up the tree-trunks.'

'I knew he'd think of a way. He's a very practical man. I hope he arranges it before it rains again.' Bernal looked out at the sky anxiously. 'He may be able to pinpoint the height at which Santos was launched out above the pavement and over on to the roadway.'

Ángel came in with a small *agenda* or address-book. 'We've been through this list of addresses and telephone numbers from Santos's office desk, *jefe*, but there's no Marisol in it.'

'He would know the number off by heart, surely,' said Bernal. 'But he must have paid the rent on the flat, if his friends are right about its being rented, or if he owned it there will be the rates and the electric bills. But he probably kept all that stuff at home, and we'll have to wait for the technical lab to send up those papers. Is there anything else of interest?'

'A lot of drafts of articles we'll have to read through. And a list of the names and addresses of all the leading politicians, including some belonging to the parties not yet legalized. He was obviously planning some features from the personal angle, because he noted down details of their wives and children, their business interests, and a résumé of their careers. It's quite a dossier.'

'That's one line we'll have to follow, Ángel, and the girl, of course, when we manage to track her down. Paco, help Elena and Ángel with the rest of the stuff from Santos's office. I've got to go upstairs for a while.'

Paco knew that by 'upstairs' Bernal meant the Secretariat, but he was too discreet to enquire about the reason for the visit.

1 p.m.

In the waiting-room of the subsecretary who had asked him to drop in, Bernal studied the elegant décor and the splendid view over the Puerta del Sol more with a sense of anger than envy. The staff who did the donkey work and the unpleasant tasks in all weathers were housed in ancient and cramped quarters scattered round the DGS building, while the subsecretaries, who were nearly all political appointees and earned large salaries from these sinecures, lived graciously on the noble floor of the old Gobernación.

The subsecretary, who now came out of his office beaming a friendly greeting, Bernal found particularly odious: a young, sleekly dressed, coiffured and manicured Navarrese, whose rapid rise in the Ministry was attributable to his charming wife's *enchufe* or influence with the wife of a former Minister.

'Come in, come in, Don Luis! Do have a *copita* of Montilla, or would you prefer something stronger? I've got some fine Havana cigars, specially imported, to offer you.'

'Thank you, Señor Secretario, but it's a bit too soon for me to take alcohol. I'll stick to a cigarette, if you don't mind.'

The subsecretary rushed round the desk to open a large gilt cigarette box containing four different brands of tobacco. 'Do have one of these. Those on the left are Egyptian. We'll have some coffee.' He gestured to his tall blonde secretary to bring in the prepared tray.

The office was imposing, with a huge Isabelline desk which bore nothing except the cigarette-box, an embossed leather writing-case, a gilt pen-stand, a crystal ashtray and, in pride of place, a large coloured photograph of the blonde wife, signed *Con todo mi amor, Loli*, which was only proper, thought Bernal, since she had got him the job. Overhead hung an enormous chandelier of Bohemian crystal and behind the desk a copy in oils of a recent portrait of Juan Carlos I which did not flatter that monarch; the artist had managed to give His Majesty a wooden-necked appearance, reminiscent, thought Bernal, of Goya's famous portraits of the royal family of his day. It made a change, though, from the sepia photographs of the young Franco which still hung outside the cells in the basement, where the prisoners couldn't have noticed any perceptible change in the treatment they received.

'This chap Santos, Bernal, have you discovered yet why

he took a dive? Was he in a state of depression?'

'We have discovered no evidence to suggest that the balance of his mind was disturbed, though we are still questioning his friends and employers, and going through his papers.'

'The Minister is anxious that the case should be cleared up without unpleasant publicity. Just a simple inquest, we thought.'

'May I enquire as to the Minister's interest in the matter? Was Santos involved in political dealings?'

'No, no, not as far as we know. But with the press, nowadays, we have to be cautious, as you will realize. The Minister is still very displeased about that series which appeared in *Diario 16* about the chief commissioner of the political brigade and his career as a "superagent".'

'Was Santos involved in that or in any similar exposé?'

On hearing this last word the subsecretary winced. 'No, no, we don't think so. But with the general election planned for June, we must try to keep on the best possible terms with the agencies and newspapers. That's why, for all our sakes, we'd like you to play this in a low key.'

'I shall do all I can,' said Bernal, 'but there is a complication. We have reason to think that Santos was murdered.'

The subsecretary went pale. 'Murdered? Are you sure? Isn't it very difficult to tell in cases of a fall from a height?'

'It was the burglary, and of course, the bloodstains on the roof tiles that put us on to it.'

'The burglary?'

'Yes, during the night.' Bernal was enjoying the spectacle of the subsecretary's discomfiture. 'Someone went over Santos's apartment after we sealed it yesterday evening. The technicians are looking for traceable evidence at the moment. We have found some jemmy-marks which will help.'

'It could be an unfortunate coincidence, then? The burglars just happening to choose Santos's apartment last night?'

'It could, if it weren't for the fact that they didn't steal any valuables, as far as we can see. Add to that the blood-stains, and the shoes . . .'

'The shoes?'

'Yes. They seem to have fallen out of the window after the body.'

'Well, well. You'll send in a full report, of course. But try to keep it all from the press, I beg you, Bernal.'

'If you think this is a political murder, Mr Secretary, I'll gladly pass the case over to the Second Brigade.'

'No, no, the Minister will want you to get to the bottom of it, Bernal, but as discreetly as possible.'

'We'll have to make some statement to the press later today. Santos's boss already knows about the fall, but was given to understand that it was either an accident or suicide.'

'Then ask for his co-operation to put out a simple statement, so as not to cause pain to the family, and all that. Dog doesn't usually eat dog, even when he's a journalist, Bernal.'

'I'll do what I can. But I have your permission to continue with the investigation?'

'Of course, of course. The Minister is relying on you.'

'Wherever it leads?'

'Yes, yes, but you'll let us see the reports as they are prepared, won't you? Especially the one you intend to send to the examining magistrate.'

'Naturally. But the magistrate at the Juzgado number twenty-five will already have been informed of the death, since he was on duty, and will expect me to keep him informed.'

'Well, perhaps it would be wise not to reveal your suspicions to him just yet. Wait until you have all the facts.'

'All the facts! *¡Ojalá!* One can see you've never been a detective, Mr Secretary! I shall have to give the magistrate some indication, otherwise he'll wonder why we are continuing the investigation after asking him for a burial certificate, and we'll have to have that today, so that the parents can arrange the funeral. We can, of course, say that we are not sure yet whether the death was accidental or not.'

'Yes, that should suffice. You could tell the parents the same thing.'

'Well, Mr Secretary, I'll get back to work and not keep you any longer from yours.' Bernal looked pointedly at the large desk, on which no papers were visible.

The subsecretary laughed heartily, but the laugh had a somewhat forced ring to it. 'It's no trouble finding time for you, Bernal, the best man we have in the Criminal Brigade. Follow this case wherever it leads, now.'

Bernal knew that he was lying in his teeth, and that as soon as the investigation touched on some raw nerve of the old or the new régime, they would be on him like a ton of bricks and pull him off the case. He would have to move with great cunning, giving the impression that he was following personal and criminal leads, while exploring thoroughly the political aspects, about which this very interview had sharpened his interest.

1.30 p.m.

The effusive farewells over, Bernal made his way back to the gloomier and grubbier side of the building where the real work was done, only to be met in the corridor by Paco Navarro, who warned him that Santos's parents had arrived.

'Ring the Magistrate at Juzgado number twenty-five Paco, and ask for a burial certificate. Tell him we are still investigating to see if the death was accidental or not. Check with Peláez first to see if he has sewn the body up and made it presentable, then you can take the Santoses to the Forensic Lab for them to make the formal identification. I'll need fifteen minutes or so with them.'

'OK, *jefe*. We still haven't tracked down the surname or the address of Santos's girl, but Prieto hasn't finished with the private papers yet.'

In the large outer office, Bernal found Ángel talking animatedly to Señor Santos, while Elena sat silently with his wife, who was sobbing gently.

Bernal invited the bereaved parents into his office and expressed his condolences. 'Señores, perhaps you would like to know that we are still not convinced that your son died by his own hand.' The ancient phrase struck Bernal as somewhat archaic, but less harsh than saying 'by suicide'. Señor Santos, who seemed intelligent and shrewd despite his advanced years, was about to ask a question, but Bernal forestalled it. 'We are still investigating the other possibilities, and I give you my word that I am determined to find out the truth. I take it you had no reason to think that Raúl was depressed in any way?'

'Oh no, Superintendent,' said Señora de Santos, who had now suppressed her sobs, 'he was always extremely cheerful. Living alone never seemed to make him depressed – on the contrary, he valued solitude for his work and for his main hobby which was painting in oils. He had many friends when he needed them, and he often dropped in to see us in Santander when he would bring friends up for the weekend. They used to take a small sailing boat out on to the estuary and sail over to Somo for a picnic.' She broke into sobs once more as she recalled those occasions.

Bernal gained the impression that the mother probably knew her son rather well. 'Did he have a special girlfriend at the moment, do you know?'

'Well, Superintendent, he tended to have a series of them,' she replied. 'Over the years I have met three whom I thought of as potential daughters-in-law, but during the last year he has not mentioned any particular one.'

Señor Santos now spoke. 'When he came home on the fifth January for Twelfth Night, he was excited about an important assignment he had begun work on. He told me it was all very secret, but when he had all the facts he would publish a series that would cause a sensation. I told him I hoped he wasn't getting too deep into political matters – that was the time when that industrialist, Señor Oriol, been kidnapped by the GRAPO extremists, you remember, and we were afraid that he would get involved. But he said not to worry, there was no danger as he was taking certain precautions. Do you think his death might be the result of that business?'

Bernal tried to conceal his extreme interest in this assignment of Santos's. 'Well, we are investigating the personal side more. Do you happen to know how much your son earned?'

'About thirty-five thousand pesetas a month basic salary, plus special fees,' said Señor Santos.

'Did he manage to furnish his studio flat out of that?' asked Bernal.

'Oh no, we bought the flat for him and let him choose all the things he wanted from our house,' Señora de Santos said. 'We have a large chalet-type house overlooking the Sardinero beach, and it's much too big now for just the two of us.' She had difficulty in controlling herself once more. 'He was our only child, you see.'

Bernal expressed his condolences again, and went on, 'There appears to have been a girl close to him during the last couple of months, but we haven't been able to track her down yet. You can't help us to find her?'

Señor Santos turned to his wife, who, Bernal now realized, was an older version of the lady he had seen in the oil-painting in her son's apartment. She said without hesitation, 'I can give you the names of the three girls he has brought home from time to time, but, as I say, I have seen no new girl-friend in the last year and a half.'

'We'd be most grateful if you could write down the names for us, and anything else you can remember about them, before you leave. I'm sorry that I cannot let you into your son's studio until our technical team has finished there, but I can assure you that every care is being taken of his possessions. I am also arranging for you to have a burial certificate this morning. As you know, under the law a funeral must take place within twenty-four hours of death, but in cases where an investigation is necessary a magistrate's certificate has to be awaited. Where are you staying?'

'We've put up at the Hotel de París,' said Señor Santos, 'just across the square on the corner of Sol and Alcalá. It's an old hotel, but comfortable and it could not be more central. We usually stay there when we're in Madrid, because Raúl's studio is so small.'

At the mention of this, Señora de Santos was on the point of breaking down again, and Bernal rose hastily and shepherded them to the door. 'I see that Inspector Navarro has returned with the burial certificate. Would it be too much to ask you to accompany him to identify your son? I'm sure it will be best to get it over with as soon as possible.'

They nodded their consent, and Señor Santos supported his wife as far as the door, where Elena took her arm, and they took leave of the Superintendent.

Bernal now called Ángel in. 'I think the political side of this case is very promising, Ángel, but we must proceed with caution. And we must try to find the girl first, just in case there was some personal revenge. After all, she is most likely to have had a key to his apartment, though it doesn't seem probable that she would have had the strength to attack him with a razor or knife and push him out of the window. But one never knows; hell hath no fury, etcetera, and she could have had an accomplice. Perhaps you'd like to take Elena out before lunch and let her see how you elicit information from your acquaintances without their realizing it. It'll be a useful experience for her and she'll be a good foil for you if you warn her not to ask naïve questions.'

'It'll be a pleasure, chief. What sort of line do I follow?'

'Well, imagine that Raúl Santos was preparing a series

of exposés about some leading politicians, and had found out something scandalous about their private lives, or their connexions with International Fascism, or with Moscow, or with any extremist organization such as FRAP or GRAPO.'

Privately Bernal had never been entirely convinced that GRAPO was genuinely a left-wing extremist group. He remembered from the long history of Francoism how easy it was for the political police to set up a phoney guerrilla group by inciting a handful of hot-heads to perform a series of limited acts sufficient to produce political tension at the right moment.

He called Elena in. 'Please accompany Ángel on a small tour of the bars and watch his methods of extracting information. You can then have time off for lunch until five p.m. when you can help Navarro with the paper work until seven-thirty or so. If you stick to normal office hours, that will help you preserve your cover as far as your friends are concerned.'

'Thank you, *jefe*. I take it you're not ordering me to have lunch with Inspector Gallardo?'

Bernal smiled and said, 'I wouldn't inflict such a thing on you, Elena. You can make your own mind up about that. But seriously, his methods are worth watching.'

'I've already noticed some of them, *jefe*. Shall I see you this evening?'

'It depends on how the work goes. If only we could trace Santos's girl . . .'

'We'll see what we can do about that,' she said, rather confidently, he thought. Well, she'd work and learn like the rest of them.

Ángel led her on to the street, treating her, much to her amusement, like a newcomer in the city where she was born.

'We'll go across to the Calle de Tetuán first, and have a snack in the Casa Labra,' he said.

She acquiesced in this arrangement and they strolled

through the dense crowds on the pavements of the Puerta del Sol and waited to cross through the traffic circling the fountains and the statue of the bear hugging a *madroño* tree, the official crest of the capital city, the irony of which was not lost on the Catalans and other provincials, who saw Madrid as the bear stealing the fruit from the rest of Spain; though the *madrileños* really had the last laugh because the small red fruits of the strawberry-tree served neither man nor beast, except, perhaps, the native bears which were almost entirely extinct.

2 p.m.

Elena had never set foot in the Casa Labra, since it was part of traditional, not fashionable, Madrid where she was normally to be found. She gazed in fascination at the treacle-brown façade of the old bar. Ángel urged her to try the fresh pieces of cod fried in batter for which the house was famous, with a *caña* of draught beer. From there they went up Tetuán, crossing the Calles de Preciados and del Carmen, and went into La Malagueña, where there was an extraordinary selection of *tapas*: *zarajo* or lamb's tripe from Cuenca, meatballs in piquant sauce, kidneys in sherry, squids' tentacles in batter, Russian salad, *boquerones* or fresh anchovies in vinegar, prawns fried on the *plancha*, cockles and mussels in their juice, small rations of *paella* . . . The latter looked excellent, and Elena chose it, with another *caña* of beer to wash it down.

She noted that Ángel was entirely at home – this was his *ambiente*, whereas she felt out of place, not least because this was an area where her mother would not approve of her being alone; the Calle de Montera and the Plaza del Carmen around the corner from where they found themselves were notoriously full of prostitutes of both sexes at most times of the day. She recalled with horror, from years before, the day when she had waited for her mother outside a shoe-shop on Montera and at least five quite respectable-looking gentlemen had asked her how much she charged. This had culminated in the incident in which a heavily painted prostitute rushed up to her and thrust three thousand-peseta notes into her hand, muttering threateningly, 'The other girls and me want you off our patch at once.' Too shocked to react, she was white and shaking when her mother emerged, but later they had laughed it off, and had the afternoon out on the proceeds.

Ángel's presence now helped to soothe her fears and she determined to enjoy herself, however much her stomach suffered in the process. Her normal life revolved round the so-called 'Costa Fleming', the elegant suburb off the northern end of the Castellana, near the Santiago Bernabéu football stadium, where her current boy-friend would take her into Mr Raf's bar to take chic *tapas* of caviare, smoked salmon and *pâté*, and some evenings they would have an Irish coffee there – Curro could prepare it better than anyone in Madrid, she thought. Now she would get to know an older, cheaper Madrid, more 'typical' than hers, and in Ángel's company she was secretly enjoying her initiation.

'Ángel, when are we going to talk to your journalists?'

'Any minute now we'll meet one. But let's have something more substantial first, next door in the Mesón Montañés. They have whole roast Castilian suckling pigs there.'

Elena winced at this suggestion, but agreed to inspect the third of these bars famous for *tapeo* or the partaking of snacks before lunch or dinner.

Bernal's thoughts were also turning to *tapas* as he sat in his office still pondering on the morning's events. He could see signs of a forthcoming clash with his superiors and the Political Brigade if he followed the Santos case to the end. He decided to confide his fears to Paco Navarro, who had now returned from the morgue.

'Paco, let's go out and have a drink. What if we go down

San Jerónimo and have a consommé and a glass of port in Lhardy?'

'That sounds great, *jefe*. It's years since I've been in there.'

Lhardy was unchanged since it was founded by a Swiss pastry-cook in 1831. The two heavy lanterns hanging over the pavement marked it out for the cognoscenti, but the modern shops which now hemmed it in meant that the uninitiated would pass by without noticing its existence. Bernal relaxed in the back-of-the-shop atmosphere, and chatted to Navarro about family matters. After a while they decided to stroll up the Calle de la Victoria, and from there made their way to the tree-filled Plaza de Santa Ana. Crossing over to the far side of the square, they went into the old Cervecería Alemana or German Beerhouse. When he had relaxed at a corner table, Bernal brought up the Santos case.

'Have you seen anything in Santos's papers to suggest a dangerous political involvement, Paco?'

'Not really. The biographical notes he was making on all the major politicians seemed to be the usual stuff one might expect in this pre-election period. Only one thing puzzled me: the words *Sábado de Gloria* on a blank sheet of paper, with three question-marks drawn on each side of them.'

Bernal pondered on this. 'Well, we both know that it's the old term for *Sábado Santo*, Easter Saturday, which is no longer a special feast-day. I suppose they used to call it Saturday of Glory thinking of the Resurrection to come on the Sunday. There are still processions on Easter Saturday in lots of towns and villages.'

'I know, chief. But why would he jot it down like that? It's definitely written in his hand.'

'We may find out more from the papers he had at home.'

Navarro now took his leave. 'I'll be back in the office at five, *jefe*. Will you be coming back?'

'I'll probably call in before eight to look at any reports

we have by then. Give my love to Remedios and the children.'

'I will, chief. See you later.'

2.30 p.m.

Bernal decided he had eaten enough for the moment and wouldn't indulge himself today in the shellfish bar on the opposite side of the Plaza de Santa Ana. He gazed depressedly at the hollow shell of the Teatro Español, burned out two years ago, with the city council showing no obvious signs of rebuilding what had been the most famous theatre in Madrid.

Since the day was still grey and chilly, Bernal caught the Metro from Sevilla station to ride the two stops to Retiro. As he let himself into the apartment, he was surprised to hear his wife talking to someone in chirping tones. At this hour she was usually to be found praying in her small oratory off the dining-room, where she had installed in a large cupboard a grotesquely painted half life-size statue of Our Lady of Sorrows, outlined in tiny coloured electric lights which she switched on during her devotions, when she would kneel on a red plush *reclinatorio*. He had earlier had battles with her over the lighting of wax candles below the statue because of the risk of fire, and he had finally got her to agree to use electric ones. Today, however, with a smell of lentil and blood sausage stew filling his nostrils as he passed the kitchen, he found her trying to reanimate an obviously moribund yellow canary, which was lying at the bottom of a small gilt cage.

'Luis, I think it's ill. It belongs to the widow who lives on the fourth floor, who has gone to Málaga to stay with her sister. She's asked me to look after it while she's away. She's provided all the bird-seed and the pieces of fish-bone for it to sharpen its beak on, and I've tried giving it lettuce leaves and pieces of apple, but it only makes half-hearted attempts to eat. Do you think it's ill?'

'I think it's dying of cold, Geñita. Find a bit of old

blanket to put round the sides of the cage to keep the draughts off it. I don't think it will live to see its mistress's return.'

'Oh, Luis, what shall I do if it dies?' she wailed. 'She'll blame me for not looking after it.'

'Don't be silly. She's given it to you half dead. What does she expect? How old is it?'

'She says she's had it for eleven or twelve years.'

'Well, then, it must be near the end of its natural life.'

'Help me to try and keep it alive until she gets back. Do you think your nice pathologist friend Peláez could help?'

'He'll be able to tell us what it dies of.'

'Oh, Luis, don't wish it dead on us!'

At least she would have something to fill her days other than the confessional box in the church around the corner, Luis thought.

'What about putting lunch up? I have to go out again.'

'Very well, Luis. Put the television on ready for the news.'

She brought in the bread shaped like a crown of thorns and a battered enamel casserole full of the lentil stew, and began to say a long and complicated grace in which he was supposed to utter the responses against the increasing volume of the television interview programme which preceded the news. With one eye on the television screen and the other on him disapproving of the unintelligibly muttered responses he was managing, she served the stew and crossed herself twice, kissing her right thumb as she completed the gesture.

'Eat up. There's plenty of stew just for the two of us, with Diego away. I hope you haven't been spoiling your appetite by eating *tapas*,' she said, looking at him sharply.

'No, no, we've been busy on that case in Alfonso XII. I've just had to interview the bereaved parents.'

'Was the boy loose-living, Luis? I'm sure he must have been to come to such a bad end.'

'He seems to have led a normal sort of life,' Bernal said.

'Anyway, we think he was murdered.'

'That just shows. Decent people don't get murdered, Luis.'

They made a pretty good effort at it, thought Luis gloomily.

'What does *Sábado de Gloria* mean to you, Geñita?'

'It's Good Saturday, of course. In the old days at home we used to bake special cakes and walk in the procession that preceded the Mass of Glory. It was the best feast-day of the year, until those cardinals in Rome decided to demote it. Why do you ask?'

'Well you see, this dead journalist jotted down the phrase on a piece of paper and I want to know why.'

'Oh, Luis, his thoughts must have turned to God at the last, and to Christ's suffering at Calvary. He can't have been all bad.'

'Well, that's one possible explanation.'

Bernal was making heavy weather of the greasy stew and particularly wanted to avoid being offered a second helping, but Eugenia's attention was divided today between the actress being interviewed on *Aquí y Ahora* and the continuing poor state of health of the canary, which was lying on its side whimpering quietly at the bottom of its cage.

After refusing some of the old, cracked Manchegan cheese she now brought out, he accepted an orange which he ate rapidly. Then he said he had to leave at once to go on with his enquiries.

'I'll have a *tortilla* waiting for you at ten,' she said.

He never ceased to be amazed at her inability to think of any dinner dish other than a somewhat burnt Spanish omelette, into which she threw all the leftovers, and there were understandably many of these.

3 p.m.
Pausing only to listen to the headlines on the television news bulletin, which mainly concerned the dismantling of

the Movement and speculation on when the large red
yoke-and-arrows emblem on the Falangist headquarters
in the Calle de Alcalá no. 44 would be taken down, Bernal
went down in the rackety lift and emerged into the cold
street once more. He called into Félix Pérez's bar for a
cortado – he only liked a dash of milk in his coffee after
meals – and a *copa* of Carlos III brandy.

Bernal took a taxi to the Calle de Barceló and, as usual,
paid it off outside the Cafetería Pablos, some doors away
from the entrance to the block where he had his secret
apartment, then strolled along the street towards the
Barceló Theatre and stopped to look at the announce-
ments outside. Making sure no one had followed him, he
unlocked the street door of the apartment block, which had
an automatic porter, and took the lift to the fifth floor and
entered the studio flat.

Here in the warmth and comfort his cares temporarily
left him. He took off his street clothes, slipped into a terry
towel dressing-gown and put on a cassette of Massenet's
Manon on the Hitachi music centre. Relaxing on the divan,
his mind puzzled over the Santos case, and stuck obses-
sively with the 'Saturday of Glory' phrase. What could it
mean? Santos didn't seem to have been a religious man or
to have done any religious features for the agency; it was
all personal or political stuff. Slowly he drifted into a
somewhat uneasy sleep.

5 p.m.

Bernal woke with a start in the darkened room, and felt for
his service revolver under the pillow. He had sensed
rather than heard the faint click of the door latch and the
soft footsteps in the hall. The cassette of the opera had
switched itself off long since, but there was a very faint
hum from the loudspeakers.

When the door opened and he saw the shape of the
person who entered, he relaxed his grasp on the revolver
and snuggled into the bedclothes once more. The figure

undressed silently, tiptoed into the bathroom and closed the door. There was a sound of teeth being cleaned, and then the delicate hiss of an aerosol scent spray. Moments later she crept into bed alongside him and he stirred from his pretended sleep.

'What time is it, Consuelo?'

She nuzzled up to him and whispered, 'Five o'clock, Luchi.'

'What took you so long?'

'We had a problem in striking the day's balance. It's all right now, though.'

'Have you eaten?'

'I had a snack in the Cafetería Pablos before coming up.'

They kissed, at first delicately, almost shyly, and then very passionately. She extended her whole nude body against his, fitting herself comfortably against his corpulence, and gradually they began to make love.

He had met Consuelo Lozano for the first time two years earlier, when he had been investigating a hold-up in the branch of the bank where she worked. They had been attracted to one another from the outset, although she was almost thirty years his junior. A shy, ungainly girl, he had thought, with the true Titian hair of the natural Spanish blonde. Blondes in the Nordic sense were rarely to be seen in the Peninsula, though there were plenty of girls who managed to appear so with the aid of peroxide. But the colour of their eyes and the sallowness of their complexions always gave the pretence away, not to mention the glimpse of the dark roots of their hair when they did not dye it regularly. Consuelo had blue-grey eyes and a pale skin. She did not bronze well in the sun, but tended to have freckles, which she loathed, with the result that she never went to swimming pools or beaches.

When interviewing her, he had discovered that she was the youngest daughter of four, the only one left at home to look after her crippled mother, who lived near the Glorieta de Quevedo. After solving the case, Bernal had invited her out for a coffee in the Dólar bar on the corner of Alcalá and the Gran Vía. She had accepted only very reluctantly, probably because she wished to bring their conversation inside the bank to a rapid conclusion, since she thought her colleagues were looking at her curiously. Shy and tongue-tied with men of her own age or younger, she got on better with older men. Bernal thought it certain that she was looking for a paternal relationship, having lost her father when she was eleven, and slowly, over many weeks, she came to accept him in that role. It had taken him six months to get her to visit his apartment in the Calle de Barceló, and on that occasion she had kissed him for the first time. He had bought her many presents, which embarrassed her, but they found a growing reliance on each other. He gave her the confidence she lacked, and she was a sympathetic and intelligent listener to his professional and family problems.

It was a year before she agreed to sleep with him for the first time and it had to be in the dark at that; he discovered with wonderment that at twenty-seven she was still a virgin. He had been entirely gentle, but awakened great depths of passion in her, so that a year later he found that she was instructing him in the further reaches of sexual fulfilment, bringing him to an ecstasy he had never experienced with Eugenia, who regarded the sexual act as about the most indecent manner of procreation the Deity could have thought of. 'Typical of a man to think of that way,' she used to mutter, rather blasphemously, Bernal considered. Nor had he felt such release with the series of street girls he had gone with throughout his married life. With Consuelo it was as though their flesh became literally one, until he could not tell which limb belonged to her and which to him. There was a sort of chemical interaction between them, which meant that nothing about her body was unpleasant for him. It seemed odourless, always with the same temperature, slightly cooler than his, and felt like soft velvet. He dozed again into a gentle sleep.

6 p.m.

Awakened by the hiss of the shower, Bernal felt for the switch of the bedside light and for his packet of Kaiser and the gold Flaminaire lighter Consuelo had given him for Christmas. He reflected with some amusement on a remark by the novelist Cela he had read in a weekly magazine, that for Spaniards the siesta was the time for *cachondeo*, or randiness. It was certainly so for him, because secret sex in the afternoon fitted best into his daily time-table. On Sundays, of course, there was more scope, and on holidays, which for the past year he had always taken with Consuelo, while his wife went to her farmhouse in the country or on her 'spiritual exercises' organized by her parish priest in some distant nunnery.

He and Consuelo never went to the theatre or to the first night of a new film, in case they met people they knew, and they ate out together in Madrid very rarely, and then only in some discreet restaurant in one of the less fashionable suburbs. They had holidayed out of the Peninsula together twice, once in Paris at Easter-time the year before and once in Venice in the summer, but they always booked their air tickets separately and did not make any sign of recognition until they got to their destination, where they had looked for an hotel on the spot. After all, adultery was still a crime in Spain, where there was no divorce, and it was punishable, for the woman involved, by up to six months' imprisonment.

When Consuelo emerged in a green silk dressing-gown, smelling of Worth's *Je Reviens* eau de toilette, he bestirred himself to take a shower while she made coffee for their *merienda*.

'I brought up some of those iced custard éclairs that you like, Luis.'

'You'll make me even fatter, Consuelito. You know

very well I can't resist them.' He had noted before that she called him Luchi before they made love, and Luis afterwards. Whether she thought the former of these names more masculine, more *macho*, he wasn't sure, but it pleased him, since no one had ever called him by it other than she. Eugenia tended to call him by the more childish 'Luisito'.

As he indulged himself in a second éclair, Bernal gave Consuelo a rapid account of the Santos case.

With her usual clarity of mind, she asked, 'Have you checked his bank account to see if he made the monthly payments for his girl friend's flat by banker's order?'

'Paco should be doing that this afternoon.'

'Surely he must have had a photograph of her? Wasn't there one in his wallet?' she asked.

'Prieto is holding all the personal stuff for his finger-printing. We should be able to get at it this evening.'

'And the *Sábado de Gloria* phrase? Have you considered that it might be a kind of password, or the name for an operation of some kind?'

'That crossed my mind,' Bernal said. 'Remember that Franco and the generals who rose against the Second Republic used the password "*Sin novedad*" – "Nothing to report", so that the phrase would pass unnoticed in telegrams and so on. I suppose the old phrase for "Easter Saturday" would attract little attention during Holy Week.'

'But that means that whatever is being planned will happen at Easter weekend,' said Consuelo, 'otherwise at any other time the phrase would be thought very odd. The date must therefore be fixed.'

'And you think Santos found out about it and was bumped off to keep him silent?' Bernal asked her.

'Well, it all sounds very far-fetched, but I suppose it's possible.'

'Not so far-fetched. Only recently, a little bird from the

Second Brigade told me, they dismantled a Fascist plot to assassinate the Minister for the Interior and they only arrested the plotters and discovered their arms factory three days before the planned date.'

'Why did they move in so late? They must have got wind of it before then,' said Consuelo.

'Of course. But one doesn't enquire too closely into the tensions within the political section. There are too many layers of intrigue, with so many of them jogging one another for the positions of power.'

'No doubt some of them wouldn't have been sorry to have an assassination to stir things up and rock the democratic boat before it's really launched.'

'I keep out of it all, Consuelo, but I'm afraid this case is going to be troublesome.' He told her about the interview with the subsecretary.

'Then they have smelled something political in it?' she asked.

'It looks like it. I'd better get dressed and go back there to see what's happening.'

'I'll have to go shopping in a minute to get some things in for mother's supper,' she said. 'Will I see you tomorrow?'

'Of course, love. I'll keep you up to date on this case. You always help me clarify my thoughts.'

'Is that all I'm good at?' she teased. They embraced passionately, and he made as if to draw her back to the divan, but she pulled away, saying, 'Now, now, Luchi. That's enough for today. You'll never solve the Santos case in bed.'

'I suppose I'd better get back. I've got a new female inspector by the way.'

Consuelo tried unsuccessfully to hide her sudden rush of jealousy.

'Is she pretty? I know your penchant for young girls.'

'Oh, come off it, Consuelo, she's a fine product of the Régime, straight from the police school and trained in the latest anti-personnel karate. I wouldn't dare.'

'What's her name, and is she pretty?' demanded Consuelo.

'Elena Fernández, daughter of a rich building contractor, and yes, she's quite good-looking, and regards me as a father and head-of-state figure rolled into one.'

'That's because of your likeness to the late Caudillo, of course. I can't imagine what I saw in you.'

Consuelo was much more left-wing in her opinions than Luis, and twelve years in a bank had made her bitterly anti-capitalist, especially since she worked in the director's office and had witnessed some of the shady dealings that had gone on under the dictatorship and the flight of capital to numbered Swiss accounts that had taken place 'since Franco's illness and which had accelerated after his death.

'Don't worry, Consuelito, she's not my type; only you are, you know that. Anyway, Ángel's taken her in tow, at my behest.'

'God help the poor soul, then, unless they taught her in the police school how to handle wild animals.' Consuelo knew of Ángel only from Bernal's accounts of him, and she pictured him as a voracious beast as far as women were concerned.

'I think she will be able to manage him, from what I've seen so far.'

'We'll see. Perhaps you'll have the first scandal of a pregnant lady detective.'

'Now, now. She knows what's what. Her friends will have told her which chemists sell the pill under the counter.' Bernal completed his dressing and put on his overcoat. 'I'll see you about four tomorrow, then. Look after yourself, and don't let them pinch your bum on the Metro.'

'Now, Luis, you know that doesn't give me a thrill. In any case I'll walk up Fuencarral and do my shopping on the way. I'll clear up here first.'

'See you tomorrow then, love. *Cuidadito* – take care.'

7 p.m.
In the office in the DGS building, Paco Navarro was puzzling over Prieto's interim report on the fingerprints found in Santos's apartment. The women's prints they had found, other than the cleaning woman's, were too blurred and partial to be of use; certainly there was no right index print good enough to be checked against the central files of the Documento Nacional de Identidad, a task which in any case would have taken many days or even weeks. There were some good prints of a right-hand glove, of cotton weave, which they had found on the inner side of the terrace door in Santos's studio and in the next-door apartment as well. Some oil from the door-hinge had got on to this glove, Prieto's report explained, and they would be able to match the prints against the glove itself or any other prints from it left at the scene of any other break-in. But the likelihood was, thought Navarro, that the burglar would have destroyed or thrown away the gloves afterwards.

He listened to Ángel and Elena chatting across the room as they went carefully through the papers from Santos's apartment.

'Found any receipts or bills connected with Santos's other flat, the one he was keeping Marisol in?' he asked.

'Nothing yet, Paco,' answered Ángel.

Just then Elena uttered an exclamation. 'I've found a photograph at the back of the wallet. Could this be Marisol?'

Paco went over to look as Ángel said, 'Yes, I'm pretty sure that's the brunette I saw him with, though it must have been taken some years ago, I'd say.'

The girl in the photograph was posed in a white one-piece bathing-costume, with her back arched against a palm-tree – perhaps taken on holiday in Benidorm or

Alicante, Paco thought.

'Take it down to Photography, Ángel, and get them to make enlargements; say ten copies.'

'OK, Paco. Elena could go on looking through the rest to see if she can find an address or telephone number. Santos's friends said that Marisol lived in the Calle de Lavapiés, but it's a long, steep street and the houses are like warrens. I hope we don't have to do a door-to-door to find her.'

'Well, we may have to,' said Paco. 'I'll help Elena with the rest.' He gazed in dismay at the drawerfuls of papers Prieto had removed from the studio in Alfonso XII.

The phone rang and Navarro went over to answer it.

'*Dígame. Sí, sí.*' He listened intently for a while, then replied, 'Many thanks, Varga, for all your efforts. We look forward to having your written report some time tomorrow.'

Bernal entered briskly as he was putting down the phone.

'Good evening, Elena. Anything new, Paco?'

'Elena found a photo, probably of the girl Marisol, which Ángel has taken to get enlarged. I've asked for ten copies.'

'Have you been round to Santos's bank?' asked Bernal.

'Yes, *jefe,* and I've got photocopies of his bank statements over the last two years. It looks as if he or the girl paid the rent in cash each month, since there's no record of any regular payment. I've also been on to his doctor, who says Santos never suffered from depression as far as he knows, and only ever had minor ailments. He's sending us a copy of the medical record.'

'Well, that doesn't get us far,' said Bernal.

'Varga has just rung,' said Paco, 'to say he found bloodstains under the leaves on the upper branches of the two trees outside Santos's apartment. There are only minute stains, because the leaves are only just breaking out of bud and didn't provide much shelter from the rain.

He's done two of the blood tests, and those stains, as well as the ones from the roof tiles, correspond to Santos's blood group, O Rhesus positive. He's doing the MN, Hr, and P Factor tests on the samples now, as a final check. The stains on the trees are level with the upper part of the sixth floor, but he thinks there could have been more higher up, which the rain washed off, because of the downward spray effect of the ones he found.'

'He's a good man. The best technician we've got, Paco.'

'Prieto's interim report on the fingerprints is here, *jefe*. You'll see it helps to confirm the route taken by the burglars, but it's not conclusive about whether there was more than one burglar, or whether he or they were distinct from the earlier assailants.'

'We'll see what Varga turns up when he has time to look at the rest of the technical evidence. He'll have looked into the door locks with an illuminated probe to search for signs of carbon or scratches on the levers. Did he say anything about the jemmy-marks on the terrace door?'

'No, chief. He's probably not got round to checking the file on those yet.'

Ángel now returned and greeted Bernal. 'We should have the photographs in half an hour, *jefe*. Shall we start a house-to-house enquiry in the Calle de Lavapiés tonight?'

'Well, if you and Elena feel up to it, we could give it a try for an hour or so. We'll start at the top and work downwards, you and Elena on the west side and I'll do the east side. Most of the porters are likely to be in their lodges, since it's a cold evening, and we may be lucky and find her straight away. Make a note of the buildings which have an automatic porter or where the porter is out, so that we can return tomorrow morning. I suggest that you and Elena go there separately, and that you spin a yarn about Marisol being your cousin, whose exact address you don't know, and whose mother is ill in Cáceres, so that you have to find her urgently. I'll do the other side in the normal way, showing my warrant card. We could meet at about half past eight in that bar half-way down Lavapiés, where there's a tiny square with old-fashioned lanterns. The bar's painted green, and I think it's called Jesusín's.'

'OK, chief. We'll take a taxi to Tirso de Molina.'

'Well, for six pesetas each you could go on the Metro. It's only one stop, you know, and you'd save the Group's expenses a bit.'

'Yes, come on, Ángel,' said Elena, who was thrilled with the prospect of some action for the second time on her first day. 'It'll be fun and we'll blend better with the crowds going home from work.'

'Righto, if you can stand the crush on Line 1.'

'I'm game,' she said. 'It's just as bad on the buses that go up the Castellana.'

Over lunch Ángel had elicited from her that her home was in the elegant suburb of El Viso, just off the upper end of the Calle de Serrano, and he privately thought she would find the tightly-packed company on the Metro Line 1, direction Portazgo, rather different from travelling in the Microbus 6 up the Castellana, even if there was standing room only on it. Still, she was keen to try anything, or almost anything, he thought. He was still smarting from the sharp rebuff she had given him after his first advances to her after lunch, during their *sobremesa* chat.

Bernal sent Ángel and Elena on ahead, so that they wouldn't emerge in his company at Tirso de Molina Metro station. Not only was there a chance that people would recognize him as a policeman, but it was also the quarter where he was born, so he was well known to many of the older people. As he fought through the crush to get out of the tube-train, he checked that his revolver was safely tucked away in his shoulder holster; there were many pickpockets in the Metro crowds, and it would be ludicrous to have his service gun pinched.

7.30 p.m.

Out under the still bare trees of the square now, Bernal

buttoned his overcoat up to the neck in the chill of the night air, in which he could feel a faint warning of rain to come – that Madrid air, famous for not being able to blow out a candle, yet it could kill a man. He walked a short way down the Calle de la Magdalena and made for the corner of the Calle de Lavapiés, beginning his enquiries at the first house on the left.

This quarter was to *madrileños* what Cheapside was to Londoners: it was the original home of the artisans and working-men of the old city. Lavapiés had been famous in the seventeenth century for its bun-shops, and in the eighteenth and nineteenth for the style, wit, haughtiness and popular elegance of dress of its *manolos* and *manolas*, so often depicted by Goya in his drawings and by Ramón de la Cruz in his prose sketches. Their modern descendants were the *chulos* and *chulas*, who fell somewhere above the working class and below the middle class, but in a real sense outside these social strata; they had their own *modo de ser* or way of being. The women tended to shun churches and priests, yet they had little statues of the Virgin in their houses; their religion was really a form of superstition passed on from mother to daughter, without any formal instruction. They walked along the streets in a proud manner, looking neither to right nor left and ignoring in a devastating way any man who dared to call out or whisper a *piropo* or compliment in their ear. Their houses tended to be furnished in execrable style, but were enlivened with bowls of plastic flowers and a canary in a tiny gilt cage in the window.

The *chulos* had a distinctive hair-style and a sleek, almost effeminate dress. In the past century, Bernal remembered reading in one of his books on old Madrid, they could be made friends for life with a Havana cigar and a short chat about bullfighting. Today they were a kind of hustler, who would offer their sexual favours to anyone they happened to fancy if the price was right, and they were always on the margin of petty theft and violence.

In a sense they and their ancestors the *manolos* had been hippies long before hippiedom. They worked at manual tasks in the mornings, and emerged like peacocks or birds of paradise in the evenings to throng the central streets of the capital.

Bernal had no luck in the first few houses, but then one of the concierges recognized him. Dressed in peasant black, she sat behind her half-door watching television and darning socks, while keeping a sharp look-out for the activities of her residents. Before he could produce his warrant card, she exclaimed:

'Luis Bernal! *¡Caramba!* It's years since you've been back to see us! I knew your mother so well. Poor soul. How hard she worked in that bar to bring you all up. And you've all done so well. Are you still an inspector? No, I bet you're a *comisario* by now.'

'Yes, Señora, they've promoted me.' He tried hard to remember her name.

'I knew they would. What can I do for you? I hope none of my people is in trouble.'

Bernal produced the photograph of Marisol. 'Have you ever seen this girl in the district?'

'What has she done?' asked the old woman sharply. Bernal remembered the code of the working class; they would never grass on one of their number unless they actively disapproved of the crime they were supposed to have committed.

'Nothing, as far as I know, Doña Pilar.' He hoped he had recalled her name correctly. 'But her boy-friend has been found dead and we're trying to break the news to her if we can find her. All we know is that she lives in this street.'

'I see. Well, she's never set foot in this house, but I think I've seen her in the bakery down the street a couple of times. Quiet girl, not a *chula*, you understand, nothing bright about her. Rather subdued, as though she had a problem. Lots of make-up she wore, but these young people, you can't tell if they're whores or decent girls these days.'

'Do you happen to know what she's called?'

'Marisol, the baker's wife calls her. You could ask when you get down to the square.'

'Well, many thanks, Señora. You've been a great help. It's nice to be back among real people for a while.'

'Don't forget us, Luisito, in all the high-up circles you move in now.'

Bernal thought she had a pretty extraordinary idea of a detective's life, but he didn't press the point.

The other *porteras* further down the street were able to add nothing to what old Doña Pilar had told him; in most cases they knew, or admitted to knowing, even less.

8.30 p.m.

As he approached the corner of the alleyway known as Ministrales Chica, Bernal could see no sign of Ángel and Elena on the other side of the street, which was totally deserted now, though the bars lower down were doing a good trade. As he crossed in front of the dark entrance to the alley, a sixth sense caused him to wheel to the left just as a dark figure threatened him with a flick-knife. 'Give me all the money you've got. And your watch.'

'What did you say?' gasped Bernal.

The young *chulo* repeated his demand with growing signs of panic, looking nervously up and down the street.

Bernal, who happened to be smoking a Kaiser, quickly pushed the lighted cigarette into the youth's face, brought his knee up into the other's groin and grabbed the wrist that held the knife, twisting it away with an agility remarkable even to himself. The *chulo* screamed from the sudden pain, dropped the knife and pulled away. He ran up the alley and turned into the Calle de Ministrales.

Bernal found himself panting and shaken. He did not attempt a pursuit. Why had he reacted in that way, and not by pretending to open his coat and jacket for his wallet and then producing his revolver? Instinctive aggression, he thought; a product of the anger the youth had provoked in him. He realized he hadn't wanted only to defend himself, but actively to commit violence on his attacker. It was this realization, more than the assault, that now made him shake. He hastened down the street to the small triangle lit by elegant Isabelline lamps mounted in threes, into which electric bulbs had been installed. Under the lamplight he could see that his right hand was bleeding from a superficial cut from his struggle for the knife, which he had picked up afterwards by the blade. Prieto could get prints from it, he thought, and they could track the youth down in a matter of days, or hours, if he had a record.

He wrapped his handkerchief around his palm, and still holding the knife by the tip of the blade, went into Jesusín's bar, where Elena and Ángel were chatting over a coffee.

'Any luck?' he asked, with as much calm as he could muster. They looked in astonishment at his hand and at the knife.

'What happened, *jefe*?' asked Ángel anxiously.

'Oh, one of the local *chulos* tried to hold me up for all the money I was carrying and my watch. I took this from him, but he got away.'

'Have a glass of brandy, *jefe*. I'll ring for a car to come and fetch you. You need to get the hand cleaned and bandaged.'

'No, don't make a fuss, Ángel. I'll go into the chemist's down the road and he'll dress it for me.'

Elena said, 'Shall I wrap the knife in a napkin? We may get prints from it.'

'Elena, you're forgetting all your training and talking like an amateur. You must never wrap an object in cloth or paper if you want to get prints from it. They'd get rubbed off by friction during the journey to the lab. You must suspend the object by a string, in a box if possible.'

Elena looked crestfallen. 'Sorry, I forgot, chief. But how will we find a box?'

'Ask the barman. He'll have some old carton or other, and a piece of string.'

Bernal downed the cheap brandy and the colour flooded back into his face. 'I'd better have a coffee as well. *Póngame un cortado, por favor.*'

'Yes, sir. Are you all right?' asked the barman, looking at Bernal's hand.

'It's just a surface cut on the palm, that's all. Will the chemist's be open?'

'He should be, sir, until ten. He's on late duty this week.'

'We'll go with you, *jefe*,' Ángel said. 'But let me ring for a car.'

'All right. Tell the driver to come to the corner of the Plaza de Lavapiés. We'll stroll down as far as there not to attract any more attention. Did you find out anything about the girl?'

'No, *jefe*. Though one *portera* said she had seen her walk past a few times, with a little dog on a lead, which does confirm that she lives in the district.'

'I got the same answer from an old *portera*, who remembered me from when I was a child.' Bernal drank the hot coffee, and suddenly felt better. 'Let's get off to the chemist's, then. I think we'll leave this enquiry until tomorrow morning. I don't want either of you to get knifed in a doorway. You two can get off home in a taxi.'

'But we can't leave you alone, *jefe*,' said Elena with concern. 'Remember I'm trained in karate and ju-jitsu.'

'You still have to face the real thing, Elena, and I'm not going to expose you to that. Your father would never forgive me. Ángel, see the girl home, now.'

'OK, chief. But we'll walk down to the chemist's with you. The car should be waiting for you at the corner of the square, and it's only a few yards to walk. We'll take the Metro if there's no sign of a taxi.'

'You should find one coming up the Calle de Valencia,'

Bernal said, picking up the box the barman had provided and in which they had suspended the knife. 'I'll see you both in the office in the morning.'

9 p.m.
In the DGS building, Bernal took the carton to Prieto's laboratory and was surprised to find it in darkness. Surely the man hadn't finished all the reports for him so quickly? He tried the door and found it unlocked. Entering, he switched on the light and placed the carton on Prieto's desk, scribbling a hasty note to ask him to check the knife handle for prints; though he feared they would fade considerably during the night.

In his own office he found a note from Navarro on top of a report from Varga. The burglars who had entered Santos's apartment had used a skeleton key to get into the next-door studio, but no skeleton key appeared to have been used on Santos's door. His murderers must therefore have had a key of their own, otherwise they could not have double locked the door on leaving. He still hadn't found out how they had left the building without being seen, Bernal reflected. He put the report away in his filing cabinet and locked it. He glanced at his watch, which he had come so close to losing in the attack on him; nearly 9.20. He decided to call it a day. Putting out the lights and locking the outer door, he shouted goodnight to the downstairs *gris*, who was pouring himself some hot beverage from a Thermos flask. 'Good night, Superintendent. You'd do well to take a taxi. It has started to rain.'

'There never are any when it rains,' said Bernal gloomily.

9.30 p.m.
He was lucky, however, and got home in a few minutes.

Eugenia was still worrying over the canary. 'It's no better, Luis. It's shivering more than ever.'

'Light the electric fire, Geñita, and put the cage near it

on the floor.' He struggled out of his damp overcoat. 'It's going to be a wet night.'

She noticed the bandage around his hand. 'What have you done to your hand?'

'I cut it on a knife. It's not a deep cut, and the palm usually heals quickly. A chemist dressed the wound for me.'

'Shouldn't you have an injection, just in case?'

'I think it will be all right. If I don't feel well later, I'll call the police surgeon.'

'He could look at the canary for us at the same time,' she said.

There was nothing like getting one's priorities right, he thought.

'I'd be the talk of the place if I called him out for that, Eugenia.'

She switched on the television news, and went off to the kitchen to make the usual *tortilla* of leftovers.

'Shall I warm up some of the lentil stew for you?'

'I don't think I could face it, thanks. Just a small piece of the omelette. And bring some of that red wine from Cebreros.'

The rain splashed against the windows and the pots on the terrace. Just an evening like any other, Luis thought.

TUESDAY, 5 APRIL

8.30 a.m.

The canary had had a bad night, and Bernal was glad to get away from Eugenia's wailing and take his usual second (and real) breakfast in Félix Pérez's bar.

If he could be said to have a local, it was this old bar, which seemed not to have changed from the Madrid of his youth, apart from the television set which had been tucked away high overhead in the gloomy area above the door. On top of the ornate till there stood a coloured pottery statue of a man making the rude gesture of crossed fists, one raised in a menacing way, with the warning inscription below, that always made Bernal smile: '*Quieres fiado, ¡toma!*' – 'You want credit? Up yours!'

He realized that he himself was a paradox, like most men over forty: he had a strong urge to make his own living quarters modern and comfortable, but he liked his bars ancient, unpretentious, and above all 'unrefurbished'.

As he emerged on to the street, he noticed that the sticky buds of the chestnut-trees that edged the Retiro Park opposite were showing the first signs of green life. Quite soon now they would burst forth into huge white candles.

Bernal decided he wouldn't join the crush on the Metro; the rain had stopped during the night and there were faint signs of spring in the grimy air. He realized that the attack on him the night before had left him nervous and slightly sick. A stupid little incident, common in that neighbourhood and in many other suburbs of the city – yet it niggled him. Why should the *chulo* have picked on him? Well, he was old, short and well-dressed – a typical target for petty hold-ups. His sudden counter-attack must have left his assailant feeling more frightened than he.

He walked briskly down towards the noble five-arched Gate of Alcalá, and recollected having seen, in his late teens, this eighteenth-century arch festooned on either side with three large vertical red banners, bearing the hammer and sickle and the portraits of Marx, Lenin and Stalin respectively. Or was the third one Bakunin? He couldn't remember now.

He wondered whether there wasn't a real chance of history repeating itself, but he doubted it. The Régime might have had its head chopped off, but its grindingly-thorough machinery still operated in every walk of life. The truly massive police organization, with its three branches of Policía Armada, Guardia Civil and Municipal Police proportionately the largest in any Western country, still watched, still reported, still took brisk action; the new Government had even pumped in money for the latest in arms, vehicles and equipment. So long used to giving a single, intense loyalty, the forces of law and order hardly hesitated to transfer it to the man who appeared to be in command, however zany and inexplicable his actions might seem. It was even conceivable, thought Bernal, that the higher echelons of the police might begin to sense that they would yet get a 'democratized' Spain that had not really changed at all, just as France had been an apparently free country on and off since the Directoire, or England since the Restoration.

Walking down the slope of the Calle de Alcalá as it ran towards the Plaza de la Cibeles, he glanced into the windows of the Café Lion, formerly the haunt of ancient scholars and bullfighting fans, which was still dead at this hour. He recalled that it had been in the meeting-hall under this old café that the Falangist anthem *Cara al Sol* had first been sung. Opposite the side of the main Post Office now, a grandiose and ugly wedding-cake which gloried in the name of Palacio de Comunicaciones, he reflected that this square, with the statue and fountain of the Great Mother goddess Cybele in its centre, was really the arterial hub of the modern city.

Waiting for an illuminated little green man to signal his passage across the Paseo de Calvo Sotelo he was horror-stricken as he was every day at how the fine northward vista of trees and fountains along the Paseo towards the Plaza de Colón was now spoilt by the unfinished twin towers of the Colón building. The Plaza de Colón itself was in the process of an ugly reconstruction in triumphal Fascist style. Bernal felt glad to be approaching old age, with the likelihood of not living long enough to see his Madrid totally rebuilt. It could still offer unexpected forgotten corners of its history, though.

He reached in safety the corner of the War Ministry, which occupied the elegant Palace of Buenavista, and he transversed Alcalá through the brand-new pedestrian subway, taking breath on the escalator which brought him up outside the Banco de España. A little way up the street he paused to buy a packet of Kaiser cigarettes at the *estanco* and took his first inhalation of black tobacco of the day, hoping he would manage on less than two packets for once. He checked his watch against the neon digital clock which surmounted the Bellas Artes building, and noted that the temperature was still shown as 8°C.

As he entered his office he found Paco and Elena already at work on the remainder of Santos's personal effects. Bernal greeted them, and they both asked how his hand was and how he felt.

'I feel grand, really. More annoyed than anything else. Have you come across anything of interest?'

'Not yet,' said Paco.

Ángel came in at that moment and Bernal suggested that he and Elena go down to the Calle de Lavapiés and complete the door-to-door enquiry.

'If we draw a blank, shall we try the neighbouring streets?' asked Ángel.

'Yes, especially those off the Plaza de Lavapiés.'

The two young inspectors left, glad to be out and doing something.

Paco asked Bernal, 'Have you seen this advert in the morning paper?'

He handed him one of the Fascist dailies, whose circulation had fallen considerably with the success of the liberal daily *El País*. The advertisement read:

SÁBADO DE GLORIA (SATURDAY OF GLORY)

All ex-combatants are requested to gather at the tomb of Generalísimo Franco in El Valle de los Caídos this Easter Saturday. A funeral Mass for the Caudillo will be sung at 12 noon. Special coaches will leave the Plaza de Oriente at 10.30 a.m. No charge. Medals and uniforms will be worn.

¡Arriba España! ¡Viva Franco!

Bernal thought the final war-cry of 'Long Live Franco!' particularly odd. He asked Paco, 'Has the Minister of the Interior permitted this gathering?'

'Apparently so, *jefe*, on condition that no funeral address or eulogy will be spoken. No cabinet minister will be attending, but the Caudillo's widow and family are expected. The ex-combatants asked for permission to hold a rally in front of the Royal Palace, but this has been refused. They shouldn't cause any problems, up there in the sierra.'

Bernal asked, 'Has the ex-combatant organization put this advert in all the newspapers?'

'No,' said Paco, 'only in the right-wing ones. I understand that coaches will be coming from all over the Peninsula, but the Movement won't be paying for them this time. It's rumoured that the Argentinian, Italian and Chilean Fascists are putting up the money.'

'I hope the Government knows what it's doing,' said Bernal. 'Are the Cabinet leaving Madrid on holiday at the weekend?'

'Only a few of them. The President, the Minister of the Interior and the Defence Minister will be staying on. So will the King.'

'Perhaps it's just as well, under the circumstances. It wouldn't take much to produce a *coup d'état*.'

The phone rang just then and Paco Navarro picked it up. 'Yes, yes, I'll tell him. He'll no doubt come down at once.' He put down the phone and looked gravely at Bernal. 'Prieto wants you to go down and see him. Some of his Liftprints from the Santos case appear to be missing. He swears they were there last night.'

'I'll go down at once. I wonder if he's had a chance to examine the flick-knife and check it out for prints.'

9 a.m.

Prieto looked angry and worried at the same time. 'Superintendent, someone's been tampering with our prints. I've questioned all the assistants and they claim not to have moved anything. But we've lost some of the Liftprints from Santos's apartment and the gloveprints. Fortunately I sent the film I took of them to the Photographic Section to be developed overnight, but it's worrying that the originals are missing.'

Bernal was relieved. 'Well, we've got photographic copies and perhaps whoever took them didn't realize that. Get over to Photography and make sure they haven't lost or spoilt them. By the way, did you find the flick-knife I left in a carton on your desk and my note?'

'A flick-knife? No, no, I haven't seen it. Listen, you chaps, who was the first in this morning?'

A pale, nervous youth spoke up. 'I was, *jefe*, but I found the door unlocked. I thought the cleaners had left it like that.'

'Did you see a box or carton on my desk?'

'No, chief,' said the pale youth. 'Your desk was clear. The mail hasn't come yet.'

Bernal was greatly disturbed by this lack of internal security. 'Look, Prieto, get on to Security and report this at once. They will look into it and question the watchman and the cleaners. The flick-knife is not part of the Santos case, so don't worry about it. Make sure you get Photography to make second copies of all the prints and send the spare set up to me. I'll call in to see how Varga is getting on.'

Varga's technical laboratory was in a basement and was full of the most extraordinary-looking apparatus and testing devices. There were separate laboratories for blood and physical analyses and a whole Institute of Toxicology. Varga was working with apparent clarity amid this confusion, and greeted Bernal cheerfully; 'The trees were the limit, Superintendent, the limit! I hope you haven't got any more strange requests.'

'No, not today, at least not yet, Varga. Sorry about the trees. I forgot you have no head for heights. But your report on the stains you found clinches the murder theory. Has the forensic lab done the final blood cross-checks?'

'Yes, and the stains all correspond to Santos's blood. Of course they might correspond to a couple of hundred other people in Madrid, but with the new Rhesus tests now able to establish eight separate groups, and the MN, Hr, and P Factor as additional checks, we can narrow the type down very closely. Your theory about the door locks is probably right. Remember that there are at least three ways of locking a door from the outside to give the impression that it was locked by a suicide from within, but all these methods leave traces: carbon or soap in the lock, scratches on the levers or key when the *ouistiti* half-moon forceps are used, or a matchstick or some similar object on the floor inside in cases where the key is still in the lock. My first reaction to a locked-door suicide is to suspect murder.'

'You've done a marvellous job for me, Varga. But look after the evidence carefully and take copies of the photographs where you can.' Varga looked serious as Bernal told him of the tampering with Prieto's Liftprints. 'I'll see to it, Superintendent. It looks fishy. Do you think it's someone inside his department?'

'Could be. But I don't want to kick up a fuss or have them all investigated yet, until I've got further with the case. Take all the care you can, meanwhile.'

'I shall. Good luck with your enquiries. By the way, the jemmy-marks don't correspond to any on the Central files.'

'Well, hang on to a copy of them, in addition to the one you lodge in central records. We don't want any more mysterious disappearances of pieces of evidence.'

9.30 a.m.

On the way back to his office, Bernal called into the police cafeteria for a coffee and was pleased to see there an old colleague who worked in Central Records. Inspector Esteban Ibáñez was born in the Antón Martín quarter like Bernal, and they had been friends from childhood. He had never possessed Luis's drive or success in solving difficult cases, and early on had opted to go into Records, for which he had a phenomenal memory.

'*Hola*, Luis. You've no idea of the problems we've been having with the change of régime. The political records are being gone over by the high-ups, who won't even let us see what they're doing, and I'm sure that a lot of our stuff is being taken away or destroyed.' An extremely orderly man, he was obviously incensed at these incursions into his territory. 'But I've got a good memory, as you know, and I'm keeping account of the names that are suddenly being given clean sheets. And it's not only the political files. A lot of the Fraud Squad stuff is being cleaned out as well.'

Bernal felt that Esteban was one of the few people he could trust in the whole DGS. On impulse he asked him, 'What does *Sábado de Gloria* mean, Esteban?'

Ibáñez looked at him hard. 'Why do you ask?'

'Well, the journalist Santos whose death I'm investigating jotted the words down on a piece of paper we found in his desk.'

'And he had found out nothing else about it?'

'Not as far as we can see, but we're still going through his papers.' He told Ibáñez about the burglary in Santos's apartment after his fatal fall.

'We've heard whispers, Luis, about a Fascist plot. You know that four German Fascists were arrested only three days before they were going to assassinate the Minister of the Interior? They've already been allowed to leave the country quietly for Germany. But that's not the end of it. There are Argentinians, Santo Dominicans, Chileans and Italians as well. Alicante seems to be a popular gathering point for them. Something's up, Luis, I can tell you, but I don't know exactly what yet.'

'But the name of this plot, if it is a plot, suggests it's all going to happen this coming Saturday, doesn't it? And you've seen this advert in the morning paper, haven't you?'

'Yes, Luis. It's probably the way of rallying the troops, And it's rumoured that the Government is going to legalize the Communist Party shortly. You've read in the papers, of course, that the Supreme Court tossed the ball back into the Government's lap by ruling that they had no jurisdiction in any administrative matter such as legalizing political parties. The council of ministers is meeting on it this afternoon in the Moncloa Palace.'

'What about the President's personal security?'

'He organizes it himself. Wise chap. Our Minister has also taken extra precautions since the business of the Germans.'

'They can't take enough precautions under the circumstances. We don't want any more celestial journeys.'

Ibáñez he knew was referring to the assassination of the deputy premier Carrero Blanco in December 1973, whose car was blown over the rooftops by a bomb laid under the Calle de Claudio Coello. The perpetrators had never been brought to trial.

'Keep in touch over this, Luis. I'll help all I can, you know that.'

Bernal told him about the prints missing from Prieto's department and Ibáñez looked grave.

'Take care, Luis. Remember that the allegations about the "parallel" police may not be just left-wing imaginings. I've heard strong rumours that someone high up has diverted a large chunk of the funds to set up a secret police within the police with a view of taking over the country if the Government moves too far to the left.'

'If I turn up anything more, I'll give you a ring, Esteban.'

'Don't do that. Come round and see me and we'll have a drink somewhere quiet.'

Luis knew he was thinking that the lines would be tapped.

'Righto, Esteban. Nice to see you again.'

10 a.m.

Paco Navarro was answering the phone as Bernal got back.

'It's Ángel, *jefe*. He's on to the mysterious Marisol, he thinks. He wants us to go and meet him in the Calle del Ave María and he suggests that he send Elena back here to hold the fort.'

'You had better wait for her here, Paco. Call a car for me and I'll go down there at once.'

'He says he'll meet you on the corner of Ave María and Tres Peces.'

That was towards the upper end of Ave María, Bernal remembered; this was childhood territory for him.

'I'll ring through to you, Paco, as soon as we've flushed the girl out. I'll keep Elena to bring her in with us, I think, but I'll see what the circumstances are first.'

As his driver negotiated the narrow streets around Antón Martín and turned into the Calle del Ave María, Bernal recalled that in the reign of Philip II the street had been notorious for its tumbledown houses infested with whores. When some of the dwellings were demolished, the corpses of murdered clients had been found in the wells of some of them, causing the onlookers to exclaim 'Ave Maria!' Bernal noticed that some of the older buildings had been pulled down and neat blocks of flats of similar height and frontage erected in their place, though there was one block, now boarded up, on the right towards the top of the street, which looked as though it had escaped even Philip II's demolition order.

Bernal spotted Ángel and Elena outside a house and told the driver to stop and park further down the street. Ángel said, looking grave, 'You'd better come in and hear the porter's story, *jefe*.'

10.30 a.m.
The porter was a deaf, frightened old man, who exclaimed on seeing Bernal's warrant card, 'Oh Superintendent, it's so lucky you've come. I've been wondering whether to call your people. It's the smell, you see. And the dog howling. The residents have been complaining.'

'This girl Marisol, now,' said Bernal pointing to the photograph. 'Where does she live?'

'Eh, eh?' Bernal repeated the question more loudly.

'I've been telling this young man. That's María Soledad Molina, who lives here on the first floor left. That's just upstairs above my quarters. She's a quiet girl, keeps herself to herself, paints herself a good bit and goes out late at night, but I understand she's a dancer in a club behind the Gran Vía. A well-dressed young man visits her nearly every day.'

Bernal produced a photograph of Raúl Santos and the porter said at once, 'That's him! That's her boy-friend. I think he has a key to her flat, because I've seen him take it out of his pocket when he comes in. He gives me a generous tip from time to time, to look after his girl, he says.'

'When did you see him last?' Bernal shouted out the

question in the quiet of the porter's lodge, with the feeling
that all the neighbours were listening on the staircase.

'Over a week ago. A week yesterday it must have been.
He was carrying a black attaché-case, like you are carrying. Haven't seen him since.'

'When did you see her last, Marisol, that is?' Bernal had
begun to realize that the porter could lip-read, so he moved
his lips in an exaggerated way instead of shouting so
loudly.

'Saturday lunchtime, it was. She was all dressed up and
carrying a small suitcase.'

'Do you think she was going away?'

'She may have been,' said the old man, 'but she often
carries a suitcase to her work. She makes her own costumes
for her turn, you know. She's got an electric sewing
machine up there.' The porter obviously considered this
to be a sign of considerable affluence.

'Have you a key to her door?' Bernal mouthed.

'No, no. We've tried knocking, because her little dog was
barking and whining. She leaves him in when she goes
out, except to take him for a walk in the mornings and late
afternoons. It's not fair on the little thing really. She
shouldn't have gone away and left him locked in, if that's
what she's done. And the awful smell the neighbours have
complained about. The poor little animal must be doing
its business all over the floor.'

Bernal went up the one flight of stairs to Marisol's door.
The stench there was overpowering and familiar to him,
and it wasn't that of canine excrement.

He strode down the stairs and called Ángel. 'Ángel, go
through the patio and see if there's a way in round the
back. Don't actually go in if you find a window open.'

'OK, chief. You think something's happened in there?'

'I'm sure of it, from the smell. I'll send Elena back and
get Paco here.'

He asked the porter to let him use his telephone and
dialled the office.

'Paco, listen. I think we've got another corpse on our hands, but we can't get into the apartment. The porter says that Santos had a key, so bring his key-ring from among his personal effects. Tell Varga to bring tools and his usual equipment, as well as half a dozen surgical masks. The smell is appalling. Then come down yourself with Varga. I'll ring Peláez at the anatomical lab. I'm sending Elena back now in a taxi. She can hold the fort in the office.'

'Right, *jefe*. I'll get things organized.'

Bernal dialled the number of the Instituto Anatómico Forense.

'Dr Peláez, please.' There was a pause. 'Peláez? Bernal here. I think I've got another one for you, in an advanced state of decomposition. We haven't been able to get in yet, but I know by the smell. I thought you might like to have first go at it, before anything is touched and before fresh air is let into the room, to help you with calculating the temperature of the cadaver. You'll need a mask. It'll be overpowering in there.' Bernal gave him the address.

'You stay out of there, Bernal,' said Peláez. 'You know you'll faint on the job. Have you sent for Varga?'

'Yes. He'll be on his way.'

'Well, let him and me go in alone first. That way your people won't trample over everything and destroy the traces. He and I are old hands at working together.'

Bernal sighed with relief and gratitude. 'Righto, Peláez. You'll have this one on a clean sheet.' This turned out to be a most inappropriate remark, as events proved.

Bernal saw Elena in the hall and said, 'I'd like you to go back and look after the office for me. Paco is on his way here.'

'I could stay and take shorthand notes, *jefe*,' she said eagerly.

'I know you could. But Peláez and Varga will have a pocket dictaphone, and it's going to be very unpleasant.'

'Is that smell . . .?'

'Yes, it is. I hope it won't be a thing you'll ever have to get used to.'

She turned white. 'Very well, *jefe*, I'll look for a taxi.'

'Good girl. We'll be back in a couple of hours, I hope. In the meantime, get on to the Gabinete Central de Identificación and ask them to look up María Soledad Molina. We don't know her second surname yet. And give Inspector Ibáñez in Central Criminal Records a ring. Tell him it's an enquiry from me. Ask him to see if she had any criminal record.'

'I will, chief. See you later.'

11 a.m.

Ángel now returned from his reconnaissance of the rear of the house. 'There's a window giving on to a flat roof, which is the roof of the porter's kitchen. It's shut, chief, but I can see faint scratch marks around the latch. We probably could get in that way.'

'But we may destroy vital evidence if we do. We'll wait for Varga and Paco. Paco may have the key to the door from Santos's effects.'

'How long do you think she's been dead, chief?'

'Well, we don't know whether it's her body, but I'd swear there's a putrefying human corpse in there. Can you hear or see the dog from the back window?'

'No, chief. But how many days might it be? If there's no water within its reach, the creature will have died.'

'We'd better be careful opening the door. The dog may be rabid by now,' said Bernal.

'Shouldn't we inform the local chief inspector at the Central Police Station, *jefe*? After all, it's on his patch.'

'Not yet. We don't want Arévalo and his troops trampling all over our scene of crime. And we haven't got a *corpus delicti* yet, have we? We'll wait until Peláez and Varga go in, then we'll tell him. That's why I used the porter's phone instead of the radio in the car. They'll be listening in, and they don't know we're here yet.'

Paco Navarro now arrived with Varga and his men in the technicians' van. 'Here are Santos's keys, chief. Shall we try to open the door?'

'First let's wait for Peláez. He'll be annoyed with us if we let the temperature in there fall suddenly. It will make it harder for him to judge the time of death. Check with the porter about the heating arrangements. There appears to be a primitive form of central heating. I've seen the boiler and the pile of coal in the patio. Peláez will want to know if it was off at night and when it was stoked up in the morning. The porter's very deaf, so you'll have to be patient and mouth your questions. I'll talk to the neighbour in the flat opposite Marisol's. She must have seen her most. Ángel, you'd better go back to the office or you'll blow your cover altogether. They have good memories for our faces in this district. Help Elena finish the Santos papers. There'll be more stuff from here later on, worse luck. Perhaps Marisol won't turn out to have been such a voracious reader or as assiduous letter-writer as her boyfriend.'

'Righto, *jefe*. We'll wait for you in the office. I'll take the Metro from Antón Martín.'

Bernal went up and rang the bell of Flat 1 right. The door was opened carefully on the chain and a middle-aged woman looked suspiciously out. 'What do you want?' she demanded.

'Police,' he said, showing his warrant card.

'What's wrong? It'll be that bitch opposite. Knew she was a bad lot. No better than she ought to be, with men in there at all hours.'

The commotion was causing other female neighbours on the floors above to lean over the banisters in curiosity, and Bernal asked if he might go in.

'Oh very well, but I'm in the middle of scrubbing the floor.'

She shut the door in order to undo the chain and then opened it wide. 'Come in, come in.'

She ushered him to a chair in the hallway. The flat was poorly furnished but was kept clean by hard scrubbing, to which her hands bore patent witness.

'Now this María Soledad Molina, has she been here long?' asked Bernal.

'Less than a year. Don't see much of her, since she sleeps all day. Then puts loud records on the gramophone at all hours of the bloody night, after she comes in from her so-called work.'

'Does she often bring men in at night?'

'Only ever seen one,' she admitted, 'he seems too good for her. A *señorito* he looks, of good family, you know what I mean. Amazed he puts up with the slut. And that dog she has. Never stops howling. It's been off its head since Saturday, but that porter doesn't hear a bloody thing. I've told him a dozen times to do something about it, but the bugger doesn't care what goes on here, as long as he gets a fat tip. This used to be a decent house, once upon a time.'

'Is this the man you've seen?' Bernal showed her the photograph of Santos.

'That's him. The spitting image. He looks sort of frightened on' this, don't he?'

She hadn't consciously realized that she was looking at the photograph of a corpse, but she shivered instinctively.

'What's he been up to, then?'

'Nothing criminal that we know of. But we're trying to find the girl.'

'Ain't she in, then? Mind, I haven't seen her since Saturday lunchtime, when she went to get bread and took that little dog out for a pee.'

'Well, thank you, Señora, I've no more questions for now. You've been very helpful.'

'I hope you'll be able to do something about the smell. It's a bloody disgrace.' Bernal muttered soothing words, saying he thought it would be cleared up soon.

'I hope to God you're right, Inspector. Can't stand much more of it.'

11.30 a.m.

Peláez was arriving as Bernal emerged.

'Hadn't you better send for some *grises* to keep these women in order, Bernal?'

'I thought I'd give you and Varga a clear run before ringing the Centro Comisaría. I'll see to it now.'

Varga had just finished inspecting the door-lock of Marisol's apartment with an illuminated probe.

'The key's in the lock on the inside, Superintendent, and the tip of it has fresh scratches on it, suggesting it was turned with an *ouistiti* from this side but that someone wanted us to think that it was turned on the inside. I'll just get a soft plastic tool to push it out, and then we can use Santos's key from this side.'

'Be ready to catch a small dog, which may be desperate after two or three days in there,' said Bernal.

After a few minutes' manipulation, Varga succeeded in pushing out the other key and inserted Santos's.

'It's double locked, Superintendent.'

'It seems the hallmark of our criminals,' said Bernal, 'always trying to make us think it's a suicide behind locked doors.'

'Well, if the local boys had got here first, they would have broken down the door and thought just that,' said Peláez.

Varga opened the door gingerly, while one of his men with gloved hands held a net across the base of the door. But no dog emerged, only the ghastly, sweet smell of human putrefaction.

'Put your masks on,' said Bernal to Peláez and Varga, 'the rest of us will wait here.'

Varga put his surgeon's mask in position, switched on a powerful hand-lantern and moved slowly across the floor of the small hall, examining the floor closely for tracks. The door into the living-room was closed. He called to his assistant to bring the net in.

'Careful now, the animal might rush out.'

'We'll close this outer door for the moment,' said Bernal. Peláez got his thermometers out of a case: one for the room and the other for the rectum of the corpse when they found it.

There was a silence, and the sickening smell became overpowering until Bernal felt faint. He pulled the mask over his mouth and nostrils. How extraordinary they must look to the women up the stairs, who watched in utter silence, as though they had divined, by some ancient folk sense, the discovery the police were about to make. They could hear Varga talking, presumably describing what he saw for his dictaphone.

Finally there was no scuffle, no desperate dog trying to get out, only a tiny, bloodstained ball of white wool at Varga's feet, scratching at his shoe with one paw. He picked the creature up and opened the outer door.

'It's all right. The dog's half dead with fear and thirst.'

The miniature white Highland terrier, for such it was under the dried blood that smeared its wide tartan collar and its front paws, legs and muzzle, gazed at Bernal with a look of something like shame and terror in its eyes.

'Give it some water,' Bernal said, 'and put it in the van to take back to the lab.'

The dog lapped some water from a saucer provided by the porter, and began to whimper softly.

Bernal heard Varga gasp in horror in the inner room and order his assistant to stay at the hall door. Peláez went forward saying, 'Leave this to Varga and me. We're more used to it than you people. It's our job after all. And you may be sick all over the evidence.'

The rest of them waited for a long time. Then they could see white flashes as Varga took pictures of the scene. He emerged at last, visibly white and shaking.

'You'd better sit down,' said Bernal. 'Come down to the porter's lodge and have a slug of brandy from this flask.'

Varga told him, 'I've never seen anything like it in twenty years, chief. She's lying on the bed, dressed in what looks like a wedding dress. She's already in the black state, so she looks like a negress. And worst of all –' he paused and swallowed hard – 'the dog's had a go at her right arm and shoulder, and has torn the flesh away. So she's covered in dried blood on that side. No doubt being shut in for two or three days he got desperate, and as his mistress slowly rotted, started eating her. There's an electric fire still on in there, which accounts for the rapid putrefaction; there are bluebottles on the torn flesh laying their eggs. They're usually dormant at this time of the year, but the heat and the smell brought them out at once. In another day their eggs would have hatched. I don't know how Peláez does it. He's taking the temperature of the corpse now, humming a tune from a *zarzuela* operetta all the while. There's a box of Seconal tablets on the bedside table.'

'You'd better stay here for a bit, or take a stroll outside until you feel better. You've taken all the photographs?'

'Yes, chief. But there'll be samples to take.'

'Leave that to Peláez and his assistant for the moment. They're more hardened to these things. I'd better ring Inspector Arévalo at the Comisaría del Centro. It's my duty to inform him of the discovery of the cadaver, but he'll soon have the place swarming with *grises*. The smell may put him off going in there and trampling on the evidence.'

'I'll go back, *jefe*, before he gets here, to take all the samples I can and have a look at the scratches on the window-frame when Peláez has finished with the body.'

'Well, only if you feel up to it.'

12 noon

Peláez came down the stairs to the lodge, which the porter

had vacated for them, just as Navarro put down the phone after talking to the Central Police Station. Bernal asked Paco to question all the neighbours who were in apart from the bad-tempered woman on the first floor. Peláez seemed less bouncy than usual and looked weary.

'It's a complicated one, Bernal. Rigor mortis has passed off, the blue-black stage has occurred, and insect infestation has begun. When was she last seen alive?'

'Last Saturday around midday.'

'Well, we'll provisionally put the time of death back as far as possible to that *terminus a quo*. Of course, the electric fire being on has meant a high room temperature, of something like 30°C, and the dog's interference with the cadaver's right shoulder and upper arm makes it more difficult. There appears to be no sign of cuts or external injury. The box of thirty Seconal tablets now contains only six, but we don't know how long since she went to the chemist's. There's no sign of sexual molestation, though she was well used or experienced, let us say, sexually. I have taken samples of all body secretions and I'll want the bed-sheets to be brought with the cadaver. The striations do not show that the body was moved after death, apart from the pulling outwards of the right shoulder by the dog. I'll need to send to the toxicologist 500 grammes of cerebral matter, 300 grammes of liver and one of the kidneys, and 200 grammes or so of muscle, because the blood is entirely congealed. I'd better send one of the lungs in case she inhaled some poison. It will take time to undertake all the tests. I'll examine the stomach contents before they go to the toxicologist, to try to calculate the time of death more closely. Let's say for the moment between midday on Saturday and 6 a.m. on Sunday.'

'Clearly before her boy-friend Santos took the jump in Alfonso XII on Sunday evening?' Bernal asked.

'Ah, that's the connection, is it? Yes, I'm sure that her death preceded his. Were they going to get married, do you know? She's wearing a skimpy sort of white wedding outfit.'

'I've no idea,' said Bernal. 'We'll look into it.'

'Well, we'll call one of our ambulances now and we'll take the cadaver down to Santa Isabel. Mind to collect all tablets and medicines you find. And all food and drink and the leftovers. This poor dog will have to be put down, I'm afraid. After all, however unwillingly, it's eaten human flesh while it was shut in there for nearly three days. Unfortunately the door to the kitchen was shut; otherwise it could have got at some of the food she had left out and at the dirty washing-up water in the sink. It could have managed on that without cannibalizing its mistress. In any case, I'll have to look at its duodenum contents to see what objects it may have swallowed. I suggest you get some deodorants sent here after the body's been removed and the samples collected.'

'Thank you for all you've done, Peláez. It's a particularly horrible business.'

'Not at all, Bernal. I told you I was waiting for a really challenging one. The cause of death may have been the Seconal, or something else.'

'Something else?'

'Oh, I forgot to tell you. She was a drug addict. Probably heroin, applied with a glass dropper inside the left elbow. Over a considerable period of time, I'd say. You'd better look for the stuff and the dropper. She'll have hidden it somewhere.'

As Peláez was leaving, a white patrol car arrived with siren screaming, and two local inspectors and three *grises* jumped out. Bernal went out to greet Inspector Arévalo and to explain how they had come upon the dead girl. Arévalo looked annoyed at this incursion into his territory, but said that he would of course have called in the DGS at once. Bernal privately thought this unlikely, and the forensic examination would have been fairly arbitrarily done by the local police surgeon if the case had been treated in isolation.

'Arévalo, I haven't been in there myself yet, since I thought it was better for the medical and technical experts to make the preliminary examination. Perhaps you'd like to accompany me now.'

Arévalo seemed to regard this as his rightful role in any event. Bernal thought he would change his mind on entering the dead girl's flat. In the doorway Arévalo grudgingly accepted a surgical mask from one of Varga's assistants, Bernal put on his and they went in with the aid of a powerful lantern.

'Please don't touch anything yet, Arévalo. We're still waiting for Prieto to come and dust for prints. Apparently there was a break-in through the window of the kitchen.'

'A break-in? So it isn't just a question of an overdose?' asked Arévalo.

'We can't be sure yet, until Peláez tells us more. She's been dead since Saturday or early Sunday, he thinks, which accounts for the stench.'

Bernal tried to control his nausea as they entered the principal room, which was really both living-room and bedroom. Marisol presented a grotesque sight, her face black, with the nostrils collapsed, and her eyes wide open and staring, but with contracted pupils, which puzzled Bernal. The Seconal should have dilated the pupils. It must have been the heroin, he thought. He checked that there was no sign of a glass dropper, spoon or drug container near the bed or under it. Varga had not mentioned finding such things, so they would have to await the detailed search after the body had been removed. The right shoulder and upper arm had been savagely torn by the dog, and there the flies were busiest. The white dress looked to be too skimpy for a wedding dress, since it was cut in a V-shape up to the thighs, although the lace veil was genuine enough.

'Arévalo,' he said. 'Does that look like a wedding dress to you?'

'Not really, Comisario. It looks more like a thing striptease artists wear in the finale of their shows. She was a dancer in a night-club, wasn't she?'

'Yes, I think you're right. But why would she go to bed in it?'

'Perhaps she'd been trying it on. Look, there's some of the white satin material near the sewing-machine in the corner there,' Arévalo pointed with his torch.

'But she'd have taken it off before getting into bed, surely,' objected Bernal.

'Perhaps she felt tired, Comisario, and just lay down for a while and then took the sleeping tablets.'

Bernal did not find this convincing, for a woman would hardly lie down in a new dress she was making, wherever it was subsequently to be worn.

'Let's go out and get some fresh air, Arévalo. We've made the required inspection of the cadaver.'

They decided to have a cigarette out in the street doorway, while one of the *grises* tried to keep the inquisitive neighbours upstairs from coming down and the other two guarded the door to the flat and the main door.

An ambulance arrived, and a car bringing Prieto and his assistant at the same time, but Bernal asked them to wait until the corpse had been removed. He impressed on the ambulance attendants that they should not touch anything inside. Varga volunteered to superintend the operation of the lifting of the body since Peláez had already left. The air of expectancy among the neighbours who were mainly women increased, and their murmuring stopped. There was an 'Ah!' of disappointment as the attendants brought the body out enclosed in a purple fibreglass tube, so that there was nothing for the craning necks to see. Only one sob, followed by the nervous laugh usual on these occasions, broke the deep silence. The ambulance departed and the tension subsided.

The ambulance men had sprayed the mattress on the bed with strong disinfectants and had left some full aerosol sprays inside the doorway of the flat. Prieto and his man now went in to dust for prints and they began putting on the lights as they finished dusting and photographing the light switches.

Bernal called Varga. 'I want you to go in now and to search for a glass dropper and anything that might contain heroin. Prieto can then dust them for prints.'

'OK, *jefe*. I've got over the nausea now, and the smell will start to fade as soon as we can open some windows. By the way, I've looked at the jemmy-marks on the window from the outside, and they seem similar to the ones in Alfonso XII, but more discreetly done. May be a case of the same instrument with a different person using it. But he lost a tiny piece of his trousers on a nail as he climbed up.'

He showed Bernal the tiny patch he had carefully placed in a cardboard sample box. The cloth looked curiously familiar and it suddenly came to Bernal that it could be from the trousers of a policeman's uniform.

12.30 p.m.

Bernal explained to Arévalo his suspicions about María Soledad Molina's death and its interrelation with that of Raúl Santos which had occurred on the Sunday evening.

'There's no doubt that they were lovers, and both met their deaths under suspicious circumstances. I hope you'll let me look after the wider investigation, while you, of course, attend to the details of the girl's death, which occurred in your district.' Bernal was careful not to mention the political aspects.

Arévalo seemed to bow to the inevitable. 'I'll be glad on this occasion to call in the central DGS officially, because of its relation to the case in the Retiro District which you are already investigating, and we shall co-operate in every way.'

'Thank you, Arévalo, that will simplify matters a lot.'

Bernal knew Arévalo as a textbook policeman of the old school: never brilliant, but slowly efficient as he followed the rule-book. Bernal thought that he was probably very right-wing politically, but orthodoxly so.

Arévalo asked, 'Do you think the man Santos murdered the girl first and then did away with himself?'

'It would be a sensible theory, if it weren't for the probable times of death in each case and for the break-in through the kitchen window here. Why should he have made a forcible entry if he had a key in his pocket? There's no special bolt on the door by means of which she could have shut him out. It's true the dog doesn't seem to have impeded the intruder, but we don't know yet how the poor creature was handled. Peláez will tell us after he has done autopsies on the girl and on the dog.'

'On the dog?' queried Arévalo.

'Oh yes, it will have to be put down and an autopsy done. In any case we can't let it live after it has partaken of human flesh.'

Arévalo blanched at hearing this detail, and said, 'Well, we can let the experts get on with their job. I'll keep a guard on this apartment. No doubt your man will be back this afternoon to superintend the detailed search. I'll make a formal report to the duty magistrate.'

Bernal said, 'Perhaps you could ask him if he'll agree for the case to be passed to the Juzgado number twenty-five which was the court on duty on Sunday, on the grounds of closely related cases.'

'Very well, Comisario. I'll see to it. Can I take you back to the Gobernación in my car?'

'It's very kind of you, but I have a car waiting for me. We shall see each other later, no doubt.'

'I look forward to it.' Arévalo uttered the courtesy

without great enthusiasm.

1 p.m.

Bernal found Elena and Ángel finishing the examination of Santos's personal effects. Elena said, '*Jefe*, have a look at this book of matches I've found.'

Bernal noted the name of the night-club it bore, the Sunrise, with an address in the notorious Calle de la Ballesta behind the Gran Vía.

'It may be the place where she worked,' he said. 'You could call round there, Elena, on your own, and enquire after Marisol Molina, as though she were an old friend of yours. But put a bit more make-up on before you go in to make it more convincing.'

'I'll go at once, chief. Do you think they'll be open?'

'No, but there's sure to be someone there, cleaning it out or something. Take a photograph of her in your handbag in case you need it. Try to put on an *extremeño* accent. Are you a good mimic?'

'I was thought to be at school. I often used to get punished for it.'

Ángel chipped in, 'Mind you don't get taken on to fill Marisol's spot in the strip-show.'

Elena put out her tongue at him. Bernal said, as she was leaving, 'Try to find out whether she showed up at all on Saturday, and if not, whether they made any enquiries about her absence. Did Inspector Ibáñez ring back from Central Records, by the way?'

'No, not yet. He said he'd do all he could.'

'Well, good luck, Elena, on your first solo assignment. Only use your warrant card and police pistol in a real emergency.'

'Yes, *jefe*, I'll remember. Isn't this exciting?'

After she had left, Bernal asked Ángel to ring the Drugs Brigade.

'Ask Estupefacientes whether they have any record of

María Soledad Molina. Do we know her second surname yet?'

'Yes, chief. It's Romanos.' He picked up a file card and read it out aloud. '*María Soledad, born 3 July 1957 in Montijo (Badajoz), unmarried. Third child of José María Molina Barba, bricklayer, and María Josefa Romanos Ponce, kitchen maid.* As you know, *jefe*, we haven't got any word on criminal antecedents yet. She came to Madrid over two years ago. Her official occupation, according to the Documento Nacional de Identidad, is that of barmaid.'

'Well, she advanced a bit from that,' said Bernal.

The phone rang and Ángel answered it. 'It's for you, *jefe*. The Secretaría is calling.'

Bernal made a face and took the phone. 'Yes. Good day, Mr Secretary. Yes, we have found Santos's girl-friend, dead in a flat in Lavapiés. Could be a drugs overdose, but there's been a break-in there as well.'

There was a short silence as Bernal listened to what the Subsecretary was saying. Then he went on, 'Well, of course I suspect that the cases are interlinked. It may be a matter of two murders now. Peláez will help us find an answer.' He listened again for a short while. Then he said, 'I really don't think, Mr Secretary, that we can pass it off as a suicide pact; the press are sure to smell a rat. Yes, I know the preliminary report mentioned a tiff between them ten days ago in a bar.' The Subsecretary had obviously been doing his homework.

'No, I agree. No statement to the press about the girl yet.' Bernal suddenly felt a desire to counter-attack. 'Have you any news about our own internal security, Mr Secretary?'

There was a silence. Then Bernal went on, 'You know, the interference in the Fingerprints Section last night with certain pieces of evidence relating to the Santos case. Yes, yes.' He listened for a while. 'Well, I hope you will be able to get to the bottom of it. It undermines all we try to do if we cannot be sure of our own security.' He put the phone down with some satisfaction. 'That should keep them quiet up there for a day or two, Ángel. They're always nervous when some internal matter may be laid at their door.'

Ángel smiled approvingly. Bernal went on, 'I'd like you and Elena to be here this afternoon to pack up the Santos stuff and clear the decks for the effects from Marisol's apartment. I doubt whether there'll be much in the way of papers. It's really like the apartment of a dressmaker or modiste. Lots of rolls of cloth and sewing materials. It's lucky we've got Elena to look through it for us. Paco can stay over there and sort out the stuff for sending with Varga's men.'

'OK, *jefe*. I'll ring through to Paco via the porter's phone.'

'Good. I'll be off to lunch now, during the lull. See you later.'

1.30 p.m.
Elena walked up the Calle de Montera in great excitement, and crossed the Gran Vía through the José Antonio Metro station underpass in front of the Telefónica building. When she had walked down the Gran Vía as far as the Sepu department store, she turned into the side-street of Gonzalo Jiménez de Quesada and stopped to reinforce her make-up in the reflection of the display windows of the Sepu. Looking quite common now, she thought, with very heavy glossy lipstick and thicker eye-shadow, she turned left into the Calle del Desengaño. She had wondered why it was called the Street of the Dis-appointment until a friend in the Faculty had told her of the legend of two sixteenth-century rakes who one night followed a veiled shadow of a lady into this street only to find that it was a well-conserved mummy, dressed up in red velvet.

With the street's present reputation, she thought its

name might well be applied to the fate of so many working-class girls from the outer suburbs and the provinces who came to this quarter in the hope of making large sums of money by prostituting themselves, and who usually ended up poor, addicted to drugs and socially ruined.

Elena turned into the Calle de la Ballesta, the Street of the Crossbow, where youths had once practised archery and nowadays indulged in a quite different kind of sport. She noticed that some of the bars and clubs already had their touts outside trying to attract the lunchtime idlers in, and she was careful not to look at any man directly until she spotted the Sunrise Club further down the street. She looked nervously at the photographs pinned up outside and soon spotted two of Marisol wearing two different skimpy outfits: in one a man wearing only a pair of star-spangled briefs was lifting her into the air with her legs spread apart in a somewhat ungainly posture; in the other she was leaning forward over the audience, baring her ample breasts and about to give her all – at least to judge by the position of her hands.

Elena wondered whether she hadn't come in a coat that was a wee bit too elegant for this quarter. She would do what she could.

The door of the Sunrise was ajar, and she gingerly drew aside the crimson tasselled curtain and entered. An old woman was cleaning the floor with a broom and a barman was wiping glasses behind the bar.

'We're closed, love,' he said.

'I know,' said Elena, 'but I'm looking for a friend who works here, who said she'd meet me yesterday, but she didn't turn up. She's from the same village as me.' She hoped neither of them was from Extremadura, but she did all she could to drop her s's and d's in the appropriate places.

'What's her name, love?' asked the man.

'Marisol Molina.'

'Oh, she didn't turn up on Saturday night, and the boss
is furious with her,' he said. 'He's sure to give her the sack.
She'd promised to put on a new finale, in a sort of white
wedding dress, to give the customers an extra thrill. She
said it unzipped down the front and left her in the altogether
with only the veil on. Real kinky it was going to be. "The
Bride of Lavapiés", he billed her as. Only thing is, she
didn't show up, and we had to watch that ancient fat piece
from Triana, Sofía she calls herself, imitating Lola Flores,
which the customers have seen in every club round here,
and they groaned and stamped their feet and tried to get
their money back. That's why the boss was so mad.'

'Did she come in on Sunday?' asked Elena.

'We haven't seen her since, love, and it's surprising she
hasn't come for her wages. The boss says she'll have to
come crawling on her knees for her money, and then he
won't give it to her. Say, are you interested in having an
audition yourself?'

'Oh, no thanks,' said Elena hastily. 'I've got a steady
job as a waitress.'

'Well, you dress pretty good for a waitress, love,' he
said eyeing her coat, which had cost 10,000 pesetas in the
Corte Inglés.

'I work in a posh restaurant,' she said pertly.

As she was leaving, the old woman followed her out.

'Maybe Marisol's ill and needing this, love,' she said,
taking out a small envelope from her apron pocket. 'You
know where she lives, don't you, my dear?'

'Yes,' said Elena, 'I've got it written down somewhere.'

'Well, since you're from her village, I can trust you to
take this round to her. It's just some headache powder
that she often asks me to get for her.'

'Oh, I will,' said Elena. 'I'll go right now. I've got the
afternoon off today.'

'Thank you, my dear, she'll really appreciate it.'

Elena was glad to get back even to the contaminated

air of the Gran Vía after the pollution of the Calle de la
Ballesta.

2 p.m.
Bernal sat alone in the Cervecería Alemána in the Plaza
de Santa Ana, sipping his third *caña* of beer. He looked
out at the children playing under the leafless trees
in the square without really seeing them, as he tried to
visualize what had happened in Marisol's apartment. It
all depended on what she had died of. If it was an overdose of barbiturates, it could have been self-administered,
by accident or intent. The time of death was crucial.
She would hardly have taken sleeping tablets accidentally
in the afternoon. The burglary could have taken place
some time afterwards, but it seemed too much of a
coincidence. Alternatively, she could have died of an
overdose of heroin. She was an addict, as the marks on her
arm proclaimed, and she might have shot up too strong a
dose. This was more likely on the face of it, since she
would probably have injected herself some time before
going out to work in the club and the state of the pupils
of her eyes also suggested it. The third possibility was
murder by the intruder or intruders. Peláez would help
him decide.

Then there was the dog. Why had it not barked, or even
attacked the intruders? Of course, the neighbours would
have paid no attention, since it barked frequently when it
was left alone. Nevertheless terriers had a sharp temper,
in his experience, and could be expected to defend their
owners against an assailant. Had it been shut in the
kitchen? But they had found it with the corpse in the main
room, with the doors to the kitchen, bathroom and hall
firmly shut. Then the piece of cloth Varga had found.
What if it turned out to be from a police uniform? Did
this tie in with the interference with Prieto's fingerprint
files? If it did, it might imply that the two burglaries and
the internal security failure in the DGS were the work of

some parallel police organization whose activities were quite unknown to him. Did it also imply that the murder of Santos could be laid at its door? Or were there two separate operations going on? Had the *chulo*'s attack on him been meant as a warning? He sighed heavily as he realized how little he knew. He was sure the Secretaría knew more than they were letting on to him.

Bernal didn't have any appetite today for *tapas* and he paid the old waiter for the beer with a fifty-peseta piece and strolled out into the square. He hailed a taxi in the Carrera de San Jerónimo and went home to lunch, still feeling too insecure to walk as far as Sevilla and catch the Metro to Retiro station.

2.30 p.m.

In their apartment Eugenia was nowhere to be seen, and Bernal felt sure she was in her cupboard oratory, praying for the canary. Nor could he see the birdcage anywhere. He called out and Eugenia emerged, clutching her rosary beads.

'Oh, Luisito, the canary died at ten-forty-two this morning,' she wailed. At least she was a precise witness, thought Bernal. 'I've put the cage in our bedroom.'

'In the bedroom? What for? Do you realize we may catch psittacosis, or whatever disease canaries have? Anyway, it will have tiny fleas, and they'll jump on to the bed.'

At this she hurried to retrieve the cage. 'I'll have to keep it until the neighbour returns,' she said. 'Oh, what will I tell her?'

'Don't be silly, Geñita. Wrap the thing in some newspaper and put it in the rubbish bin. The dustman will collect it in the morning.'

'Oh, it would be like hiding a murder, Luis.'

'Well, you didn't kill it, did you? The refuse man won't even notice it.'

'Oh no, Luis, I can't do that.'

'Then find some airtight box and put it out on the terrace, for God's sake.'

'All right, Luis. I'll get your lunch now.'

'Well, scrub your hands first, before touching the food.' He knew her country ways and slipshod hygiene of old.

Lunch turned out to consist of *sopa de ajo*, a greasy mixture of olive oil, stale bread and garlic, into which she had broken a raw egg at the last moment, and this had congealed into strings. Rather like a very inferior sort of Italian *stracciatella*, Luis thought. He ate what he could of it in silence, and then she produced a plate of eggs poached in wine glasses and turned out in little mounds, surrounded by slices of *jamón serrano* or mountain ham from her village and covered with freshly-made tomato purée. This was one of her better dishes, though it was served almost cold, and Bernal made the most of it.

She asked, 'What case have you been on today?'

He told her briefly about the dead girl Marisol, and the grotesque discovery of her corpse which they had made.

'Oh Luis how horrible. I take it she led an evil life?'

'Yes, you could say that.' These cases simply served to confirm her general impression of human society and the price it paid for turning away from God. Bernal still looked forward to the day when he could investigate some ripe ecclesiastical scandal, to try and shake some of her *idées fixes*.

3 p.m.

Pleading pressing business in the office, Bernal changed his suit and put on a new silk tie. After taking leave of Eugenia, he descended to the street which a pale sunlight was bravely attempting to warm. He stopped at Félix Pérez's as was his custom to take a *café cortado* and a *copa* of Carlos III brandy. Then, calling a taxi, he made for his other flat in the Calle de Barceló.

Consuelo was already there, making herself a snack in the kitchen. '*Hola*, Luchi, you're early today.'

'So are you, love,' he said, embracing her from behind and straining round to kiss her.

'Hey, you'll make me spill the soup,' she said. 'How are you getting on with the Santos case?'

She looked grave as he told her about their discovery of Marisol's body and told her about some, but not all, of the macabre details.

'It's horrible, Luchi. Do you think she was murdered too?'

'Peláez will tell us, I hope, this afternoon. I'll have to get back by five to see him.'

'Well, that doesn't leave us much time, does it? I'll just get some of this soup down me. We had an easier morning in the bank with so many people already closing their businesses for a long Easter break. The rush was really on Saturday and yesterday, when they were all wanting cash to pay the travel agents for their five days in Benidorm or Palma. What have you done to your hand?' She had spotted on the palm the piece of sticking plaster with which Bernal had replaced the chemist's bandage.

'Oh, I cut it lifting one of Eugenia's pots, which fell to pieces in my hands. It's been dressed by a chemist.'

'Well, mind you don't get tetanus in it.'

Bernal had decided not to tell her about the *chulo*'s assault on him in the alley and the missing flick-knife.

4.30 p.m.

As they were dressing, Consuelo asked him, 'Have you got any further with *Sábado de Gloria* and what it means?'

'Apart from the possibility that something is being planned to take place on Easter Saturday, no.'

'Have you thought of the initials it makes, SDG? I just thought idly that it might be a variant of DGS, the General Directorate of Security.' She had a crossword mind, which often looked at things acrostically or anagrammatically, Bernal remembered.

'It's a bit far-fetched, though Varga did find a piece of

cloth outside the girl's flat that looked as though it got torn off the trousers of a policeman's uniform.'

'There you are, you see,' she said triumphantly. 'It's all a Fascist plot of some of your extremist colleagues. No wonder it's going to be difficult to solve, with them breathing down your neck and able to interfere with the evidence. Which of your people can you trust?'

'Well, all my group, except for the new girl, Elena. She's a staunch Francoist. Do you think they planted her on me?'

'I expect so,' she said with relish, secretly happy that this piece of possible sexual competition would be cast under a shadow. 'And the others? Are you sure of them?'

'I'm quite sure of Navarro and Ángel, and the other two, Carlos Miranda and Juan Lista, have got the week off. In any case, I could trust them with my life.'

'How about the technical people?'

'Well, Varga and Peláez are old friends, and professionals to their fingertips. So is Esteban Ibáñez in Central Records. Prieto in Fingerprints is the doubtful one, and it's there we lost one piece of evidence and had others tampered with, though he swears he doesn't know how it occurred.'

'What about the people on top?'

'It's difficult to say. The Minister himself, of course, is one of the staunchest members of the new Government, and he himself may not be sure who to trust in the Secretaría and among the first-rank commissioners. Most of them were appointed long before his time. If I had some firmer evidence of a political plot in this case, I'd go to the Chief Commissioner and hand over the case to the socio-political branch, the Second Brigade as it's now called. That would be the proper thing to do, by the book, as it were. But the difficulty is that some of them may be involved in a private capacity, and would be able to quash the whole enquiry in order to allow the plot to come to fruition.'

'I'm frightened, Luis,' she said. 'Didn't you tell me that there was a plot to assassinate the Minister a couple of weeks ago?'

'So Esteban told me, but the Second Brigade arrested the four German conspirators three days before the date they had planned to carry it out. And they've been spirited out of the country since, so they'll never come to trial. The problem is that International Fascism has been able to operate without control during the whole of the dictatorship, and it's going to be an uphill task to bring its members to heel. The country's crawling with exiles from Cuba, Santo Domingo, Mexico and Argentina, and immigrants from Italy and France; there are still some who got out of Germany at the end of the war. A terrible hotch-potch. Remember we and the Portuguese provided the Fascists' paradise for over forty years, and now we've got the Fascist exiles from Portugal as well. While the Portuguese tried to undo the Gordian knot overnight, it's going to take years of our kind of democracy to clean it all up, if we ever manage it without another general coming to "save" us.'

'Do be careful, Luis. Go direct to the Minister, if you have to.'

'But they'd all come down on me like a pack of wolves if I did that – breach of protocol, lack of use of normal channels, etc. Just imagine the fuss there'd be.'

'Well, think carefully before going to the commissioners. They may be all Francoist diehards.'

'I'll be careful, Consuelo. Don't worry, now.'

'Of course I'll be worried, love. Ring me and let me know how things are going.'

'Yes, I will, if there's any news. I must go back now, to see Peláez.'

5 p.m.
In the office Bernal was met by a breathless Elena, who told him in a rush of what had happened in the Sunrise

Club, and of how Ángel had sent the envelope containing the white powder she had been given by the old woman to the Instituto de Toxicología for analysis. He was pretty sure it was heroin, from its bitter taste on the tip of the tongue.

'Should we tip off the Drugs Brigade to raid the club, *jefe*?' she asked.

'Not yet,' said Bernal. 'It would hamper our enquiries. Paco can go round there later and talk to the manager officially about Marisol's job and her absence on Saturday. Estupefacientes will have the place on file, for sure, because it will be one of those clubs that changes its name and manager twice a year, while the owner keeps well out of sight. They know what goes on in all those clubs and will be after the chief supplier, not the small-time pedlar.'

Ángel broke in, 'Did she tell you they offered to take her on to fill Marisol's spot in the show, *jefe*?'

'Oh, come on, Ángel, you promised you wouldn't tell the Superintendent.' Elena blushed scarlet.

'You must have done a good job with your make-up, Elena,' said Bernal.

'Thank you, chief, that's the only compliment I've had today.'

Dr Peláez arrived, looking very pleased with himself.

'Well, Bernal, you brought me out to a classic case. I've opened her up and there's my preliminary report. As you'll see, there are no external marks of violence, apart from the injection-marks in the left arm and the damage done by the dog. My initial finding is death by a massive dose of heroin, more than fifteen decigrams, I'd say, but we'll get the exact figure later from the toxicologist. I've sent him part of the brain tissue, one lung, one kidney and a sample of muscle.'

Elena blanched at these details.

Peláez went on, 'I can't see any sign of barbiturate poisoning. I don't think she had taken any that day. Oh, the time of death. The stomach is virtually empty, which implies that she had died some two to six hours after her last meal. The leftovers in the kitchen and what you found out from the neighbours suggest she ate lunch between one and three p.m., let us say, which would put the time of death between four and ten p.m. on Saturday. The amount of putrefaction, accelerated by the electric fire, is consistent with that sort of time-scale. I can't be more precise, I'm afraid. She was in poor physical condition, because of her heroin addiction, and the sudden massive dose, much more than she can have been used to, would have caused unconsciousness, and then respiratory failure within an hour or so of the injection. You realize that most of the heroin powder sold only contains between five and eight per cent of the pure drug and it's usually mixed with lactose or powdered milk. Someone must have given her an almost pure powder, either by mistake or with intent to kill her. It's difficult to say where they could have got hold of it, except from a main supplier, because the small-time pedlars only receive it in the diluted form. That is one very puzzling aspect.'

'Did she inject it herself?' asked Bernal.

'Well, we didn't find a glass dropper, or a spoon and matches near the bed. But in theory she could still have had the strength to hide the injecting apparatus before she became unconscious. If it weren't for one thing.'

'What's that?' asked Bernal.

'Well, that's the second puzzling aspect. As I told you, I've sent one lung to the toxicologist, just in case a poisonous inhalant had been used. I cut open the other myself and noticed a faint smell of ether. Now I don't keep any ether in the dissecting room, and none was found in the flat. This suggested to me that she had been made unconscious by an assailant, and that he then injected her with a lethal dose of heroin. We'll wait to see what the toxicologist reports.'

'What about the dog?' asked Bernal. 'It wouldn't have acquiesced in his mistress's being chloroformed.'

'I thought of that, and my assistant and I put it down humanely. Then I dissected it and examined one of the lungs, but there was no sign, of course, because he had lived on for three days and had not been injected, as far as we can see. I've sent the other lung over to the toxicologist in case he is able to find a trace of ether. The dog's stomach contents are of human tissue, of course. It's possible that the poor creature only brought himself to touch her during the last day of his captivity. Anyway, dogs prefer rotting flesh.'

His three listeners shuddered at this remark, but Peláez was quite unaffected.

Bernal said, 'Let's try to imagine what happened, Peláez. A ring on the door bell during the evening, when she's trying on the new dress for the show. She shuts the dog in the living-room to stop it running out. She opens the door without looking through the grille first, perhaps thinking it's her boy-friend, coming to make it up. There's no telephone in the flat, so he can't ring her before coming round. The assailant, or let's say two assailants, then make a grab at her with a pad impregnated with ether, and she becomes unconscious. They hear the dog barking inside, and one of them takes the pad and opens the living-room door slowly, catching the dog with gloved hands and putting him out for the count. Then they carry her to the bed and look for her glass dropper, mix a strong solution of heroin, or they may have brought it ready mixed, and inject her with it – a dose sufficient to kill her.'

'Why may there have been more than one assailant, Bernal?' asked Peláez.

'Because we didn't find any marks on the tiled floor of her having been dragged, and she was still wearing rubber-soled slippers when we found her. So she was put out of action and carried without any scuffle at all.'

Ángel now objected, 'But chief, what about the break-in through the kitchen window? Couldn't they have entered that way?'

'Very well, let's hear your reconstruction, Ángel.'

'The assailant, or perhaps more than one, broke open the kitchen window with a jemmy. The dog barks and she goes in to see what's happening. At that moment she's trying on the new dress for that night's show, perhaps to make final adjustments to it. One assailant chloroforms her, while the other deals with the dog. They carry her to the bed, inject her, and then search the apartment.' Elena looked at Ángel with admiration. 'But what are they looking for, *jefe*?' asked Ángel.

'We'll come to that in a minute,' said Bernal. 'First let's examine your explanation carefully. The kitchen window is very small. They would have taken some time to scramble through it. Yet the dog hears them at an early stage. Marisol goes to investigate. On seeing the first man coming through she would have had time to run to the door and down to the porter's lodge to telephone for help. Furthermore, the dog would have had a go at them before they got fully in.'

'Then she was sleeping,' said Ángel, 'or lying on the bed drugged, and the dog was shut in the living-room with her.'

'But she wouldn't have lain down in the new dress; the satin would have got creased,' objected Bernal. 'And why would they have needed to use chloroform if she was drugged? How does your reconstruction relate to what happened in Santos's apartment the following day? Remember that we are pretty sure there were two sets of intruders there.'

'So you think the first intruders came in by the door and drugged her, with fatal effects,' Ángel went on, 'and the second intruders got in later by the window and found her already dead, or dying.'

'That seems more likely,' said Bernal.

'But what was the motive in each case?' asked Peláez, who had got deeply interested in the theoretical reconstruction.

'That's what we're not sure about,' said Bernal. 'It's likely that the first intruders, the assailants, took the key from Marisol's handbag and placed it in the lock on the inside when they left, one of them turning it twice with an *ouistiti* or similar instrument while the other kept watch on the stairs. They went to this bother to make it look as though Marisol had shut herself in. They also took from her bag the key to Santos's apartment, which they were to use the next day. The second intruders, the burglars, had no key to either apartment. That is why I postulated that Marisol opened the door to the first intruders, thinking perhaps that it was Raúl coming to make it up after their tiff.'

Ángel looked puzzled. 'If the first intruders did all this to find some valuables or documents,' he said, 'who were the second lot and how did they find out what had happened?'

Bernal replied cautiously, 'They may have been keeping tabs on the first lot, keeping them under discreet surveillance, as it were. They too were perhaps interested in looking for something, probably the same thing as the first intruders.'

'But why did the first lot kill in each case?' asked Ángel.

'Perhaps because they thought Marisol and Raúl knew too much. They may have threatened Santos, or even tortured him to try to get him to talk, but the effects of the fall he suffered would have covered any marks of violence he bore. Anyway, they may just have threatened to push him out of the window, and when he wouldn't talk, did so.'

'But did either lot find what they were looking for?' asked Elena.

Bernal shook his head doubtfully. 'How can we tell, unless we find it, or them? The trouble is, we don't know exactly what to look for.'

'By the way,' said Peláez, 'didn't Varga find a piece of cloth? How does that fit in, Bernal?'

'I think one of the second lot of intruders got it torn from his trousers when climbing in or out; it's just possible that the dog could have torn it off, or loosened it enough for it to fall off later, since he would have recovered sufficiently from the ether by the time the second lot arrived, and would have been frantic, perhaps, at his mistress's condition. Varga will find out if there is canine saliva or teeth-marks on the patch of cloth.'

5.30 p.m.

Dr Peláez said he had to go off to see if he had any new customers, and as he left bumped into Paco Navarro in the doorway.

'You look tired, Navarro, you need a rest.'

Navarro said, 'Thanks a lot, doctor, you've made me feel a lot better! The smell down there has got me down. Even though it's faded a lot, it clings in one's nostrils.'

'I haven't noticed for years,' said Peláez cheerfully. 'Don't hesitate to call me if you find any more. *Hasta pronto.*' He waved a vigorous goodbye.

'What's happening down there, Paco?' asked Bernal.

'Prieto's nearly finished. Varga and I found the injection kit wrapped in a polythene bag and suspended in the lavatory cistern. Varga's got some of the drug from the dropper, and Prieto found a good clear print, which looks to be too big to be Marisol's. It may be our first good lead. I've asked him to rush a photo of the Liftprint over to get a check made on it.'

'That's the best news of the day, Paco. What about the stuff from the girl's apartment?' asked Bernal.

'Varga is bringing it up. Fortunately there'll hardly be any documentary stuff to go through, it's mainly dresses and dress materials, and a few popular magazines.'

'Elena, you can look at it for us,' said Bernal. 'There won't be any need for you to go to the apartment. I want you to search all the seams of the garments carefully, in case something was hidden.'

'Of course I'll do it, *jefe*,' said Elena.

'Paco,' said Bernal, 'go down and fetch a copy of that print from Prieto. We don't want it to get lost, do we?'

'I understand, chief.'

'Then we'll have a spare copy should they lose it in Identificación Criminal,' said Bernal.

'I'll go right away.'

The phone rang and Elena answered it. 'It's the Secretaría, for you, Superintendent.'

'I'll take it in my office,' Bernal said.

The same subsecretary as before came on the line.

'Ah, Bernal, is that you?'

'Yes, Mr Secretary.'

'Shocking business about this girl-friend of Santos's. Just been reading the incidents report on it. Was it murder?'

'It's a difficult one, Mr Secretary, since she was a heroin addict. We're still investigating.'

'Well, keep in touch. I liked the brief press hand-out about Santos's death. Neatly done. Call in for a chat tomorrow, if you like.'

'I shall be glad to, Mr Secretary, if there's something concrete to report.'

'Good luck, then, Bernal. *Hasta mañana.*'

'Until tomorrow.'

He pondered over the import of this call, so soon after the previous one. It was certainly strange that they were getting so uptight over the death of a dancing-girl.

Paco now returned and came into Bernal's office.

'I managed to get a photocopy of the fingerprint out of Prieto. He was very reluctant to let it go, I thought. Went on a lot about protocol and the rules.'

'Let's have a look at it,' said Bernal. 'H'm. It looks like part of a right thumb and right index finger. Probably a man's. I'll tell you what, Paco, get another photocopy made of the partial right index finger and take it round to the Documento Nacional de Identidad. Ask for Inspector Cambronero. He's a friend of mine from the old days, and he may be able to run a discreet check on it against the main national files. It'll probably take some days. Prieto will send the original Liftprint to Identificación Criminal and they'll check it first against the criminal fingerprint file, which they'll manage to do overnight, probably. Nothing like being ahead of the system, is there?'

'And it will prevent any tampering with the evidence, eh, chief?'

'I see you've realized what's happening in this case, Paco. Someone up there doesn't like us going into it too far.'

'Varga's on his way up, *jefe*. He says he's got a few things to tell us.'

'Good. Tell Elena and Ángel to come in and listen to what he'll have to say. Elena might be able to rustle up some coffee. You can go round to the DNI afterwards.'

6 p.m.
Varga had found out much that was of interest.

'First of all, the attack on the girl, Marisol.'

'How can you be sure she was attacked?' asked Bernal.

'I found some rubber scuff-marks on the wall of the hallway and on the door leading into the living-room. There was also a tiny piece of cotton wool inside the main door, which the lab is checking.'

'They may find traces of ether,' said Bernal. 'Peláez smelled it in one of her lungs.'

'I see. Then there were almost certainly two of them, since they would have had the dog to cope with.'

'Do you think the dog ripped a piece out of the trousers of one of them, Varga?'

'Not really, no. Possibly from the trousers of one of the later intruders, when they forced the kitchen window.'

'You are sure there were two lots of intruders?' asked Bernal.

'Pretty sure,' said Varga. 'There are signs they went out by the window as well as coming in that way, so why

would the same lot have gone to the bother of using an
ouistiti on the main door, when they could have locked it
from the inside before leaving by the window?'

'How do you reconstruct the movements of the first
intruders, then, Varga?' asked Bernal.

'While Marisol was still unconscious from the ether,
they searched the apartment, and found her injection kit,
which one of them prepared with almost pure heroin. The
tiny traces in the glass dropper have already been con-
firmed as that by the lab.'

'Good going,' said Bernal. 'And then?'

'Well, before injecting her, they may have tried to
torture her after she came round.'

'Torture her?' Ángel said. 'But Peláez didn't find any
marks.'

'I know,' replied Varga, 'but there are three cigarette
burns, two on the right shoulder of the white satin dress
and one on the bed-sheet below it. As you'll recall, *jefe*, the
right shoulder of the dress was pulled down, and that gave
the dog the piece of bare flesh to chew.' Elena shuddered
at this. 'I'm sorry, Inspectora,' said Varga, 'but that's how
I see it. The dog eliminated the evidence of the torture. I
don't think it's possible, from the position of the burns,
that she could have burnt the dress and sheet accidentally,
by smoking in bed, although the assailants might have
imagined we'd think that. I've sent all the cigarette ends
from the ashtrays to the lab for them to run a saliva test.
We'll then know the blood groups of the smokers if they
were "secreters", and most people are. You know that it's
often easier to find the group from a saliva trace than from
a dried blood sample, chief?'

'No, I didn't, but go on,' said Bernal.

'Well, Marisol seems to have smoked Virginia tobacco;
the packet at the bedside was of Winston. But the ashtray
contained one stub of Rex, which is black tobacco. Those
are the saliva traces I'm most interested in.'

'What if the partial fingerprints on the glass dropper

and the blood group of the smoker can be pinned on the same person, Varga?'

'That would be unlucky for us in a way, because the courts would accept the fingerprint evidence alone, as absolute proof, whereas it would be nice if the saliva on the cigarette end were from the other assailant, who didn't leave any fingerprints, though he left glove-prints on various bits of furniture. Trouble is, they're messed up by the glove-prints of the later intruders. But if you find the gloves, we'll have a go. Has Prieto checked the glove-prints against those found in Santos's apartment?'

'Not to my knowledge,' said Bernal. 'He's dragging his feet a lot on this case.'

'Doesn't he always?' asked Varga, with professional rivalry.

'Well, go on, Varga, what next?'

'When the assailants had searched the apartment for whatever they were seeking, presumably in vain, apart from the injection kit, they waited for her to come round. There are tiny signs of disturbance of the dust in the drawers and cupboards, the lining papers have been lifted and so on, but it was carefully done.'

'No way of distinguishing between two separate searches, of course,' objected Bernal.

'No, but two were made, to judge from the way the glove-prints overlie one another,' answered Varga. 'When she came round, they may have threatened her, to get information of some kind, using lighted cigarettes on her right upper arm and shoulder.'

'But were they successful, Varga?'

'How can we tell? They gave her the overdose of heroin then. She may have co-operated in that, of course, since she was probably desperate for a fix by then. She would have thought the dose normal since the powder would look the same, the only thing being that there was next to no lactose in the last fatal injection.'

'Perhaps,' said Elena, 'they offered her the injection as a

reward and the lighted cigarette as a punishment?'

'Well reasoned, Elena,' said Bernal. 'A desperate addict might not feel the pain of the cigarette burns very much, despite the very high burning temperature, but she'd do or say anything for a fix.'

'But perhaps she didn't know anything and couldn't help them,' said Paco.

'That was probably it,' said Bernal, 'except she may have blown the gaff on her boy-friend's whereabouts, so they went on the next day to deal with him. What about the second intruders, Varga?'

'Well, they are almost certainly the same lot as the burglars in Alfonso XII. The jemmy used on the kitchen window has left identical marks, but it was probably wielded by the other man, or a different man. One of them may have run into trouble with the dog, who may have been responsible for the patch of cloth torn from his trousers, apparently. The lab is checking the patch. Curious thing is, the material is identical to that used in the uniforms of the Policía Armada.'

They all looked at him in astonishment, except Bernal.

'But who could get hold of a police uniform?' asked Elena.

The others looked at one another, momentarily surprised at the innocence of the question, but Bernal got over the pause by saying hastily, 'Oh, that's not difficult, Elena, and it would have made things so much easier for them if they went about dressed as policemen. That may be why they weren't noticed either in Ave María or Alfonso XII. Anything else, Varga?'

'Well, only the dog. Whereas the first intruders probably put him in the kitchen after chloroforming him and shut him in there, the second lot found him there and he probably woke up to find them coming in through the window. They may have secured him there or in the bathroom while they searched the flat. They certainly shut him up in the living-room when they left, but that wouldn't have been difficult, because he is likely to have stood guard over his mistress, who would have been dead by then.'

'What about the time-scale, Varga?' asked Bernal.

'Well, from what Peláez said at the scene of the crime, I should have guessed that the second lot of intruders went in some time after ten p.m. on Saturday. There would have been less risk then of being spotted when people were having their dinner and watching television. They got in over the back wall into the yard, and it's no height up to the girl's kitchen window. Since the porter's deaf, there was no chance of his hearing them, though they may not have known that, of course. I found rubber-heel marks on the back wall, but the rain since Saturday night has obliterated all other traces.'

'You've done a thorough job, Varga, and we're all immensely grateful. We only have to wait for the report on the lab tests now. And for Prieto's on the prints. I'll walk down with you. Elena, perhaps you'd go on helping Ángel to look through the stuff from Marisol's apartment. Paco, you'll perform that little errand for me, won't you?'

'Yes, chief. I'll go right away.'

'I'll see you back here in an hour, then. *Hasta luego.*'

'*Hasta luego,*' they chorused.

6.30 p.m.

Bernal walked down to the street with Varga.

'Let me invite you to a drink or a *merienda*, Varga.'

'Fine, *jefe*, I've got a bit of time in hand.'

In the bar the technician opted for a white coffee and Bernal took the same.

'I'm worried about this case, Varga, not least because of the internal security leak last night in Prieto's department. That, together with the patch from a policeman's trousers, makes me think that the second intruders in both apartments were there in some semi-official capacity and they're keeping us in the dark about it.'

'Or they may be the *incontrolados*, chief, the extreme right-wing groups, or even the parallel police. You know that a number of our colleagues are rumoured to be involved.'

'But who is organizing it, Varga? It would have to be someone high up.'

'Well, one hears about the internal tussles up there between the *profesiónalistas* and the *militaristas*, with the Minister trying to hold the ring.'

'Yet there must have been some sort of contact between the murderers and the burglars,' said Bernal. 'Otherwise, how could the burglars have known that Marisol had been attacked and her apartment searched? We didn't find out until this morning.'

'The second lot may have been keeping the first lot under surveillance, chief, and went in afterwards to see what had occurred, which suggests that they are some sort of security force.'

'Well, that fingerprint, if it can be identified, will enable us to track down one of the murderers, which is my chief professional concern,' said Bernal.

'We may have the answer tomorrow,' Varga said.

Bernal thought it best not to confide in him about Paco's errand to Inspector Cambronero in the Documento Nacional de Identidad.

'We'd better be getting back, Varga. I ought to prepare a preliminary report.'

'Before you go, *jefe*, you'd better see this. I thought I'd keep this piece of evidence until we were alone,' said Varga, taking out a small buff cardboard box from his pocket. 'It hasn't been dusted for prints yet, because I was reluctant to let Prieto see it, so please don't touch it. I found it in Marisol's flat, near the bed.'

Bernal took off the lid of the box, and stared at the small metal badge, which bore the letters DGS in the form of a monogram in red on a black background. He remembered Consuelo's remark of that afternoon, and realized it could be read SDG, since the letters were superimposed one upon another; *Sábado de Gloria* – 'Easter Saturday'.

'Have you ever seen anything like it, *jefe*?'

'Never,' said Bernal. 'It's not an official badge of the Dirección General de Seguridad, and it's so small, it would just fit into a buttonhole on a lapel.'

'That's probably why it fell out when they were torturing or injecting her. Clearly it belonged to one of the assailants.'

'How can we get it checked for prints, Varga?'

'Well, it's probably too late now, they'll have been effaced. But I'll have a go later on, when my staff have gone home. I've got an old Liftprint set in the lab which Prieto doesn't know about.'

'I'd be very grateful, Varga, it's worth a try. And will you photograph the badge for me?'

'Better than that, I'll hand it over to you in the morning.'

'Yes, but not in front of my staff, apart from Paco.'

'I understand, *jefe*. I think the whole thing's a mess when we can't work properly for lack of confidence in our colleagues.'

Bernal was on the point of telling him about the *Sábado de Gloria* business, but he thought better of it. There'd be time later to put Varga in the picture if it proved necessary.

'We'd better go back, Varga, and clear up what we can for today.'

'Yes, chief, I'll see how the lab technicians are getting on with the various tests.'

On the way back, Bernal bought a copy of the left-wing evening paper, *Diario 16*, which he folded carefully and pushed into his overcoat pocket. 'I wouldn't like the *grises* at the door to see me carrying this, Varga, but it's essential reading since that series it ran on Comisario Conesa the week before last.'

Varga laughed and said, 'Be careful carrying even

El País, chief. A few days ago the Antidisturbios riot police were hitting people with their truncheons in Callao if they saw a copy under their arm.'

7 p.m.
Bernal found that Paco Navarro had already returned from the Documento Nacional de Identidad, and was helping Elena and Ángel finish the search of Marisol's possessions.

'We've found photographs of her family, *jefe*,' said Elena, 'as well as letters from her mother. Here's her home address in Montijo.'

Bernal looked at the sad, blurred snapshots of a middle-aged couple in ceremonial peasant dress, apparently taken at a local fiesta.

'Would you telephone through to the local police, Paco,' he asked, 'and request them to break the news to her parents and arrange for them to travel to Madrid to make the formal identification? Then you should get off home. You've had a hard day.'

'Thanks, *jefe*. I'll ring them now. But what about the preliminary report for the examining magistrate?'

'I'll dictate it now. Have you found anything else, Elena?'

'There's an empty envelope, similar to the one the old woman gave me in the Sunrise. We'd better send it to the toxicologist to see if there are any traces of heroin in it. Apart from that, there's only this key, which Varga says doesn't fit any lock in her apartment.'

Bernal looked at the key with interest. It was small but of high-grade manufacture, probably a security key, he thought.

'I'm just checking the rest of the sewing materials,' Elena said.

'Well, after you've done that and packed the stuff up again, you and Ángel can get off home while I dictate the preliminary report.'

The stenographer arrived, a super-efficient matron in her early fifties, bristling at being called at so late an hour, but clearly a martyr to her duty. Dictation was not Bernal's forte, and the stenographer's fierce appearance did not help matters. Nervously he began to stutter an account of the discovery of Marisol's corpse while the matron took it down with ease and clear signs of disapproval of his inefficient dictation.

In despair he moved to the window to avoid her gaze, and settled into a better rhythm, as he turned his eyes unseeingly down to the last-minute shoppers in the Calle de Carretas and the office girls streaming out on their way to the Metro in Sol.

When he had finished, he asked the stenographer whether she would be able to have it typed that evening.

'Oh yes, Comisario, in half an hour it should be ready for you to check.'

'Thank you so much. I'll wait for it, so that the magistrate can have it by the morning.'

She hurried out, without acknowledging Elena's or Ángel's presence in the outer office. They had now finished repacking the household effects in the large boxes Varga had brought, and got ready to leave.

'Have you time to take *tapas* with me, Elena?' asked Ángel.

'I'm sorry, I can't this evening. I've got a date later on,' she answered, noticing his disappointment with some satisfaction.

'Perhaps tomorrow evening, then,' he said.

'We'll see.' She waved good night to Bernal.

'You needn't stay, Ángel,' said Bernal. There's only the report to check and sign.'

'All right, chief. I'll see you in the morning. Good night.'

'Good night, Ángel. Don't stay out too late.'

'I thought I'd drop in to the Sunrise later on, and see what the atmosphere is like.'

'If you wish, but be discreet.'

'I will, *jefe.*' He put on a smart suède jacket and spent some time checking his appearance in the small mirror by the coat-rack. The vanity of youth, thought Bernal, running his hand through what was left of his hair.

While he waited, Bernal lit a Kaiser and read the headlines in *Diario 16*. 'USA needs Spanish bases until 1990' ran the largest of them. Then, 'Political Parties: decision next week; all expected to be legalized except the Republicans'. 'Danger of war in South Africa', and a large photo of the Press building of the Francoist Movement which had recently been abolished, accompanied by speculation on the future of the Movement's newspapers. On an inner page there was a gruesome photograph of embalmers at work in Los Rodeos airport in Tenerife, fitting together the limbs of the hundreds of crash victims before embalming them, with row upon row of coffins stretching away behind them. The accompanying text contained a denial by the Madrid Funeral Services that they were charging 200,000 pesetas each for embalming the more difficult cases, and a statement that they only charged between 25,000 and 50,000 depending on the state of the cadaver; even this scale of charges seemed rather high to Bernal. He must tell Peláez that he was in the wrong business.

Two small news items tucked away at the bottom of page seven caught his eye: the morning before, on 5 April, the President had consultations in the Moncloa Palace with the Defence Minister, who was also first Vice-President, and the Ministers of the Army and Navy. In the afternoon he had received the second Vice-President and the Ministers of Justice and the Interior. There was also a statement that the President would probably remain in the capital over the Easter weekend. The second, even smaller, news item stated that the King had received the Minister of the Interior in the Zarzuela Palace on the same day.

Bernal wondered what their discussions had been about. They must have considered questions of security. He looked at his watch – almost 7.45 – and supposed that the meeting of the Council of Ministers was almost over. Had they taken the plunge and legalized the Communist Party and some of the other left-wing parties? He guessed that some of the diehards would be fighting a rearguard action, raising the spectre of La Pasionaria's imminent return from Moscow. If they had made a firm decision, he hoped they would pick a quiet moment to make the announcement.

The matronly stenographer now returned, and Bernal hastily folded *Diario 16* and hid it in a drawer of his desk. He invited her to sit down while he read the report through. It was brief, but gave the salient points to the magistrate. She had typed it well – better than most of the younger secretaries would have done – and he signed it and sealed it in an envelope. She helped him heat the wax and affix the official seal, and said she would dispatch it for him.

'Thank you very much, Señora. I'm so sorry to have kept you working late.'

'Not at all, Comisario, glad to have been of service,' but her tone of voice did not suggest that she was particularly glad. She took her leave and Bernal locked the carbon copy in his filing cabinet.

8 p.m.

Emerging into the torrent of humanity that poured into the Puerta del Sol at this hour, with lottery-ticket sellers crying out that they had just two numbers left for the *gordo* or 'fat' prize in the weekly national draw, and the newspaper sellers calling out the names of the papers almost unintelligibly, '*Informaciones! El Pueblo!*' The bars were packed, and the street corners crowded with young people waiting for their date to turn up – it was a miracle how they ever found one another in the crush.

Bernal decided to go straight home, but knew he'd never find a taxi at that time. He descended into the Sol Metro, passing the beggars on the steps. Many of them appeared to be gypsy children, who had been dumped there by their parents for some hours. Most of the blind lottery-ticket sellers had gone, ready to hand in their unsold coupons in the Calle de Prim before the daily drawing of the three-figure number at nine o'clock. This daily lottery for the blind was supported by millions of his countrymen, who usually picked their number with great superstition.

The sight that moved him most was an elderly woman dressed in black, sobbing her heart out half-way up the Metro steps.

'Can I help you?' he asked her.

'It's my daughter,' she said.

'But can I help you? Do you need money?'

'No, no!' she sobbed uncontrollably.

'Can I help you up the stairs?'

'It's my daughter,' she repeated, not really seeing him.

'But what's wrong with her?'

'My daughter!' she said again hopelessly.

Bernal was relieved when a well-dressed middle-aged lady stopped and asked him, 'What's wrong with her?'

'She won't say. She only mentions her daughter. She won't accept any money.'

'Leave her to me,' she said, 'I'll see if I can help her.'

Bernal felt liberated. How typical and shameful it was for one to think that other people's problems could be solved with a small gift of money; otherwise, one wanted to avoid the inconvenience and embarrassment of getting involved. He looked back at them; the well-dressed lady was helping the inconsolable old woman up the steps.

There were long queues at the ticket-windows and old women were selling tickets at ten pesetas which they had earlier bought for six. Everything in Madrid was obtainable if you paid a higher price, he reflected. Fortunately he had change and took a six-peseta ticket from the automatic machine and passed through the turnstile. The tunnel leading to Line 2, direction Ventas, was full of hurrying figures and the large metallic door swung across and prevented Bernal from catching the train standing at the platform. As soon as it blew its whistle and left, the metallic door swung open and he was propelled on to the platform. He moved along to the rear end, since this would be nearest to his exit at Retiro. Three, four minutes passed and the crush behind him reached enormous proportions.

Two trains had come in from the opposite direction and had virtually cleared the platform on the other side. He wondered why the intervals between trains were not the same in each direction. The signal at the far end on his side had changed to green some time before, when the train he had missed had left the next station, Sevilla.

Now there was a rumble and the overhead lights flickered as the ancient red and cream train trundled towards the station. Just as it emerged from the tunnel, Bernal felt a powerful jab in his back. Someone was trying to push him off the platform. Straining with all his might and catching on to the man next to him, he resisted the pressure until the carriages were flashing by and slowing down. Just as suddenly the pressure on his back ceased, and looking round quickly, he saw only two young girls chatting to one another at the front of the throng. The man on his right looked at him oddly and was about to say something as Bernal said, 'I'm awfully sorry. They were pushing me from behind.'

The man said, 'That's all right.'

But crushed in the train now, Bernal suddenly felt nervous. Had someone really tried to push him under the train? He supposed that a person standing behind the young girls could have put an arm between them to propel Bernal forward. Or someone on his left; he'd not had a clear view on that side. He looked carefully at the people surrounding him in the carriage; they all seemed perfectly innocuous. The two girls were still alongside him, talking about their boy-friends. He thought it probable that the person who had pushed him had hung back when the train doors opened and made his escape with the many passengers who had got off the train.

Before the train stopped at Retiro, Bernal squeezed his way to the door; hardly anybody would alight here and he needed to be near in order to get out. Up in the night air now, he decided he could do with a drink. He turned into Félix Pérez's and asked the barman for a Larios gin and tonic.

'You look pale, Don Luis.'

'I've had a hard day.'

The proprietor courteously offered him some green olives on a wooden spoon, which Bernal accepted, and then put a canapé of *bonito* fishpaste on a little saucer in front of him.

9 p.m.

As he finished his second *gin tonic*, Bernal felt lightheaded and a little sick. He was suddenly very surprised to see his wife passing by in the street. How she had changed in forty years, he mused; when he had first seen her sitting side-saddle on a black horse in the annual fair in her village, he had been overcome by her dark, arrogant features, so typical of northern Spanish women. Now those high cheekbones and that long straight nose had shrunk into a beak-like profile, not dissimilar, he suddenly realized, to that of Franco's widow. On the rare occasions when he accompanied her on some outing, their joint resemblance to the late dictator and his wife must give the passers-by quite a shock.

Paying for his drinks, he left hastily and overtook Eugenia before she reached their house. He noticed she was carrying an osier basket containing a trowel.

'Geñita, where have you been?'

'Luis,' she said, looking round rather guiltily, 'it's you. Oh, I had to go over to the Retiro and bury the canary. I couldn't bring myself to put it in the waste bin.'

'But Geñita, you haven't gone into the park in the dark?

You might have been attacked.'

'Well, I didn't want the neighbours to see me. I said a few words over the poor creature, Luis.'

'It's a good job one of the park police didn't bump into you. He would have been scared out of his wits at finding you kneeling over a recently dug little grave.'

Eugenia was unconcerned about this. 'I think Doña Pepita – you know, the owner of the canary – will be pleased I've given it a proper burial.'

Las cositas de la vida – the little things of life; how absurd and yet how welcome they seemed after someone had tried to push you under a tube train, thought Bernal.

There followed the usual boredom of television-watching and a *tortilla* for supper.

'I'm going to have an early night, Geñita. I've had an exhausting day.' He realized he felt sapped of energy from the nervous reaction to the incident in Sol Metro station. First the *chulo*'s attack the night before, then the push in the back. Did someone think he knew too much, or was he getting too close for their comfort? He was exasperated by the lack of evidence of motive in this case, and he was convinced that there had been two sets of intruders, the murderers, followed by the burglars. Apart from not knowing why the murderers had murdered, he didn't know why the burglars had burgled.

As he finished cleaning his teeth, the phone in the passage rang and he unhooked it.

'*Dígame.* Oh, Diego, are you having a good time?' He called Eugenia to tell her that their younger son was calling. 'How's the weather in upper Aragón? Is there still enough snow to ski at Candanchú?' He listened to his son's enthusiastic account of the holiday. 'Have you got enough money? I'll send you some if you need more.' He listened to the reply. 'All right. Ring me later in the week if you do need any. Here's your mother.' He handed the phone to Eugenia, whose chief concern turned out to be whether Diego was attending Mass regularly.

His son's cheerfulness and *joie de vivre* lifted Bernal's spirits and he went back to watch 'Esta Noche . . . Fiesta', a variety show televised from Florida Park, a night spot in the Retiro, just across the road from where he was. At least the interviews with the actresses in the audience would be amusing, even if the pop singers weren't up to much.

WEDNESDAY, 6 APRIL

Bernal woke from a fitful sleep to the sound of Eugenia rattling cups in the kitchen. He shaved hastily to try to beat the insurance agent on the floor below this morning, but the latter managed to send up a blast of foul air just as Bernal was combing his hair. He dressed with care, and looked out through the terrace window at the grey morning. There were sure to be showers later, he thought.

Eugenia called him to have breakfast, which consisted of the usual undrinkable coffee and fried stale bread. He dunked one piece of it into the coffee, and since she was sitting opposite him, did what he could to drink it down.

'I'll have to go early, Geñita, I'm expecting the technical reports on the Santos and Molina killings.'

'Take an umbrella, Luis, it looks like rain.'

'You know I'll only lose it on the Metro.'

He pulled on his overcoat and checked his service revolver with more care than usual.

'I'll expect you about two-thirty, Luis,' Eugenia called out.

'I'm not sure. I expect so. *Hasta luego.*'

In the Calle de Alcalá he bought a copy of *El País* which he read slowly over his second breakfast in Félix Pérez's. The headlines referred to telephone tapping of his ministers by the previous President, Arias Navarro. The article was culled from the London *Economist* of the previous day, and claimed that Arias used to listen to the most interesting of the tapped calls each morning. It was even suggested that the Franco Régime had tapped the King's telephone from 1970 onwards, when he was still Prince Juan Carlos, of course. Bernal particularly relished the translated remark of the English journalist that 'in

hell, it's reliably reported, the cooks are English, the
journalists are Russian and the policemen are Spanish'.
There was even special mention of the DGS's computer-
ized system of political files. The most interesting revelation was that under Carrero Blanco's Vice-Presidency, a
special anti-subversive group had placed men in the key
ministries to prevent a military coup. Bernal hoped that,
if this was so, they would function in favour of the current
President.

He paid for his coffee and croissant, and decided to wait
at the bus stop for a bus or taxi, whichever came first. The
bus won, and he pushed into the crush on the back step. It
was slower than the Metro, but safer, perhaps.

8.30 a.m.
In the outer office he found Paco Navarro already opening
the reports that had arrived.

'*Buenos días*, Paco.'

'*Muy buenos, jefe.*'

'Has Prieto sent a report?'

'Two, chief. The final one on the two apartments in
Alfonso XII and the preliminary one on the flat in Ave
María. I haven't had time to read them yet.'

'Anything from Varga?'

'Not yet, chief.'

Elena came in as Bernal started reading the first long
report from Prieto, and she greeted him warmly.

'Elena, could you ask the main desk if they've heard
from the Montijo police about Marisol's parents?'

'Yes, chief, I'll ring down to see.'

Bernal turned to the second of the reports with more
attention, since there was nothing in the first that he
didn't know already. Prieto would go no further than to
say that some of the glove-prints in Marisol's apartment
resembled some of those found in Alfonso XII; he wasn't
prepared to state that any were identical, because they
were partial and smudged. He was doing further tests on

some of them, however.

Bernal called Paco in. 'Has any report come in from the Criminal Identification Department on the fingerprint found on the glass dropper?'

'No, chief, not yet.'

Ángel now blew in, looking as cheerful as ever, despite the late night he had probably had.

'I went to the Sunrise a little after midnight, chief. It's the usual sort of strip-joint cum clip-joint, full of middle-aged men in mackintoshes. No obvious sign of drugs being distributed. Perhaps it's only among the girls who work there. Lots of them get trapped by drug-taking into that sort of work. I sat at the bar and chatted up the barman about the various girls. He volunteered information about Marisol, how I'd missed seeing the real star of the show, who had walked out last week and hadn't come back. He said she was too good for that sort of work and he hoped she'd got out of it. He didn't say anything about her addiction, of course. The manager looks a tough character. I'm sure I've seen his mug on the criminal files. I'll check it later, if you like.'

'Yes, do that, Ángel, we may need to call him in for questioning, though Paco could go round there for a formal chat with him first.'

Elena came back from the phone. 'The main desk says that Marisol's parents are arriving about now on the night train, chief. They've been told to take a taxi and come straight here.'

9 a.m.

The Molinas looked as though they had come out of the past. The husband, dressed in dark countryman's clothes with an old black beret, which he took off and screwed in his hands in Bernal's presence, seemed old enough to be Marisol's grandfather, so wizened and weatherbeaten was his face from a lifetime spent working in the sun. His wife looked many years younger, but had allowed her figure to go, like the majority of working-class Spanish women after marriage, and she had a pale and unhealthy complexion, probably the result of always working indoors. She bore the signs of having wept continuously, and was about to weep again as Bernal offered them chairs and asked Elena to bring in some coffee.

'I am so very sorry about your daughter's tragic death. We are still investigating to see what happened exactly.'

'It was as though she were no longer our daughter,' said Señor Molina harshly. 'She sent us a little money each month when she first came to Madrid, but she hasn't even written to us for the past eight months.'

'Oh, Inspector,' wept Señora de Molina, 'she was a good girl and in our home town there was nothing for her. No job that would bring in much money. So she saved up enough for the fare and came here, something she had always dreamed of doing. She thought the streets would be strewn with carnations for her – like that old song said – and that she'd meet a nice husband who would look after her.'

Bernal could see that the father, like so many people of peasant stock, stated the matter in economic terms – the loss of income from the girl's earnings – while hiding his real feelings. The mother was of a romantic inclination – the daughter no doubt inherited it from her – which had probably been fed by reading cheap novelettes.

'When did she die, Inspector?'

'On Saturday evening, we think.'

'On Saturday? And she wasn't found until yesterday?' she said, horror-stricken.

'I'm afraid that's so.'

'And what did she die of?'

'An overdose of drugs, I'm sorry to say.'

'Oh no!' the mother wailed. 'She didn't take her own life, did she?'

'We don't think so. The drug was stronger than she can have known.'

'Then it was accidental?' asked the father.

'We're still investigating that,' said Bernal cautiously. He thought they would have to be told more, before they heard it in the magistrate's court. 'I'm afraid she fell into bad company, and was taking illegal drugs, no doubt to calm her nerves. She must have spent a lot of money on them, which is probably why she stopped sending you some of her earnings each month.'

'Can't you arrest these people she fell in with?' demanded Señor Molina.

'We are trying to identify them,' said Bernal, 'but her boy-friend is also dead.'

'How did he die?' asked the father.

'He fell out of a window the day after Marisol's death.'

'Oh, was he so upset by it that he took his own life?' asked Señora de Molina.

'We're still not sure about that,' said Bernal. It seemed better to leave them in ignorance of the real events for the moment. 'I'm sorry to have to ask you to do this, but would you accompany me to make the formal identification?'

'Yes, of course, it is our duty, and we naturally wish to see her,' said Señor Molina.

'Ángel,' Bernal called, 'will you ring down for a car? Will you come with us, Elena?'

'I'd be glad to, chief.'

'Where are you staying, Señor Molina?' Bernal asked.

'We haven't thought about that,' he replied.

'Well,' said Bernal, 'you'll need to arrange the funeral and you'll have to wait for the magistrate's certificate to proceed with it. Inspectora Fernández will help you find a clean *pensión* or small hotel not too far away.'

'Thank you, we'd be glad of that.'

9.30 a.m.
The driver of the Seat 124 took them sedately down the Carrera de San Jerónimo and along the Paseo del Prado

to Atocha Square. Negotiating the narrow streets behind the disused Hospital Provincial, he drew up in the Calle de Santa Isabel, where there was the usual cluster of bereaved relatives waiting to claim the bodies of their loved ones from the Laboratorio Anatómico Forense. At the desk, Bernal showed his warrant card and asked to see Peláez. He soon emerged dressed in his dissecting robes and took Bernal into his office, while Elena took the Molinas to the waiting room.

'I've brought María Soledad Molina's parents to do the ID, Peláez,' said Bernal. 'I haven't told them much about the circumstances, except that there was an overdose.'

'I've tidied her up and she's been embalmed, Bernal. They mustn't look at more than the face, though, so I'll only open the fridge drawer a little. The face doesn't look too bad. I'll take them in now. You and the Inspectora can wait here.'

Bernal smoked a Kaiser as he waited silently with Elena. After a short while, the parents emerged looking devastated. The mother was in a state of semi-collapse. Elena took charge of her while Señor Molina signed the official deposition. Elena said she would take them by taxi to look for a place to stay, but Señor Molina said that they would like to find somewhere near there. 'We'll be close to the station, and our daughter, and it's our sort of quarter, with country people coming and going.'

'You could ask the receptionist if she knows of a clean *pensión* nearby, Elena,' said Bernal. 'You'd better keep the official car in case you have to go further afield.'

'No, *jefe*, I'll call a taxi if need be, but there's sure to be some lodging near here.'

'All right, then, I'll leave them with you. You might help them sort out the official forms for the funeral. They'll feel terribly lost.'

After they had left, Peláez took Bernal back into his office.

'There's something you ought to see, Bernal.'

He took the bloodstained collar of Marisol's dog out of a drawer.

'Listening to your theory about the case yesterday, I wondered what the intruders had been looking for, so I checked the things I still had here belonging to the Molina girl. Look behind the collar, at the seam.'

Bernal examined the back of the dog collar, which was rubbed by wear. The seam was partially unpicked at one end, and the edge of a piece of paper was visible.

'Here's a pair of forceps, Bernal. I thought I'd leave it there until you arrived.'

Bernal opened the seam a little more, and slowly slid the paper out.

'Have you a pair of small tweezers, Peláez? There may be prints on it still.'

Peláez took a pair of surgical tweezers from his pocket and Bernal unfolded the long strip of folded paper without touching it with his fingers. 'It's a receipt for a bank safe deposit, Peláez. This needs looking into at once. Have you got a large envelope?'

'Here you are, always ready to oblige. Should have been a detective myself.'

'You are, Peláez. The most important one we've got.'

'Have a brandy or an *anís* before you go?'

'No, I'd better get on with this.'

'All right, Bernal, hope you can solve it today. Then we can start on another.'

'Let's hope it's not like this one, Peláez.'

'You'll get my final report when I've had word from the toxicologist. I'll enclose his report with mine.'

10 a.m.

Remembering the security key found among Marisol's effects, Bernal told the driver to take him to the DGS building and there to wait. Bernal made his way to Varga's lab first and talked to him alone in his office.

'Have you got that fingerprint kit handy, Varga?'

'Yes, chief. I didn't find anything on the badge. You'd better have it to keep.'

'It didn't seem very likely, did it? I want you to examine this.' He handed Varga the envelope Peláez had provided. 'It contains a bank safe-deposit slip which Peláez noticed rolled up inside the collar of Marisol's dog. We may find Santos's prints on it.'

Varga went to fetch a board and the kit, and stretched the paper flat with special clips. He blew a small quantity of the dusting powder on to the sheet and brushed it gently. After pulling down the window-blind he switched on an ultraviolet lamp. They could see a number of smudges and part of what looked like a thumb-print.

'I'll just get the fixed-distance camera, chief. Then I'll do the back of it.'

The reverse of the sheet was even more promising, with partial prints of an index finger and a middle finger. Varga completed the photographing, and cleaned the dust off the sheet with a brush.

'I expect you are going round to the bank to open the box, chief.'

'Would you come with me, Varga? I'll go upstairs first for that security key you found, in case it fits the safe deposit box. If not, you may have to force it.'

'I'll gather some tools together and wait for you in the hallway, *jefe*.'

'Good man. In the meantime keep the roll of film of the prints safe and we'll get it developed later.'

Bernal told Paco Navarro about Peláez's discovery and gave him the address of the bank. 'Varga will come with me, in case we have to force the box open. I'm taking the key we found among Marisol's things.'

Varga was waiting for Bernal in the hall and they set off in the official car to the bank on the Gran Vía. There Bernal presented his warrant card and asked to speak to the manager, who came out at once to receive them.

'Señor Director, this receipt was found among the

possessions of a deceased person whose death I am investigating. Here is a copy of the death certificate.' Bernal had taken the precaution of bringing the magistrate's certificate for Santos in case the bank should prove difficult. 'I wonder whether you could produce the safe deposit box for us?'

'Of course, Comisario, come into my office and I'll send down for it at once.' He pressed a button on his desk and an elderly employee entered. 'Please fetch up the box to which this number refers.'

He offered Bernal and Varga cigarettes, which they accepted, and Bernal asked him whether Santos had an account at the bank, since it was not his regular bank.

'I'll just check, Comisario. What was his full name?' Bernal gave it. The manager picked up the phone to make the enquiry. 'They'll ring us back. It's quite in order, of course, for someone to deposit a strong box even if he is not a regular customer, so long as we can be present when something is deposited or removed. We like to have some idea of what they're putting in, naturally.'

'Do your customers bring their own boxes, or does the bank supply them?'

'They most commonly bring their own, but we have a standard issue which they can hire if they wish.'

'Do you keep duplicate keys?'

The manager was cautious. 'We might be able to obtain a replacement key from head office for one of our own boxes if the customer were to lose the original, but they do not usually leave us duplicate keys to their private boxes.'

'Can you tell if a box is one of your own?'

'Oh yes, it would have a number on it. The customers often have their names painted on, but we always tie a numbered label on the handle, which corresponds to the number on the receipt.'

'And usually you will only produce the box for the owner of it?'

'That is so. Only on receipt of a signed authorization by the depositor would we produce it for his agent, except under circumstances such as the present ones.'

The phone rang and the manager picked up. 'Yes, I see. Thank you.' He put down the phone. 'Well, Comisario, this man Santos did not have an account with us.'

The elderly employee now returned with a somewhat ancient strong-box. The manager checked the number on its label against the receipt.

'It's not one of ours. I take it you have a key?'

'Yes, but we're not sure if it fits.' Bernal took out the security key from an envelope and tried it in the lock. It would not turn.

'You'd better try, Varga.'

Varga examined the lock with an illuminated probe and then the key. 'This is for a different lock, chief. Shall I try to get this open?'

'If the manager has no objection.'

'No, no, Comisario. You will have to see what's in it. May I see the key?'

'Of course. You may be able to help to identify it.'

As Varga opened his attaché case, which was packed with an impressive array of tools, the manager inspected the key.

'It is certainly a strong-box key, of recent date, but not from our bank. We don't use this manufacturer. Perhaps you can find out for which banks it was made, Comisario?'

'Yes, we'll certainly do that. Of course it will be difficult to find out where the strong-box is held without finding a receipt.'

'Well, not so difficult. Each branch will have a special list of strong-box depositors, which can be checked, but that depends on this man having used his real name. Though it is likely that he would have done, because no bank would accept a deposit from a stranger without asking to see his *carnet* of identification.'

'That is most helpful, Señor Director, thank you for

enlightening us,' Bernal said.

Varga was now manipulating the levers of the lock and suddenly it sprang open.

'Thank heaven your colleague works for the police, Comisario,' said the manager, 'or we should not feel secure.'

Inside the box lay a stout buff envelope, sealed with wax. There was nothing else.

Bernal said, 'We need to check for fingerprints before opening the envelope. Have you any objection to our taking the box away with us?'

'Not if you sign a receipt for it,' said the manager, smiling.

'Does only one of your staff deal with this type of deposit?'

'One or two of them, usually. Would you like me to call them in?'

'Yes, please. The date on the receipt is only ten days ago and they may remember him. I have a photograph for them to see.'

The manager called in the staff concerned, a lady in her forties and a young man. 'These are the members of my staff who deal with the customers who wish to deposit in our safe.'

Bernal shook hands with them and introductions were made.

'The employee you have already met,' the manager went on, 'is the person who actually descends to the vault to fetch the boxes.'

Bernal showed the photograph of Santos to the employees in turn. The lady remembered him. 'Quite recently it was, perhaps the week before last. He brought a box in and asked to deposit it. I told him about the scale of fees, checked his *carnet*, and asked him to open the box so that I could inspect the contents. I lifted out an envelope and by the feel and weight of it I realized it contained documents. So I was satisfied it could be deposited.'

Bernal now showed her the box and the envelope inside it. 'Yes, that looks like it.'

'You definitely touched the envelope, Señorita?'

'Oh yes.'

'In that case it will have received your fingerprints last, if you returned it to the box before the customer locked it.'

'Yes, I suppose it did.' She looked disconcerted by this realization.

'It doesn't matter, now that you've identified the depositor from the photograph. Thank you all so much for your co-operation. We'll get back to the laboratory now,' Bernal said.

11 a.m.

Bernal accompanied Varga to his laboratory to superintend the opening of the envelope. Varga got his fingerprinting kit out, but the thick folded sheets yielded next to nothing.

'It's special paper used for high-grade printing, chief, and has a very dry surface. I don't think we'll get more than these smudges.'

And so it proved. There was nothing worth photographing.

'Let me see the contents, Varga.'

'It seems to be a sort of timetable, *jefe*. It's headed *Sábado de Gloria*.'

'What?' exclaimed Bernal. 'Let's have a look.'

He was soon engrossed in reading an extraordinary plan, which seemed to be the meanderings of a madman.

SATURDAY OF GLORY

12.00 hours. Mass at the Valle de los Caídos.

12.45 hours. The Caudillo will be presented to the ex-combatants.

13.00 hours. The President will be seized in the Moncloa Palace, the Infante Felipe taken in the Zarzuela Palace as hostage to secure the co-operation of the King and Queen, and the Ministers of the Gobernación, Defence and the Armed Services arrested and taken to military barracks. Special units will take control of the Telefónica, radio and television studios and transmitters, and the other key points indicated on the map. All other telecommunications will be immediately controlled by our troops, who will bear the SDG symbol on stickers placed on their helmets. Simultaneously, the key points in Barcelona, Bilbao, Seville, Córdoba, Málaga and other cities will be secured. Only those officials displaying the special SDG badge in their lapels are to be trusted and obeyed. Radio and television programmes are to be allowed to continue normally, but no word of the takeover is to be broadcast. As little display of force as possible is to be made in the streets.

18.00 hours. The Caudillo will be brought by special train to the Estación del Príncipe Pío, thence by car with full military escort to the Palacio de Oriente. He will enter by the Puerta del Príncipe.

22.00 hours. Radiotelevisión Española will announce, on the pre-recorded videotape and radio tape, the successful completion of the takeover and the arrangements for Easter Sunday.

SUNDAY OF THE RESURRECTION

08.00 hours. The marshals will take up their positions in the Plaza de Oriente to control the onlookers.

10.00 hours. The Caudillo will appear on the Royal Palace balcony, alongside the King and Queen. The public will give the usual salute by waving their handkerchiefs.

14.00 hours. Victory march-past along the Paseo de la Castellana, at which the Caudillo and their Majesties will take the salute.

¡Viva Franco! ¡Arriba España!

Bernal read the document in utter astonishment. Was it a hoax? Or did they really intend to disinter Franco at El Valle de los Caídos? Or was the 'Caudillo' mentioned some replacement of the old dictator? Without speaking, he passed it to Varga, who also read it in silence.

When he had finished, Bernal asked him, 'Do you believe it?'

'I wouldn't have if I hadn't seen one of the SDG badges.'

'Even with that piece of evidence, up there in the

Secretaría they'll still think it's a hoax, or, if they're involved, will say that it is,' said Bernal.

'What can you do about it, *jefe?*'

'Try to find some of the names of the plotters. There's none with this timetable or map. Do you think this map is a military one?'

'It could be a police map, reduced in size,' said Varga. 'Do you think Santos was intending to publish all this?'

'Almost certainly. He was probably waiting to fit all the pieces together and win a tremendous scoop, but he left it too late.'

'Do you think he infiltrated the organization?' asked Varga.

'How else would he have got hold of a printed copy of the detailed plan? There must be a list of names in existence, which we have to try and find quickly. Otherwise we shan't know who to trust, for a start, and we need it to convince the powers-that-be to take the *coup* seriously. If we show them this, they'll just laugh at us. I'll get back upstairs and start calling the banks to see if there's another safe deposit box.'

12 noon
Bernal found that Elena had just returned, after finding a *pensión* for Marisol's parents.

'I'm sorry to give all three of you a tiresome task,' he said. 'We need to ring every branch of every bank and ask them to check their list of safe-deposit customers, to find out whether they are holding a strong-box in Santos's name. Let's take the telephone directories and choose a bank each. They'll close at two o'clock but the staff may be there later than that. Oh, one final thought. We'd better ask about two possible names: Raúl Santos López and María Soledad Molina Romanos. It could be in her name, since we found the key in her apartment.'

Paco said, 'I'll ask the main desk to give us four lines for the next two and a half hours. They've just been on to find out if we'd like another case to investigate.'

'I hope you held the duty officer off for a bit, Paco. We've got enough to do with the present one.'

'He's managing for the moment, he says, but hopes we can take something over the weekend.'

'We'll see,' said Bernal.

It was a laborious business, not least because many of the managers were rightly cautious about giving the information, and insisted on ringing back to make sure that it was the DGS that was calling. Others were out, no doubt having pre-lunch *tapas* with important clients, and their deputies were reluctant to act in their absence. Bernal remembered the earlier manager's advice and rang the Barcelona manufacturers of the key they had found in Marisol's flat. They weren't of much help, since they supplied eight banks and sold the boxes to the public. Spain had more banks than any other European country, and the largest of them had an inordinate number of branches. After 2.15 they found more and more of them closed for the day and got no answer to their calls.

2.30 p.m.

'Well, it's probably worth the effort,' said Bernal. 'We'll go on with it tomorrow morning if we don't come up with any other solution.'

'What are you hoping to find in the box?' Elena and Ángel asked him, almost in unison.

'What the intruders were looking for,' he said. 'When we see the contents we may be able to arrest them.' He did not think it politic to show them the documents he had found, but asked Navarro to stay behind when he sent Ángel and Elena off for lunch.

'Paco, take a look at this. Varga and I found it in the safe deposit box in the bank in the Gran Vía.'

Navarro read it in silence and growing signs of astonishment.

'Do you believe it, *jefe*?'

Bernal showed him the SDG badge. 'Varga found this under Marisol's bed.'

'But it's incredible. Are they really going to dig up Franco?'

'Well, that sort of thing's happened before. Remember that every year on St Ferdinand's Day, the mummified corpse of King Ferdinand III is exposed to public view in Seville Cathedral. I saw it one year and he's incredibly small, and ironically, for a Moor-slayer, has blackened face and hands; the shining eyes must be glass. He still grips his sword and holds the orb. It's an extraordinary sight, considering he died in 1252. Then there's General Perón carting Evita's embalmed body around in a glass-topped coffin. He kept her in an attic in Madrid for years, and it's even said he took her on holidays with him, along with the second wife. That mummy was his re-entry visa into Argentina. It's hard to calculate what effect the sight of the mummified body of the Caudillo will have on the crowds in the Plaza de Oriente. But remember we're the descendants of a people who persuaded themselves in the sixteenth century that their eleventh-century hero El Cid rode into battle against the Moors after his death, propped up in the saddle. Didn't you see the Hollywood epic? It was very well done, that scene.'

'They may get away with it for a day, or a couple of days,' said Paco, 'and I see they're choosing Easter Sunday for the symbolic value of the Resurrection, but not longer, surely.'

'So they'll sanctify the whole zany business and mix it in with the religious processions. Once the initial shock effect has worn off, they won't have to worry about the symbols. It will have given them time to consolidate their position and liquidate the opposition, which won't be able to organize on a holiday weekend, especially with the telecommunications in the usurpers' hands. They can bank on the fact that most people in positions of power will be out of town and, anyway, may be favourably disposed towards them.'

'We must try to stop it,' said Paco, and Bernal was relieved to hear his reaction, 'but how can we without the names?'

Bernal thought about the problem. 'Even if we get an identification of that fingerprint from the glass dropper that was used on Marisol, and arrest her murderer, it would take us too long to penetrate the organization through him.' Bernal was struck by a sudden thought. 'I'll ring Martín at Retiro. It's worth another look at Santos's apartment.'

Martín was on duty, and agreed to meet Bernal at the flat at 4.30.

'You'll look after things here for me this evening, Paco?'

'Of course, chief.'

'I'll just go down and make some photocopies of this curious document before I leave,' said Bernal. 'They'll have gone to lunch by now and I can use the machine myself. I'll leave you a copy, Paco, but don't show it to anyone yet.'

4.15 p.m.

After a lunch of rather hard chickpeas and cold halibut at home, Bernal took his usual *café cortado* and a brandy in Félix Pérez's, then strolled down towards the Puerta de Alcalá. A light rain had begun to fall. Since he was early for his appointment with Inspector Martín, he decided not to go through the pedestrian subway to reach the Calle de Alfonso XII, but crossed Serrano and then the lower part of Alcalá on the west side of the Plaza de la Independencia. Perhaps it was some instinctive dread of being isolated or trapped in the underpass that made him walk the long way round, a remnant of his feeling in the underground station the day before.

He met Martín in the main doorway of the apartment block and they went up in the elegant lift. Bernal was glad to see that there was still a uniformed *gris* at the door of Santos's studio.

'I want to have another look round, Martín,' said Bernal. 'There is something we still can't find, possibly a receipt for a bank safe deposit box. It isn't among the papers brought from here or from Santos's office. Perhaps he hid it somewhere.'

He told Martín about Marisol's murder, but not about the *Sábado de Gloria* documents. For the next hour and a quarter they searched the entire apartment very thoroughly, but found nothing further.

'One thing has puzzled me, Superintendent,' said Martín. 'It would have been likely that someone in Santos's position would have had a car, but we didn't find any car keys. Were there any motoring documents among his papers?'

'That's an excellent suggestion, Martín. I'll ring through to Navarro to see if they listed any in the inventory they made, if this phone still works.'

It did work, and Bernal was soon talking to Navarro. 'Paco, Martín and I have found nothing here. Were there any car papers among Santos's things? Insurance documents, garage bills and so on? You'll have a look. If you find a registration number, Martín could help us look for the car, since it's likely to be parked or garaged somewhere in his district. Good. You'll ring back to Martín at Retiro? Very well, I'll tell him. I'll see you about seven, Paco. No other reports in? I see, not yet. *Adiós, hasta luego.* Well, Martín, Navarro will ring you. It's urgent to find the car. It may contain important clues.'

'Would you like a lift back to Sol in my car, Superintendent?'

'No, that's all right. I've another errand to perform first. I shall probably be in touch later about the car,

Martín. If you find it, I'd be grateful if you'd call me before examining it.'

5.45 p.m.

As Martín went off in his official car, Bernal walked back along Alfonso XII towards the Plaza de la Independencia. He could look for a taxi coming down Alcalá, he thought, if he crossed to the other side of the square where the bus-stands were. He waited for the little green man to appear in the traffic lights, and crossed to the central reservation. With the light still in his favour, he began to cross the last section when suddenly a large black Cadillac roared down from the exit of Serrano and deliberately, it seemed to him, tried to knock him down. With a surprising athleticism, he ran for the kerb and the protection of the trees as the driver tried to straighten the wheel to correct the car's crazy course. Before it reached Cibeles and turned northwards, Bernal managed to glimpse the number plate. He leaned for a moment against a tree to get his breath, and jotted the number down on his cigarette packet. The newspaper seller in the kiosk on the corner asked him if he was all right.

'Yes, only winded,' said Bernal.

'It's shocking the way they disregard the traffic lights,' said the *quiosquero*. 'Many an accident I've seen on this corner over the years. You're lucky to be all right.'

'Yes, I suppose I am,' answered Bernal.

He looked for a taxi and spotted one coming with the green '*Libre*' sign up inside the windscreen. 'Take me to the Calle de Barceló, please.' He was about to pull out a cigarette when he saw the notice placed on the dashboard: 'We live in a polluted city. Please don't pollute this taxi by smoking'. Bernal thought the first part was certainly right, and replaced the packet of Kaiser in his pocket.

He pondered on the two, perhaps three, attempts on his life. Why had they been so inefficiently carried out? Unless they had been meant to fail, intended only as warnings, to put him off pursuing the case.

In his studio apartment, he found Consuelo making coffee in the kitchen. 'Sorry I'm so late today, love. Everything happened at once.'

He kissed her and told her of most of the day's events, and showed her the *Sábado de Gloria* document. She read it through, looking very serious. When she had finished, she said, 'It seems incredible, but the right wing have so much lost touch with reality that they're capable even of dreaming up this rubbish. Do they think we're going to be governed by a stuffed mummy?' She turned the sheets over. 'Where are the names of the people involved in this insane plot?'

'That's the problem, love.' He told her how they had rung all the banks they could before they closed, without tracking down any strong-box in the name of Santos or Molina. 'Where else could one deposit a strong-box except in a bank, Consuelo?'

She thought about it. 'Well, the Caja de Ahorros and savings banks don't offer such a service. There are branches of foreign banks, of course, but that's less likely.' She had a sudden thought. 'What about a lawyer's office? They often keep wills and important documents.'

'I'll ring through to Paco and ask him to find out who Santos's lawyer was. He must have used a law firm when he bought the flat in Alfonso XII.' He dialled the number. 'Paco, is that you? Bernal here. Have you checked on his car? I see. What about his parents? They're probably still in the Hotel de París, and could tell you for sure if their son had one, even if they don't know the number of it. While you're looking through the papers again, see if he had a lawyer, yes, a lawyer. He may have left documents with him. I'll be in shortly. Don't forget to ring Martín if you discover the car number. His men can scour the Retiro District for it first. *Hasta luego*, Paco.' He rang off.

'If you find the list of names, Luchi, where are you going to take it, and this plan?' asked Consuelo.

'That depends on the list of names. At least I'll know who not to take it to.'

'Yes, that's true. But I think you should take it to the top, and I mean to the very top.'

'I'll think about it, love. We may not find the names. What do I do then?'

'You'll simply have to take it to the Interior Minister, irrespective of protocol, on the grounds of extreme urgency.'

'We still have two days to forestall it,' said Bernal. 'Let's wait a little longer.'

'If you wait too long they won't be able to react in time, especially not on a holiday weekend.'

'I'd rather have some names to show them. Otherwise they'll say it's all a hoax.' Bernal drank the coffee and munched a chocolate éclair. 'I agree about fairly rapid action, though, or this SDG group may try to put us out of action, should they suspect we are on to them.'

'Do it soon, Luis,' she urged, as he was leaving.

7 p.m.

Bernal took the Metro back to Sol from Tribunal Station; it was only two stops on the busiest part of Line 1 and he kept well back from the edge of the platform until the train came in.

He found Elena and Ángel completing another search of Santos's papers. They told him they could find no car documents or anything relating to a lawyer. Paco was on the phone, having apparently located Santos's parents.

'A blue Mini, yes. At least four years old? Thank you so much, Señor Santos. I understand, of course, that you can't remember the number, except that it was a Madrid registration. We're most grateful. Goodbye.'

He accompanied Bernal into the inner office. 'I've already tried the vehicle registration records of the Ayuntamiento, but they'll take some hours to find it, they say. It's much quicker, of course, to find the name and address of the owner when you've got the registration number.'

'Well, see if they can show us how quick they are by telling us who owns this car.' Bernal pulled out his packet of Kaiser and read the number out to Navarro. 'It's a black Cadillac limousine, and it tried to run me down an hour ago in the Plaza de la Independencia.'

'Are you OK, chief?'

'Yes, I jumped out of the way in time.'

'I'll ring them now,' said Paco. 'By the way, Inspector Cambronero came over with this letter for you, marked for your attention only.'

As Navarro went out to telephone, Bernal tore open Cambronero's letter. He had managed by great good fortune to identify the print of the right index finger found in Marisol's apartment. It belonged to Giancarlo Torelli, motor mechanic, born in Milan in 1935, naturalised Spanish citizen in 1971. The latest address noted for him was a lodging-house in the Calle de las Huertas.

Bernal went to the outer office. 'I'm going out for twenty minutes, Paco, to see Esteban Ibáñez in Central Records.'

'OK, chief. I'll watch over things here.'

Ibáñez had warned Bernal not to phone. He probably suspected that there was surveillance of all DGS calls, internal and external. The system had not been modelled on the Gestapo's for nothing.

Esteban spotted him from his glass-panelled office and came out.

'Just the right moment for a coffee, Luis. Let's go out to the bar round the corner.'

The bar counter was filling up with customers, but there were empty tables at the back. They sat at one of them and Bernal showed Ibáñez the note from Cambronero.

'Could you see if this Torelli has any record, criminal or political? I've now got the evidence to charge him with murder, or at least with administering dangerous drugs with intent to cause death.'

'I'll check it out at once, Luis. You know that the main records are now on computer, but I still have access to the old card-index files, which were kept up to date until eighteen months ago. I'll also run a computer check.'

'I suspect he's in a Fascist organization. You'd better see this.' Bernal handed him a copy of the *Sábado de Gloria* document, which Ibáñez read carefully.

'Mad as it sounds, I believe they intend to do it, Luis. Haven't you found any names?'

'Not yet. That's why I'm holding my hand. If I could arrest and question this Torelli, they'd think he squealed.'

'But that would put you in danger, Luis. Once you've taken him down to the cells, the inside men in this plot will find out he's detained.'

'That's why I want you to keep this copy of the document, in case anything happens to me. Then you can decide whether to go with it to the Minister, or even to the President.'

'But would they listen to a mere Inspector, Luis?'

'They're always prepared to listen to anyone. Whether they'll act on it or not is a different matter. That's why I want to get the names of those behind this business.'

'I'll get off and check this Torelli out now, Luis. I'll come up as soon as I can.'

'I'll be expecting you, Esteban. Good luck.'

7.30 p.m.
When Bernal got back, Paco Navarro waved a sheet of paper at him.

'Here's the owner of that Cadillac, *jefe*. An Argentinian subject called José Weber, with a very strange address, considering the quality of the car: Avenida de la Ciudad de Barcelona.'

Bernal knew that was the arterial highway running past Atocha Station and the RENFE offices out to the working-class district of Vallecas.

'That's in Martín's district, Paco. Ring through to him and see if anything's known about the address. Don't give him the name at this stage.' Bernal wasn't anxious for the name to be overheard on the telephone.

Elena and Ángel came into his office. 'There's nothing, chief,' she said. 'Isn't it extraordinary? If one has a car one is bound to have a record of its number.'

'Not necessarily, Elena, but one would expect to find garage receipts, which would give the number and the mileage. Perhaps he just threw them away, or kept them in the car.'

Paco came in. 'Martín is checking on that address, *jefe*.'

'Good. While you are all here, I had better tell you that we are moving towards making an arrest. The report from the DNI Paco brought me earlier identified one of Marisol's murderers and we have an address for him.' Elena looked thrilled at this news. 'But we have to move cautiously,' Bernal went on. 'I suspect he is part of a larger conspiracy. And we have a strong reason to seek his associates, because one of them at least would have been an accomplice in Marisol's killing, and probably in Santos's too, but we have no evidence yet to prove they killed Santos. The identified man is an Italian by birth, naturalized a few years ago, called Giancarlo Torelli, thought to be lodging in the Calle de las Huertas.'

'Shall we go round there, *jefe*?' asked Paco.

'Not yet. I'm waiting for more information on him. He may well be armed and dangerous, and we need to plan his arrest carefully. Paco, will you arrange for a K car with six armed police in plainclothes to get ready for when I give the word? You and Ángel will wait here, Elena. Paco and I will go into the lodging-house first, while the armed police cover the exits. Let's look at a detailed map.'

He pulled out a large-scale Instituto Geográfico map of the Centro District and hung it by its upper roller over a notice board.

'You'll see that the house is near the corner of the Costanilla de los Desamparados, which is no more than a lane, and we must make sure that there is no escape by that way.'

Elena thought that the lane had an appropriate name, 'the little slope of the Shelterless'.

'The lodging-house,' continued Bernal, 'occupies the entire second floor, and is of low category. The moment Paco and I enter, therefore, the support police must cover the possible exits. Paco, will you brief them with a map?'

'Yes, chief. They'll probably want to go on ahead and check out the terrain. The K car will be a van of some kind that won't arouse suspicion if it's parked there for a while.'

'Good, see to it now. Ángel, if Inspector Martín doesn't ring through before we leave, will you liaise with him over an Argentinian called José Weber, with an address in the Avenida de la Ciudad de Barcelona?'

'Is he the other suspect, chief?'

'I'm not sure yet. In an emergency you can contact us by radio. That will give Elena the chance to see the radio communications room.'

8 p.m.

Inspector Ibáñez arrived bearing a large brown envelope, and Bernal took him into his office.

'I've made you copies of Torelli's files,' Ibáñez said. 'He's on the criminal and political ones. Suspected of armed robbery on two occasions, but not charged. Member of clandestine Fascist organization in Italy, probably used as a gunman, but left Milan when things got too hot for him. Italian Government sought his extradition, hence the application for naturalization, which was granted. Involved in various right-wing extremist activities here: attacks on bookshops, intimidation of workers' commissions, etc. Arrested once by the political brigade, but released with no charges preferred.'

'Many thanks, Esteban. Here's another one for you. José Weber, Argentinian citizen.'

'Oh, I hardly need to look, Luis. I've just come across his name in connection with Torelli's activities. Weber's supposed to be a rich textile importer, but the business is probably a cover. I'll see what I can dig out before I go home.'

'Leave it with Ángel Gallardo if I'm not here, Esteban. The balloon is about to go up over Torelli.'

'Good luck, Luis, but he's only a henchman. Why don't you let him lead you to his bosses?'

'That thought has struck me, but I am in a position to charge him with a crime, and if I don't play it by the book they'll criticize me upstairs afterwards. But I could say I wanted to trap his accomplices, couldn't I? All right, I'll give it a try. I'll re-brief Paco and the armed plainclothesmen.'

'Keep your head down out of the line of fire, Luis. You're not as young as you were.'

'You should see me avoid murderous Cadillacs,' said Bernal grinning. 'I'd like to nail the bastard who drove it.'

He was about to go down to look for Navarro when Martín rang.

'The address in Ciudad de Barcelona is a warehouse, owned by an Argentinian called José Weber, Superintendent, but he lives in the Salamanca quarter, in an elegant apartment. We have been interested in nocturnal comings and goings at the warehouse for some time. Shall I stake it out and keep a watch on visitors?'

'If you can spare the men, Martín. We're about to descend on a lodging-house near you, in Huertas, but unfortunately it's not in your district. We still haven't got anything on Santos's car, except that it's a four-year-old blue Mini with Madrid registration.'

'We'll keep in touch, Superintendent. Good night.'

'Good night, Martín.'

Bernal went down to the briefing-room and broke in on Paco's speech to the armed police, who looked a tough and capable bunch.

'I've just received information which suggests that we should not necessarily arrest Torelli on sight. If possible we shall follow him in order to arrest his accomplices as well. Here is a photograph of him.' Bernal showed them the full-face and two profile photos Ibáñez had brought, which had been taken as a matter of routine when Torelli was first arrested.

Bernal went over the map details again with the armed plainclothesmen, and they set out to make a reconnaissance. Bernal asked Navarro to order an unmarked radio car, which they could leave with its driver in a side street, or at a discreet distance from the lodging-house.

8.30 p.m.

In the Calle de las Huertas Bernal told their driver to park some way up the street. He and Navarro walked down and conferred with the two plainclothes inspectors in the K car, which was a small laundry van, and they noted that the sergeant and the three men were covering the side alley and the street on either side of the house.

Navarro and Bernal entered the gloomy hallway, which looked as though it had once been a yard for stabling horses. The broad wooden stairs were ill-lit and deserted. The door of the lodging-house on the second floor was of massive oak. They rang, and after a pause a blowzy woman of indeterminate age, with gold-filled teeth, and wearing a stained nylon dressing-gown decorated with large pink roses on a green background, answered the door cheerfully.

'Are you looking for a room, gents? Everything's very clean here, and the food's very palatable. Only three hundred pesetas a day each, all in.'

'Could we see it?' asked Bernal.

'Of course, gents. Come this way.'

This was a piece of luck, thought Bernal, since if the suspect was listening he would relax on hearing her talk to prospective clients.

She showed them into a large bedroom with one double and one single bed, a rickety washbasin and an enormous old-fashioned wardrobe. Bernal closed the door and showed her his warrant card.

'We're police officers, Señora. Please don't raise your voice.'

'Holy Mother of God!' she exclaimed, crossing herself. 'What is happening in my house? This is an honourable house, always has been.'

'I'm sure it is. There's no need for alarm,' said Iernal soothingly. 'Have you a Señor Torelli staying here?'

'Yes, yes. He's been here over eight months and is a very quiet gentleman. No trouble. Pays his bill in advance every week. Misses a lot of meals, and doesn't ask for a refund. What's he done?'

'Is he in now?'

'I don't think so. It's early for him. The long-stay guests have their own keys to the downstairs door and to the landing door. They also have keys to their rooms, of course.'

'Could you go and see if he's in, making some excuse for disturbing him? On no account warn him that we're here. You don't want any trouble in your *pensión*, do you?'

'No, no, Comisario, I'll do what you say. Is he dangerous?'

'If you do what I tell you you'll come to no harm. Now come back and tell us whether he's there. Which is his room?'

'The one next to the bathroom. The third door on the left from here.'

She went off in some trepidation and Bernal switched off the light and pulled the door ajar. Paco drew his revolver. The landlady returned breathless. 'He's not in, I'm sure. He doesn't answer my knock and there's no light on.'

'Have you a master key?' Bernal asked.

'Yes, of course. I go in to clean the room and make the bed.'

'Then get it and take a pair of clean sheets. If he turns out to be there, you can say you forgot to change them earlier.'

'He'll think it odd,' she said, 'I change the sheets every Monday.'

'Never mind. Take towels or anything.'

'All right.'

She went off nervously along the passage, opened an airing cupboard and took out two towels. Cautiously she knocked on the door again, then opened it slowly and turned on the light.

'It's all right. You can come and look,' she said in great relief.

Bernal and Navarro followed her and quickly began to search the room, trying not to disturb anything.

'Please stay in the hall, Señora, and if he comes in, detain him as long as you can with some excuse, anything you can think of.'

'A registered letter came for him this afternoon,' she said. 'I could tell him about it and invite him into my sitting-room. That would give you time to get out and lock the door.'

'All right,' said Bernal.

The search of the room revealed nothing of interest. If Torelli was armed, he clearly kept his gun on him, and his spare ammunition in some place other than this. After ten minutes, Navarro and Bernal emerged and locked up the room. The landlady was waiting for them in the hall, in a state of great nervousness.

'Where's the letter you mentioned, Señora?'

'I've got it in here,' she said, ushering them into her

private sitting-room, which was furnished with faded chintz-covered chairs. The envelope was postmarked Alicante on the previous day.

'We'll take charge of it,' Bernal told her. 'Now, when he comes in, tell him nothing of the letter or of our visit, you understand? Nothing. Act as you always do. From what you say he doesn't always dine in?'

'Very seldom,' she admitted. 'He usually comes in to shave and change his clothes, and goes out again about nine.'

'Now remember. If you say anything about our visit, I will not be responsible for the consequences to you or to your *pensión*, you understand?'

'Yes, Comisario, I understand.'

Bernal and Navarro went down to the street, meeting no one. They went to confer with the armed plainclothesmen at the window of the laundry van.

'We'll wait until he shows up,' Bernal told the two inspectors. 'He usually goes in to shave and change and then comes out again quite soon. We'll follow him to see where he leads us. If he goes by car or takes a taxi, we'll box and cox with the van and the unmarked car, and keep in touch by radio.'

'OK, chief.'

'Please warn your men not to close in on him.'

'I will, chief.'

As they waited in their small Fiat parked near the corner of the Calle del Amor de Dios, from where they could see the entrance to the lodging-house, Bernal slit open the registered letter and peered inside with the aid of a pencil torch.

'It's money,' he said to Paco. 'About ten thousand pesetas, but no letter with it. I won't take it out, in case we can get some prints from it.'

He talked to Central Control by radio, and asked to speak to Ángel Gallardo. The radio crackled, and Ángel's voice came over.

'Inspector Martín has rung through, chief. He's put a discreet watch on the warehouse and will report any suspect movements.'

'Good,' replied Bernal. 'Will you arrange to put him in direct contact with me if there's anything urgent?'

'Yes, *jefe*, will do.'

Higher up the Calle de las Huertas, where it joined the Plaza del Ángel, the bars would be full of bullfight enthusiasts at this hour, thought Bernal, but down here, nearer the Paseo del Prado, a chill wind blew down the street and there were few passers-by. Huertas, the street of the gardens, probably those of the old Convent of San Jerónimo; none to be seen now, he reflected.

Navarro drew Bernal's attention to a figure wearing a light-coloured suède jacket, who was walking quickly down Huertas towards their parked car.

'It could be him, chief.'

They slumped down in the back seat, while their driver watched in the mirror. As he passed their car, the man did not even give it a glance. It was one of many parked on that side of the road. As he turned under a street lamp into the doorway of the house, Paco recognized him from the photograph.

'That's him, chief. I'm sure.'

After a few moments, one of the inspectors came over to speak to Bernal.

'We recognized him, sir, from the photograph. What do you wish us to do?'

'If he needs a taxi,' said Bernal, 'he's sure to walk down the street to the Plaza de Platerías Martínez. There's nearly always one free there, or he'll find one on the Paseo del Prado nearby. Therefore I suggest that we move down and park out of sight in the entrance to the Calle de Moratín, while you stay here and tell us what is going on by radio. If, of course, he walks up Huertas, which is one-way, then two of your men can follow him separately on foot; likewise, if he takes either of the alleys. But they mustn't press him too close.'

9.30 p.m.

In their new position in Moratín, Navarro and Bernal had to rely on the periodic messages from the K car, 'Nothing to report.' Finally, at 9.42, the radio crackled into life again.

'He's coming out, now wearing a fawn overcoat and a dark brown Italian-type slouch hat, pulled down over the left eye. He has turned down the street.' There was a pause. 'He's passed the entrance to Desamparados without entering it. He's walking on towards the corner of Jesús. One of our men is starting to follow. Suspect has not looked back yet.' Another pause. 'He's crossed Jesús and is walking down to where you are parked.'

Bernal noticed that a taxi had just dropped a fare on the corner of the Paseo del Prado. Would Torelli spot it and hail it? As he wondered, the hatted figure came into sight out of Huertas, running, and shouting 'Taxi!' As they watched him get in, Bernal told the driver to start the engine. He knew that unless it crossed the boulevard towards the Prado Museum, the taxi would have to turn right down the Paseo del Prado towards Atocha, because it was one-way on that side.

He picked up the radio handset. 'K thirty-two? This is Bernal. He's taken a taxi which we are following. Gather your men in and follow us reasonably closely. It's turning right towards Atocha. We mustn't lose him under the flyover that crosses the square in front of the station.'

The message was acknowledged. In the four lanes of halted traffic at the first traffic lights under the flyover, Bernal saw that Torelli's taxi was three vehicles ahead of them, in the second lane. K 32, the disguised van, was two vehicles further back in the fourth lane. Bernal spoke again into the radio and gave the K car the taxi number and its position. 'We'll be prepared for him to turn right into the Calle de Atocha, or to go down Primo de Rivera, or cross into the railway station. You are better placed to follow him if he bears left around the fountain towards Reina Cristina or Claudio Moyano.' The message was again acknowledged.

Bernal spoke to Paco and the driver; 'I've a strong hunch he's going to bear left towards Reina Cristina and then right down Ciudad de Barcelona. Let's try to get Ángel at Control.'

The driver sent out a call, and Ángel's voice came in; 'Yes, chief?'

'Ángel, can you get me Inspector Martín by direct link?'

'Yes, chief, he's near you, in a K car alongside the warehouse on Ciudad de Barcelona.'

'Excellent,' said Bernal. 'Put him through.'

'Yes, Superintendent? Martín here.'

'Martín, we're at Atocha and it's very possible that the suspect Torelli is coming in your direction in a taxi. At what point on Ciudad de Barcelona is the warehouse?'

'Soon after the junction with Doctor Esquerdo, two blocks down, on the right.'

The lights changed and Torelli's taxi turned left half-way around Atocha fountain, and was stopped by traffic lights again.

'Martín,' said Bernal into the radio, 'it's almost certain. The taxi's turning towards Reina Cristina.'

Bernal's driver managed to do the impossible, and changed lanes, coming to a halt behind the laundry van, which was now two vehicles behind the taxi. Bernal spoke to K 32. 'Watch out for the lane he takes at the lights where Reina Cristina and Ciudad de Barcelona divide.'

'OK, chief.'

The taxi took the third of the five lanes, suggesting that it was going to go straight over towards Vallecas; its driver certainly hadn't entered one of the two lanes for continuing along Reina Cristina, which bore left at this point.

Bernal spoke to the K car again. 'When he enters Ciudad

de Barcelona, we'll overtake him and proceed beyond the textile warehouse, which is soon after Doctor Esquerdo, on the right. You should move more slowly, at some distance behind him and stop well back if he stops. Retiro District has the warehouse under surveillance from K twenty-two. Do you know what vehicle that is?'

'We think it's a soft drinks lorry, chief.'

Torelli's taxi gathered speed along the emptier highway, and Bernal's driver put his foot down to pass it in the outer lane. Navarro and Bernal again slumped down in the back seat as they passed the taxi, though Bernal considered that there was little danger of Torelli's noticing the Fiat, because it was a very common car on the streets of the city. He was more worried about his spotting the laundry van, which he had walked past on his way out of the lodging-house.

After they had passed Doctor Esquerdo, Bernal's driver reduced speed and watched in the rear-view mirror. 'The taxi's slowing, chief. I think he's getting out at the corner.'

Bernal took up the radio handset and spoke to Martín. 'He's alighting at the corner of Doctor Esquerdo, Martín, wearing a fawn overcoat and a dark brown slouch hat.'

'We can see him, chief. I have men watching the back of the warehouse in case he goes in that way.'

Bernal's driver turned right into the second side street and turned in the road. He parked near the corner but out of sight.

The radio crackled again and Martín spoke. 'He's reached the front gate and is letting himself in through a small door. He's gone in.'

'Come to the corner, Martín,' said Bernal, 'and we'll have a council of war.'

Navarro and Bernal got out to meet Martín and his sergeant. The laundry van had pulled up nearby and the plainclothesmen got out.

'Is there a back entrance, Martín?' asked Bernal. 'We

don't want to knock on the main door and raise the alarm.'

'Yes, there is, and there's a window on the first floor with a light showing. We've seen three men go in. Torelli was the fourth. There's a black Cadillac parked at the back.'

'That will be Weber's,' said Bernal.

'There's no light showing through the front windows, sir,' said Martín's sergeant. 'Shall we force both doors simultaneously? The locks are of the simplest type.'

Bernal believed in teams of men sticking together. 'Martín, you take your men round to the back and force an entrance there. How are your men armed?'

'Each has a pistol, and two have sub-machine-guns. That should easily be enough.'

'Have we pocket radio sets?' Bernal asked the plain-clothes inspectors.

'Yes, chief,' said the burlier of them, 'and they are tuned in to the same frequency.'

'Well, give one to Martín and one to me. I'll give the word when to force the two doors. Have we torches?'

'Plenty of them, *jefe*.'

'Good. They may well resist arrest, and try to put the lights out of action. Keep your heads down and try not to shoot one another. Aim only at close targets when you're sure who they are. We'll enter in approximately five minutes, Martín. I'll call for them to surrender. Have you a loudhailer, Inspector?'

'Yes, sir. Press the red button when you want to speak.'

'You hold it for me, Paco.'

10 p.m.

The plainclothes sergeant worked silently with a plastic strip on the lock of the front door, and after a few minutes it clicked open. They drew their guns and Bernal edged the door open an inch, but could see no light. Then he spoke into the radio set, 'Now, Martín!'

They kicked the door wide open and rushed in, taking

cover on each side in the gloom. A faint light came from behind some large bales of cloth, which stood row upon row in the outer part of the warehouse. The two plain-clothes inspectors and Navarro switched on powerful torches, and Bernal waved them and their men to take the right side while he and Navarro took the left. As they rounded the bales into the lighted area, Bernal took the megaphone and spoke authoritatively: 'This is the police! You are completely surrounded. Drop your weapons and put your hands over your heads, or we shall shoot to kill!'

Four men stood around a table on which some dis-mantled weapons were lying. Torelli, whom they had followed, Weber the fat Argentinian, and two others. One of these, a short, dark man, was about to draw a gun when Martín and his men came up behind them, and Martín said sharply, 'Don't move! Not one of you, or I shoot!'

The short, dark man slowly lifted his hands on to his head. Suddenly, the place was plunged into darkness, apart from the light from the police torches. A bullet whistled past Bernal's ear, and he fell to the floor, dropping the megaphone. He realized that there had been a fifth man after all, who had been handily near the light-switch. Cautiously Bernal and Navarro withdrew to the cover provided by the bales on the left, while the plain-clothesmen did likewise on the right.

Then from the rear, Martín had a large portable arc-lamp trained on to the table in the centre, and an intense shooting match began, and just as suddenly ended, with a loud explosion as a hand-grenade on the table was hit. Bernal felt around for the megaphone. 'Put down your arms, or you will all be killed.' He turned to Navarro; 'Hold your fire and bring more torches up.'

In the meantime, one of Martín's men had brought another arc-lamp into play on to the centre of the ware-house, where one man could still be seen crouching under the table. 'Don't shoot, I'm coming out! Don't shoot!'

The man who spoke was not the fat Argentinian but one of the two unknown men. Torelli lay unmoving behind the table and the short, dark man lay lifeless between the table and the side wall. One of Martín's men had moved around the rear wall and discovered the fifth man, who was unarmed, and he now forced him to restore the lights.

A rapid search was made of the rest of the building. 'Where is Weber?' Bernal shouted to Martín. 'He's not with the others.'

Suddenly they heard a car engine start up at the rear of the warehouse. 'He's getting away! After him!' shouted Bernal.

Martín raced out through the rear exit, and two shots were fired. Then there was silence. Navarro went out to see what had occurred, and found that Martín had raced to his car where the driver was waiting and was roaring off in pursuit. He knew that he would report in to Central Control and ask for help to intercept Weber.

He turned to find Bernal bending over Torelli. 'Here's one of our murderers, Paco. He's unconscious and has bad burns from the grenade that went off. Let's see what the other two are carrying.'

The short, dark man lay unconscious with a bullet-hole through his right shoulder, and Bernal felt in the pockets of his jacket and pulled out the wallet he found there. 'Giovanni Cavalli, another Italian! What interesting things our Italian visitors get up to! And these two?' he asked Martín's sergeant, who had the other two men handcuffed.

'Strictly local products, chief. Here are their *carnets*. Look at these badges they were wearing.'

Bernal took charge of the red and black SDG badges, which were already familiar to him. Navarro came back from the radio car.

'I've called for two ambulances, *jefe*.'

'Good,' said Bernal. 'Search as rapidly as possible for all papers and documents and bring them out to the car. I'll have to inform the Second Brigade. These arms are a political and military matter. They'll then take over here and hold these prisoners, I suppose,' he said ruefully. 'Search their pockets, Paco, and see if there's anything that suggests that they or the unconscious man could have been our second murderer. Torelli looks to be in a bad way. But we'll charge him with murder if he recovers.'

10.30 p.m.
Bernal went out into the street and lit a cigarette. He decided he wouldn't be too quick in informing the political brigade, so as to give Navarro a chance to gather any papers that could be found, but he knew he would have to do it in a few minutes, because Central Control would have heard the request for the ambulances.

These now appeared, and Bernal directed the attendants inside. 'Which hospital will you take them to?' he asked. 'They're both under arrest as suspected terrorists.'

'In that case, we'll take them to the Gran Hospital in Diego de León. There's better security there. You'll send two of your men with us?'

'Yes, but you won't have any trouble. They're both out for the count, and one of them is badly burned by an explosion.'

Bernal went in and asked the plainclothes inspectors to send two of their men with the ambulances. He noted that they had uncovered an impressive arsenal from large crates tucked between the bales of cloth: four boxes of hand-grenades, twelve sub-machine-guns, six rifles with tele-scopic sights, and what appeared to be bomb-making equipment.

'By God, we're lucky that grenade didn't send up the whole caboosh,' said the plainclothes sergeant.

'I can see that,' said Bernal, 'and with all these bales there'd have been an almighty blaze.'

One of the plainclothesmen was pulling out a large package covered with brown paper, and Bernal told him to open it. Inside there were large red and black banners marked with the SDG monogram, just like the badges.

'What group is this?' asked the sergeant. 'It's obviously not the FRAP or the GRAPO.'

'I think it must be a new lot,' said Bernal, who now went out again to radio in from his car. 'Bernal to Control. Is that you, Ángel?'

'Yes, chief.'

'We've got them, or most of them. Two of them are injured, but none of ours. We had a bit of a shoot-out. Will you put me through to the Second Brigade?'

'Right away, chief.'

There was a pause, then a voice crackled. 'Bernal? This is the Chief Commissioner, Segunda Brigada. What is happening?'

'While pursuing a murderer, Commissioner, we've stumbled upon what seems to be a terrorist bomb-factory. I suggest you come at once.' He gave him the address. 'I'll be waiting at the front entrance.'

As he switched off the radio, Paco turned up with a handful of documents. 'That's all I can find, chief. Weber has probably gone off with the important stuff.'

'Let's have a quick look through, Paco. We must try to find a list of names of the SDG plotters before the Second Brigade take the whole thing over.'

They went through the papers by the light of a torch and the dim interior light of the car. 'Only lists of weapons here, Paco. Nothing on the plot. We can hand over these to the Second Brigade, but take a note of the arrested men's *carnets*. We can do some checking on our own account.'

As Paco finished this task, an impressive convoy of jeeps and armoured cars screamed to a halt outside the warehouse. Bernal walked down to meet the Chief Commissioner.

'We stumbled on this by accident, Commissioner, having followed a murder suspect from his lodgings.'

Just then the ambulance men emerged with the two stretchers.

'Here's our man,' said Bernal, pointing to Torelli. He gave the Commissioner a brief summary of Torelli's background. 'If he recovers, I shall be wanting to make a formal charge against him.'

'We'll see, Bernal, we'll see. I'll take charge of the matter here. It clearly falls within my jurisdiction.'

'Of course, Commissioner. Navarro has all the papers we've found here for you.'

The Commissioner took charge of them.

'Oh, I should have told you, Commissioner,' Bernal went on, 'one man, possibly the ringleader of these terrorists, escaped, and Inspector Martín of Retiro has gone in pursuit.'

'How did Martín come to be involved in this?' asked the Commissioner.

'He was co-operating with me in the arrest of Torelli. After all, we are in his district.'

'I see,' said the Commissioner, looking none too pleased.

The ambulances now drove off at high speed, with sirens screaming.

'Well, you can be getting back, Bernal. We'll take over now. I'd like to see your report in the morning.'

'Thank you, Commissioner.' Bernal went over to the plainclothes inspectors and shook them by the hand. 'Thank you for the excellent co-operation you and your men have shown.'

'It's been a pleasure working with you, Superintendent,' they said.

10.45 p.m.

Martín, meanwhile, was having his own difficulties. His driver had been able to start the heavy Seat 124 and get to the corner of the Avenida de la Ciudad de Barcelona in time to see that Weber had swung the Cadillac to the right and was leaving the city towards the south-east, in the direction of Vallecas. Martín feared that the Seat wouldn't keep up with the Cadillac on the open road, but so far they had kept Weber's car within sight.

He called in by radio to Central Traffic Control, and gave details of his position, but it was clear to them as to him that until Weber reached Vallecas, there was no way of guessing which way he would go. They said they would alert all mobiles to be on the watch for the Cadillac, and they broadcast its registration number.

Out now in the area that was not built up beyond Port-azgo, Martín could see the lights of Vallecas in the distance. Fortunately there was very little traffic and his driver was managing to close a little on the Cadillac.

'Watch out at Vallecas crossroads, Enrique,' Martín said. 'He won't stop for any traffic lights.'

'OK, chief.'

As they approached the complicated junction, Martín saw that Weber was bearing left, towards the north-east and the Autopista de Valencia. He spoke into the radio; 'Suspect making for the Valencia motorway. Please inform the patrols.'

The message was acknowledged. As they sped along the Carretera de Vallecas north-eastwards towards the motorway interchange, Martín warned his driver, 'Watch out in case he makes a feint at the junction, Enrique.'

Weber reached the first turning and started to turn right as though to go south, then at the last moment he pulled the wheel sharply round and went straight on through the underpass. Enrique had slowed slightly, so wasn't taken in, but he lost ground.

'See if he turns left to join the westbound carriageway.'

Enrique grunted. Again at the very last moment, Weber slewed the Cadillac to go left with a scream of tyres and a lot of black smoke and roared on to the motorway, just missing a heavy lorry that happened to be passing. As Enrique eased the Seat into the motorway traffic, Martín spoke to Control; 'Suspect now making for the Avenida del Mediterráneo. Have you a patrol near the M thirty interchange?'

'We are despatching one,' came the reply. Martín thought it would be much too late.

'Be prepared for him to take the Autopista de la Paz, Enrique, at the next interchange.'

'I can't get enough power to overtake him, chief. He's doing about a hundred and forty km. an hour, and we can hardly reach that.'

'Try to keep him in sight if you can.'

At the M30 interchange, Weber turned northward at the very last moment, up the Autopista de la Paz. Martín spoke again to Control. 'He's turned northward. Can you get patrols to all the access points?'

'We're doing what we can.'

It wasn't good enough, he thought. They still weren't used to the sheer speed of motorways and the virtual impossibility of blocking their exits, without causing multiple accidents. He tried to visualize the road map and the interchanges: O'Donnell, Alcalá, Mola, Arturo Soria, then Chamartín. Were there some he'd missed?

He didn't have to worry. Weber put his foot down and tried to outdistance them in the outer lane.

'He's pulling away from us, sir,' said Enrique. 'I've got my foot flat down.'

Martín spoke to Control. 'We're losing him. Have you got Chamartín covered?'

'Yes,' came the reply, 'and Arturo Soria.'

'Good. Keep us informed when he's spotted.'

Martín had a hunch it was going to be Chamartín and the mainline railway station. There was a new access road from the motorway, and once inside the station, Weber would be difficult to spot.

He spoke into the radio again. 'Warn the station police to be on the watch for his arrival.'

'Will do.'

They lost sight of Weber's car after two more minutes, but Enrique kept the Seat going flat out. They listened anxiously, then the radio crackled. 'The patrol at Chamartín interchange have spotted him coming off the motorway. They are pursuing.'

Martín sank back with relief. Enrique started to brake as they approached the turn-off, and they circumnavigated the access road to the station. As they drove up an extraordinary sight met them. The Cadillac had come to a halt vertically on a grassy bank, with its chassis resting against an ancient green steam engine, which the RENFE had carefully restored as a museum piece and placed to enliven the station approach. There was no sign of Weber, though a police patrol vehicle had stopped nearby and the patrolmen were running towards the station entrance. Martín and his driver followed them, and inside the large new departure hall Martín went to the Police Control office.

The chief inspector in charge had been in touch with Traffic Control. 'Inspector Martín? What does your suspect look like?'

'Fat, balding, cleanshaven, wearing a black overcoat and a red silk scarf. Warn your men that he is armed and dangerous.'

The station inspector rapidly gave orders. 'We've got a good chance,' he said. 'There are no trains departing for ten minutes. The biggest risk is that he'll take the line that runs underground back to Atocha. On that he could get out in the middle of the city, at Nuevos Ministerios or Recoletos. There's no ticket inspection on that stretch, of course. The other possibility is that he'll jump on the stopping train to the Escorial. The halts are not manned at this time of night. I've got men on all the platforms here, but it'll be a few minutes before they receive your description of him.'

Martín thought it would be a damned sight more efficient if all the men on the beat were issued with two-way pocket radios, as in other countries; they only got them on special occasions in this still backward country.

The station inspector came back from the telephone. 'We'll see if we can't pick him out. The station master is very upset at having that Cadillac wrapped round his old railway engine. It'll have to be repainted, he says.'

During the next quarter of an hour, five respectable, fat businessmen in black overcoats were hauled into the office for Martín's inspection. After documentation had been checked, profuse apologies had to be made. Then they had a stroke of luck. The woman lavatory attendant had been disturbed by the sudden entry of a fat gentleman, red in the face, who rushed into one of the cubicles in the gents', without waiting for her to hand him the statutory three pieces of toilet paper. Worried about losing her tip, she decided to call one of the *grises* patrolling outside. He had just been given Weber's description, and went in with her to wait for him to emerge.

When Weber came out, without an overcoat and wearing a small black moustache, the policeman thought the old woman was raving as usual. But he decided to stop the man and ask him for his *carnet*. When Weber produced a pistol, the old woman screamed, distracting him momentarily, and the *gris* was able to disarm him.

In the office, Martín pulled the false moustache off Weber's face, and made him turn out his pockets. He was then handcuffed, and the station inspector offered Martín an escort to take him back to the Retiro District station, which he accepted. Weber refused to say anything at all. Martín looked quickly through his wallet and personal effects. Behind his lapel he found an SDG badge, which puzzled him. 'What is this badge, Weber?'

'You'll soon find out.' And those were the only words they could get out of him until they got back to Retiro.

11.15 p.m.
When Navarro and Bernal arrived at the DGS building,

they found Elena waiting for them.

'Are you still here at this hour?' asked Bernal.

'I couldn't miss the excitement,' she said. 'I've been with Ángel in the radio room. He's still there following Inspector Martín's chase of the Argentinian. Ten minutes ago they had reached Chamartín station, but they had lost him.'

'Well, we've got Torelli,' Bernal said, 'who's one of our murderers, and tomorrow we'll ask for saliva tests to be made on the other three arrested men for the lab to check against the cigarette stub we found in Marisol's apartment. You had better get off home, Elena.'

'Can't I just wait to see if Inspector Martín brings Weber in?'

'Very well.'

The phone rang and Navarro answered it. 'It's Martín, *jefe*, for you.'

'Yes, Martín. You got him? Where are you taking him? To Retiro? I'll come down and meet you there. Yes, well done. A good night's work. *Hasta luego.*' Bernal put down the phone. 'They've got him, Elena. Satisfied? Now you can go home and get some supper inside you. Perhaps Ángel will take you.'

'Oh, I'm much too excited to eat,' she said. 'It's been a thrilling evening. I'll see you tomorrow at the usual time. Good night, *jefe*. Good night, Paco.'

When she had left, Bernal took the SDG badges out of his pocket and looked at them pensively. 'We're going to have a job to stop them, Paco. Let's go down to Retiro and interview Weber.'

'OK, chief.'

11.30 p.m.
But when they reached the district station in the Calle de Fernanflor, they found a chief superintendent from the Second Brigade waiting. 'Ah, Bernal. We understand from the Chamartín station police that Inspector Martín has

arrested Weber. We'll take him in for questioning, of course.'

'Of course,' said Bernal, with a sinking heart. 'You wouldn't let me question him first about the murders?'

'The Chief Commissioner says you can do that later on. The political side must take precedence. He said you'd understand.'

'Yes, I understand,' said Bernal.

Martín now arrived with his prisoner, and his face fell on seeing the superintendent from the Second Brigade.

'We'll take him, Martín, and we'll be doing the domiciliary search. Thank you for bringing him in. You've done an excellent job. This escort can return to Chamartín. My men are outside.'

Martín handed Weber over, noticing the sly, hopeful look that had crept over his prisoner's face. When they had left, Martín invited Bernal and Navarro into his office, and asked the desk sergeant to get some coffee.

'No,' said Bernal, 'let's go out for a drink. Isn't there a bar round the corner?'

'Yes, in the Calle de Jovellanos, opposite the Zarzuela Theatre. There's that old bar called Manolo's.'

'That will do. I want the three of us to have a quiet chat.'

When all three of them were seated at a corner table and had been served with *cañas* of beer and an assortment of *tapas*, Bernal gave Martín a full account of the SDG plot. Martín and Navarro listened intently, and the former read through the timetable of the plot with an expression of disbelief. But then he put his hand into his pocket and brought out the SDG badge he had found in Weber's lapel. 'This was on Weber, Superintendent.'

'Another one for our collection,' said Bernal. 'You see that we either have to sit back and let it all happen, or we try to find the names of the plotters and take the whole thing to the highest authority.'

'Oh, we must try to stop it,' said Martín without

hesitation. 'But where is the list? Where do we start looking? Tomorrow morning is our last chance.'

'Well, from eight-thirty we'll go on enquiring at all the banks to see if there's another strong-box. And there's Santos's car. We must find the blue Mini. By the morning, the Ayuntamiento should have found out the registration number.'

'I'll put all available men on to it, *jefe*,' said Martín. 'It may well be in my district. Once we have the number, we can find out when it last had a parking ticket and on which street.'

Bernal felt that he should give them both a warning. 'I think you ought to know that two, possibly three, attempts have been made on my life this week. One was definitely made by Weber, or at least by someone driving his car.' He told them how the Cadillac had tried to run him down, and also mentioned his experience in the Metro and the *chulo*'s attack on him in the street. 'All three of us may now be in danger, despite Weber's arrest. Please take care, and don't walk about alone.'

'I'll take you both home in my car,' said Martín, 'since you've sent your driver away.'

'That's very good of you,' said Bernal. 'We must get cracking first thing tomorrow.'

12 midnight
Bernal found the flat in darkness; Eugenia had obviously gone to bed. In the kitchen he discovered she had left him the usual omelette of leftovers, but it was cold and looked greasy. He decided to make do with the *tapas* he had eaten and crawled into bed alongside her.

MAUNDY THURSDAY, 7 APRIL

7 a.m.

Bernal had slept badly. Awakened at 3 a.m. by stomach pains, he wasn't sure if they were from the pangs of hunger or a nervous knotting of the stomach muscles. Anxious not to awaken Eugenia, he had reached into his jacket pocket for a Kolantyl tablet and chewed it meditatively. Then he had fallen into an uneasy sleep once more.

Eugenia now disturbed him by opening the door to her private oratory in the dining-room and beginning her daily round of prayers and housekeeping. Still half asleep, he heard her last Amens and was brought more fully into consciousness by her grinding of the mixture of burnt acorns and coffee beans. Groaning, he made his way to the bathroom and began to shave.

Well ahead of the insurance agent this morning, he dressed and looked out at the uncertain dawn. After a cold night, it would probably rain and become milder, he thought.

'Geñita, I've got to go in early this morning. I hope to clear up those two murders. We arrested four suspects last night.'

'I shall pray for you, and for them too, Luis. You know what day this is? The day of the *pedilavium*, when the feet of the poor are to be washed.'

'But is that still done in Madrid, Geñita?'

'No, more's the pity. We have godless rulers, Luis. All the old cherished traditions are ignored. And what is put in their place? Sinful activities, mindless doings,' she lamented. 'Feast-days are now an excuse for immoral behaviour.'

Bernal gulped down as little of the coffee as possible and

went to put his coat on. 'Did Diego ring up last night, Geñita?'

'No,' she said. 'I hope he's going to Mass each day.'

Luis thought that nothing was less likely, but forbore to say so.

'Santiago rang,' she added. 'They want us to go round for lunch on Sunday.'

'I'll look for some little Easter present for our grandson,' he said.

'Oh, you spoil him, Luis. He has all Santiago and Diego's old toys to play with as it is.'

'Still, I'd better get something. Perhaps an Action Man. He'll expect us to take some present or other. I'm off now. I'm not sure that I'll be in for lunch today, with all the reports to write up.'

'Very well, Luis. I'll be out at church all the morning. I can always fry you some fish if you come in.'

'*Hasta luego*, Geñita.'

Bernal stopped in the street to buy *El País* and had a quick second breakfast in Félix Pérez's.

8 a.m.

As he was leaving the bar, Bernal spotted a vacant taxi and hailed it. No point in taking chances today, he thought. When he got to the office, he found Paco Navarro already there opening the mail that had just been delivered. 'Here's a note from the Traffic Department, chief. They've tracked down the registration number of Santos's car.' He handed the sheet to Bernal, who picked up the phone and dialled Martín's number.

'Is Inspector Martín in? Not yet? Please get him to ring Superintendent Bernal as soon as he arrives. Yes, thank you.'

'There's a note from the Subsecretary, *jefe*, asking you to call in and see him this morning.'

'I don't suppose he will be in much before nine-thirty,' said Bernal. 'Anything else of interest?'

'Peláez's final report on Marisol, and the toxicologist's report. It seems that the glass dropper contained almost pure heroin, and that she was injected with a massive dose which would have soon caused respiratory failure.'

The phone rang and Martín came on the line. 'Please take down this registration number,' said Bernal. 'Do you think your men can start an immediate search? They can? Many thanks. Yes, I'll be waiting for your call.' He hung up.

Elena and Ángel now arrived together, and Bernal asked them to start telephoning the banks, picking up where they had left off the day before. 'I'll draft out a report for charges to be brought against Torelli,' he said. 'We have the final medical report now. I think we've only got the evidence to charge him with causing Marisol's death. Paco, will you ring the Second Brigade and see if they will let us have saliva tests taken on the other men arrested last night?'

Inspector Martín telephoned again and Bernal took the call in his office. 'I thought you'd like to know that I found two sets of car keys among the contents of Weber's pockets last night, chief. One of them has a British Leyland tag, and the keys are not for the Cadillac. Could they have been taken from Santos's apartment?'

'They certainly could,' said Bernal. 'In which case they may have been looking for the car as well as us. This find certainly incriminates Weber in Santos's death, though it doesn't prove that he was present in the apartment when it occurred, of course. Torelli and his accomplice probably brought the set of keys to him. Hang on to them for the time being, Martín.' He put down the phone. Frowning, he wondered whether the SDG organization had already found Santos's car and broken it open and searched it.

9 a.m.

Navarro came in and told Bernal that the upstairs office was on the phone asking whether Bernal was free to see the Subsecretary. Bernal grimaced, but said he would go.

The blonde secretary received him as warmly as ever and took him straight in. The Subsecretary looked calm, Bernal thought, but received him less effusively than before.

'Well, you seem to have cleared it up, ‎qernal. Pity your man died during the night.'

'Died?' exclaimed Bernal.

'Oh yes, haven't you heard? Torelli didn't recover consciousness and died from his burns at four-fifteen a.m.'

'No, they haven't had the kindness to inform me,' Bernal said coldly. 'I should still like to have saliva tests done on the others.'

'Ah, there is a slight problem. The Second Brigade decided to release Weber and the other two who were not injured. Not very strong evidence against them, and it was thought that more would be gained from keeping them under surveillance and seeing where they lead us.'

'Release them? But there's plenty of evidence that they had illegal arms.'

'It transpires that Weber had a licence to import them. Here is a copy of it.' Bernal was staggered by the news. He decided not to ask about the SDG banners. No doubt they had been suppressed in the official report.

'Why did he evade arrest, then?'

'Well, being a foreigner, he was naturally frightened of being deported. Well, that sews it up. Perhaps you'll be able to have a happy Easter after all, eh, Bernal? I think your group should have the weekend off. This has been a tough case.'

'Yes, Mr Secretary, they'll be most grateful. We could all do with a quiet Easter, couldn't we?' He took his leave and stormed back to his office. He thought he wouldn't tell Ángel and Elena yet, to let them go on phoning the banks, but he called Navarro in. 'They've done the dirty on us, Paco. Torelli died during the night, and they've released Weber and the others. Insufficient evidence of illegal activities. Insufficient evidence, my eye! They're all in league, Paco. We've been wasting our time,' he said bitterly. 'Who'd try to be an honest policeman in this paradise for gangsters and hired assassins, who are allowed to roam at will?'

'Are you going to tell Martín?'

'Not yet, not yet. There's one forlorn hope of his finding the car, or of Ángel and Elena coming up with a bank with Santos's other strong-box. I suppose I might as well finish drafting this report. By the way, we've all been given the weekend off.'

'A reward for our silence, eh?' said Paco.

10 a.m.

Navarro hurried into Bernal's office. 'Martín's found the car. He wants us to go to Cibeles at once and meet him on the steps of the Post Office.'

Bernal went to get his coat. On the way out, he asked Elena and Ángel to go on with the telephoning. 'If we find the strong box, we'll ring you to put you out of your misery. Have you heard? We've been given the weekend off.' They looked cheered by this news.

Navarro and Bernal took an official car and were driven along the Carrera de San Jerónimo, then left through Sevilla and down Alcalá. The day was opening out, with signs that the sun might shine later on. Outside the main Post Office, they got out and told their driver to return to the DGS. They saw Martín and his sergeant waiting for them on the steps. 'The car's around the back, Superintendent,' said Martín. 'We searched all the streets in this area and found nothing, then my sergeant thought of the cars parked inside the post office yard. Normally, only employees' cars and official vans are allowed in, but clearly the watchman didn't think anything of seeing the blue Mini there for nearly a week. Perhaps Santos had left it there on previous occasions.'

They walked briskly round the corner and through the

iron gates. The Mini was tucked in a corner, and apparently hadn't been tampered with. Martín produced the key-ring he had found on Weber, and discovered that one of the two keys fitted the door-lock.

'Don't worry about fingerprints,' said Bernal. 'The case is all but closed anyway.'

Martín looked surprised at this, but didn't comment. They found nothing inside the car, except for the car papers and documents. Then they opened the boot. Wrapped up inside a strip of waterproof cloth they saw a new-looking strong-box. Bernal produced the security key they had found in Marisol's apartment and discovered that it fitted the lock. Inside was a sealed brown envelope, similar to the one they had collected from the bank on the Gran Vía, but it was much fatter.

'Let's go over to the Bar Correos opposite,' said Bernal. 'The three of us can examine the contents together.'

Martín left instructions with his sergeant for Santos's car to be taken to the district station, and asked his driver to wait for him.

They crossed Alcalá and went down the steps into the bar, which was empty at that hour. 'Shall we have coffee?' asked Bernal. They agreed. Calling to the barman for three *cortados*, Bernal led them to a table in the far corner, where he opened the envelope. They found that the contents consisted of thirty-two typed sheets, apparently duplicated by Xerox. The first page was headed 'SÁBADO DE GLORIA' and it and the next twenty-one sheets contained a list of names, set out under a series of headings which comprised all the Ministries, the Armed Forces and the Police organizations. Bernal, Martín and Navarro turned hastily to the section headed 'DGS' and were horrified at the length and importance of the list. Bernal noted that the Subsecretary's name was included, as well as even more senior administrators and many commissioners, superintendents and inspectors. They were also shocked by some of the military names, and by the long lists from the provinces.

The remaining ten sheets revealed the details of the coup planned for the weekend: the names of those who were to arrange for Franco's coffin to be exhumed at the Valle de los Caídos on Good Friday evening, when the monks were at their evening meal; the identity of the RENFE employees who were secretly putting on a special train on the Saturday afternoon to bring the coffin and its escort to the Estación del Norte, below the Royal Palace; the police who were detailed to control the crowds in the Plaza de Oriente on the Sunday morning when Franco's 'resurrection' would take place, and the officers chosen to head the columns for the march-past in the Castellana on the Sunday afternoon. Every detail was recorded, including the arrangements in the Ayuntamiento for the erection of the saluting platform, the tiers of seats and the barriers for the military display.

The three of them read through it in utter astonishment. Martín spoke first. 'You clearly cannot take these lists to our superiors via the usual channels, Superintendent, because too many of them are involved. They'd do anything to stop it getting to the Minister.'

Bernal mused over the lists. 'You have both noticed that no member of the present Government is involved? So in theory I could take it to our Minister if I could get to him.'

'But you'd have to get through a barrage of secretaries,' Paco objected, 'and once they knew your business they'd never let you see him.'

'What puzzles me,' said Bernal, 'is that there's no leader mentioned. These documents go on as if the Caudillo were really going to come back to life, yet there must be someone they have in mind to take over as dictator ultimately, but they're keeping him carefully out of sight for the moment. Maybe that's what Santos was trying to find out before he took all this to a left-wing daily to achieve his world scoop. The newspaper wouldn't have dared print the lists, of course, because the people named would have denied any involvement. But publishing the details of the plot would have been so damaging as to cause them to call the whole thing off. Nevertheless Santos needed the names to convince an editor that it was a genuine plot. My guess is he was still after the big name when they rumbled him.'

Martín said, 'The best thing to do is to go to the President with all the documents and the other evidence.'

'The banners we saw in the warehouse seem to have been mysteriously overlooked by the Second Brigade,' said Bernal, 'but we have the badges.' He now told Martín how Weber had been released, and how Torelli had died during the night. 'Are you both agreed that I take all we've got to the President, on grounds of extreme urgency?'

'Yes. I'll come with you if you wish,' said Martín, and Navarro nodded his agreement.

'No, there's no need to put more than one career at risk. I'll telephone to the Moncloa first.' He went over to the bar and asked the barman for two *fichas* for the telephone, handing over six pesetas. At the back of the long room, he consulted the directory and dialled the President's palace.

'This is the Presidency of the Government. Can I help you?' cooed a female voice.

'I should like to speak to the President's private secretary.'

'Who is calling?'

'Comisario Bernal of the Dirección General de Seguridad.' He was banking on the telephonist not asking him his business or which brigade he belonged to. There was a pause, then a man's voice said, 'This is the President's personal aide. What can I do for you, Comisario?'

Bernal took a deep breath. 'Does *Sábado de Gloria* mean anything to you?'

There was a cough and a pause, then the aide replied,

'What is your interest in the matter, Comisario?'

'In the course of a murder enquiry I have come across certain documents that the President himself should see as a matter of extreme urgency.'

'Hold the line, Comisario, while I consult.' Bernal put the second *ficha* into the slot of the telephone, hoping he wouldn't be cut off. Nervously he lit a Kaiser and tapped his foot with impatience. Then the same voice came over the line. 'Would you come here immediately with the documents? You'd better take a taxi, not to call attention to your visit. I'll instruct the men at the gate to let you pass.'

'Thank you, I'll set out at once.' Bernal noticed that his hands were shaking as he hung up the receiver. He went back to Navarro and Martín. 'They want me to go to the Moncloa at once, by taxi.'

'We'll go with you,' they said.

'No, they're only expecting me, and there's no need for you to stick your necks out.'

'Well,' said Martín, 'let us follow you in my car in case anything goes wrong. When we see you reach the entrance safely we'll drive past.'

'Very well,' said Bernal. 'You'd better go and fetch your car from the Post Office and Navarro and I will wait outside and look for a taxi.'

11 a.m.

Navarro suggested that they should not take the first taxi they saw, but the second or third. 'Just in case we're being followed, chief.'

A number of taxis were coming down to Cibeles from Independencia, and they hailed the third one with the green '*Libre*' sign showing behind the windscreen. Bernal got in, and told the driver to wait for a moment. Then Navarro saw Martín and his driver turning round the Puerta de Alcalá and coming in their direction. 'Right, chief. Take care. We'll keep fairly close behind you.'

Bernal told the driver to take him to Moncloa. He knew he would take that to mean the Air Ministry, at the top of the Calle de la Princesa, where the University City began.

Their journey through the heavy traffic on Alcalá and the Gran Vía was uneventful, and at 11.15 they were passing the Plaza de España and climbing Princesa.

The driver asked Bernal, 'Which part of Moncloa, sir?'

'Oh, the Palace,' said Bernal.

'The President's Palace?' asked the driver, a burly man in his fifties who looked like an ex-soldier.

'Yes, that's right.'

The driver looked at his fare curiously in the mirror. 'Never taken anyone there, not since the museum was closed and the President took the place over.'

They had now passed the Air Ministry and were approaching the Arco de la Victoria, a triumphal arch commemorating Franco's victory in 1939. The traffic had now thinned out, and after they had rounded the Glorieta de Cardenal Cisneros, Bernal noticed that the University buildings set in lawns on either side had policemen with binoculars posted on their roofs. He wondered if this was a normal precaution or whether there was a special guard on the approaches to the Presidency.

As the taxi took the curve into the Avenida de Puerta de Hierro, there was a sudden crack, and the driver fought to control the wheel and bring the vehicle to a halt. He managed to stop on the grass verge, and Bernal got out. There was no other vehicle in sight. He noticed at once that the nearside rear tyre had burst. The driver got out, saying, 'That's the second puncture this week! I won't be long changing the wheel.'

Bernal then saw that the tyre had been pierced by a bullet, and he called urgently to the driver to come away from the boot and crouch down between the taxi and the grassy bank. 'Keep down, man! Someone took a shot at us! Look at the hole.'

The driver looked at him as if he were mad, then, his

former military training coming out, he said, 'It looks like the hole from a rifle bullet. Where is the sniper?'

'Probably back in that clump of trees,' answered Bernal. 'Keep down, or he may get us in his sights.'

Martín's car suddenly came into view, and screeched to a halt behind the taxi.

'Keep down!' Bernal called out urgently. 'We've been shot at!'

Navarro opened the offside rear door and urged Bernal to climb in.

'You come as well,' he said to the taxi driver, 'we'll get help shortly and you can change the tyre when the area is safe.'

Keeping below the level of the car windows, they crept round the back of the taxi and clambered in beside Navarro.

'Drive on as quickly as you can,' said Martín to his driver. Enrique had already engaged second gear. He slewed the Seat round the taxi and pulled away. As he did so, a bullet shattered their rear window, scattering glass fragments over Navarro, Bernal and the taxi driver, who were lying on top of one another on the floor. Enrique accelerated along the Avenida de Puerta de Hierro and turned into the Palace entrance.

Bernal showed his credentials to the security police at the gate and informed them of the sniper in the clump of trees further up the road. They ordered Martín, Navarro and the drivers to wait in the lodge until patrols were sent out. Bernal said to Navarro, 'Paco, we forgot to ring Elena and Ángel to tell them to stop telephoning the banks. Ring them when you can.'

Two security men now took Bernal in a small Citroën along the drive to the Palace entrance. He felt shaken up by this latest attack on him, and he tried to calm his nerves by examining the Moncloa Palace with keen interest. He thought the eighteenth-century façade looked modest but tasteful, though the grounds weren't as

wooded or as extensive as they must have been when they
served as a park for the Cardinal Archbishop of Toledo,
Bernardo de Rojas Sandoval.

The Citroën pulled up at the entrance and the guards
inspected his warrant card. He was shown through the
elegant hall to a baize-covered door. The attendant
opened it and asked him to enter. He was astonished to
find himself in a very up-to-date communications centre,
which possessed large wall-maps and the latest electronic
equipment, with a busy team working at the controls.

The President's aide came forward. 'Comisario Bernal?
I'm afraid the President has a visitor at this moment, but
he has authorized me to see you. Would you come this
way?'

He led Bernal into a small modern office. 'Do sit down,
Comisario.'

Bernal got the SDG documents out and handed them
over to the aide, who started reading through them
rapidly, tut-tutting as he came to the list of names. 'This
is of vital importance, Bernal. We knew of this extraordinary plot, of course, but this is the first time we've
seen the full lists of names. Would you mind waiting while
I interrupt the President for him to see this?'

'Not at all,' said Bernal. He was impressed by the
modernity and efficiency of everything. Perhaps they
might even be able to foil this conspiracy. The aide was
away a long time, and Bernal smoked three cigarettes as
he gazed out into the park, which fell away towards the
Manzanares, but nowadays it did not extend all the
way to the river because a public road had been cut
through it. He watched the guards with rifles slung over
their shoulders holding Alsatians on the leash as they
patrolled the grounds.

Finally the aide returned. 'The President is putting full-
scale counter-measures into effect at once. All these
people will be taken in for questioning and held over the

weekend at least. We have a counter-insurgency organization well established for this sort of thing. Thanks to you
we should be able to snuff out this *coup* today. The guards
tell me you had some trouble on the way here. They have
scoured the area, but the gunman had got away. We
shall send you back to Sol with an escort. The President
would be grateful if you would say nothing in your reports
about this matter. Rest assured that your services will not
be forgotten. You will notice some changes in your
Ministry by this evening. In the meantime, do nothing and
say nothing. Please order your colleagues Navarro and
Martín to do likewise. The guards have seen to the taxi
driver and we have recompensed him for the damage to
his taxi. You may like to know that the Minister of the
Interior is here with the President and he has authorized
me to tell you that your action in coming here was
entirely justified in the circumstances in which you found
yourself.'

'Thank you,' said Bernal. 'My only regret is that I can't
resolve the two murders I was investigating to the satisfaction of the law.'

'*Force majeure*, Bernal, *force majeure*. We have, of course,
read your preliminary reports on the deaths of the
journalist Santos and his girl-friend.' Bernal was extremely
surprised at this revelation. 'Santos,' the aide went on,
'played for high stakes and lost, but his death led you to
uncover this business. In any case, it wouldn't have been
very convenient for us if he had succeeded in passing
the information he had acquired to the press. It was
extremely fortunate that you managed to find these
documents, after others had failed, and were wise enough
to bring them straight to us.'

After others had failed? The words clanged in Bernal's
mind. Now he realized that the 'burglars' were part of the
Government's anti-terrorist squad, who had been shadow-
ing the SDG thugs.

'The girl's death,' the aide went on, 'was more fortuitous really, but she was a wretched creature anyway, wasn't she?'

Bernal had a sudden mental picture of her poor parents from Montijo.

'Yes,' he said slowly, 'I suppose she was. But can you explain to me how the plotters intended to revivify the Caudillo? Surely they can't have imagined that people would kowtow to a corpse?'

'That is what is still puzzling us, Bernal. The documents don't shed any light on it. Our teams are still questioning the plotters released by the Second Brigade, whom we have re-arrested.'

'Well, if I can help any further, I'll be available at all times.'

'Thank you for the offer, Bernal. It would be best if you returned to your office for the moment, and carried on as usual until we can round up everyone on the SDG lists. I'll provide an escort to get you out of the palace.'

12.30 p.m.

Bernal, Martín and Navarro chain-smoked as Enrique drove them through Moncloa and down the Calle de la Princesa. Ahead of them, almost touching the front wings of the car, went two motorcycle escorts and behind them was a black Seat 131 packed with five armed guards. Bernal felt that this was a little ostentatious, especially since the SDG plotters would now have nothing to gain by eliminating him and his colleagues, though they might not be aware of that yet.

Martín dropped them at the DGS building and told the Presidential guards they could return to the palace, but the chief of them insisted on escorting him to the district station in the Calle de Fernanflor.

Bernal and Navarro entered the office to find Elena and Ángel relaxing after their efforts with the banks.

'It's all over bar the shouting,' announced Bernal,

'apart from writing up the reports, of course.'

'A lot of things have come in, *jefe*,' said Ángel. 'Dossiers on Weber and Torelli, a final report from Fingerprints, and, oh, there's an urgent message from the Subsecretary who's very anxious to see you.'

'I think that you and Elena could go off now for the weekend, Ángel, but I want you in early next Monday morning. Paco will help me with the drafting of the reports this afternoon.'

'Oh, that's great, chief,' said Ángel jubilantly. 'I might slip down to Benidorm. Interested in joining me, Elena? I'll show you round all the night spots.'

'No thanks, Ángel. I've seen more than enough of one night spot here. In any case, my parents are going up to the sierra and I think I'll go with them.'

'Mind that you don't discuss anything of this case with anyone, not even with your families,' warned Bernal. 'It's turned out to have more political overtones than we imagined.'

Elena looked a little disappointed at this; she had been planning to give a colourful account of it to her parents.

'Paco,' went on Bernal, 'perhaps you'd sort through these reports that have come in ready for drafting this afternoon, while I drop in on the Subsecretary. If you wait for me, we could have an aperitif together before lunch.'

1.15 p.m.
The long-legged blonde secretary greeted Bernal, but with markedly less effusion than usual. She took him straight into the Subsecretary's office, where the Navarrese was standing, with a grim expression on his face, behind the ornate desk.

'Well, Bernal, how far have you got with your final report on this case?'

'I hope to complete it this afternoon, Mr Secretary.'

'Have you been making further enquiries this morning?

You weren't in your office and my secretary called a number of times.'

Bernal considered the matter: if the Subsecretary were to reveal that he knew Bernal had been to the Moncloa Palace, then he would implicate himself in the sniper's attack on the taxi.

'We discovered Santos's car, Mr Secretary, and I had to go down to search it for possible evidence.'

'And did you find any?'

'One or two things. Documents in the main.'

'Have you brought them for us to see?'

'They needed forensic examination and, er, other expert perusal first, in my opinion.'

'I see. I expect that you are aware, Bernal, that Santos had meddled in affairs that did not concern him? Affairs of state, shall I say?'

'I should like to know more about that, Mr Secretary, since it was probably the motive for his murder.'

'Come, come, Bernal, I think you know more about all this than you are telling me. It is our considered view that you should have handed this case over to the Second Brigade at a much earlier stage, when you first realized it had political implications. Have you any comments on that?'

'I broached this matter with you earlier, Mr Secretary. As I see it, I investigated two deaths in the normal way, and obtained evidence to show that they were both homicides. As soon as I discovered political and military materials – a veritable arsenal – I called in the Second Brigade, as you know. Very regrettably, in my view, they saw fit to release three of my suspects.'

' "Regrettably"? "Regrettably"? Your view is neither here nor there, Bernal,' raged the Subsecretary. 'You exceeded your authority! We take the decisions over detentions and prosecutions.'

'Exceeded my authority, Mr Secretary?' asked Bernal calmly. 'Perhaps you would be good enough to tell me in what way? In my opinion I have followed the procedures set out in the penal code and in our administrative handbook to the letter.'

'In your opinion? Your opinion counts for nothing! For nothing, you understand?' The Subsecretary's voice rose to a scream. 'Place your service revolver and your warrant card on the desk at once, do you hear? I am suspending you from duty until further notice. Furthermore, I don't think it's safe to let you roam the streets, at least, not for a day or two. Give up your revolver!'

Bernal pondered on this order. Technically, the Subsecretary had the power to suspend him, pending an official enquiry, if an accusation of professional misconduct was made. Would the President's counter-insurgency machinery really swing into action and succeed in stopping the *coup*? He decided to feign astonishment.

'I am frankly amazed at your attitude, Mr Secretary. I cannot think that I have conducted my enquiries in an improper way.'

'Your gun, Bernal!' screeched the Subsecretary, pressing a bell-push on his desk. 'You're finished, you understand? Finished! You have concealed evidence from us! You have passed it into the wrong hands! You, you . . .'

As Bernal slowly reached for his pistol, the door flew open and four plainclothesmen burst in, with pistols drawn. The blonde secretary stood beyond them, her face white as the sheet of paper she happened to be holding.

'Keep still! Put your hands above your head!' rapped out one of the guards.

Bernal took his hand slowly from his coat and raised his arms. Two of the plainclothesmen moved cautiously forward, but to Bernal's surprise and the Subsecretary's amazement, they suddenly went behind the desk and handcuffed the latter's hands behind his back.

'What in God's name are you doing? You fools, it's him, Bernal, you should be arresting!'

One of the guards turned back the Subsecretary's left

lapel and revealed the SDG badge nestling there.

'We want to ask you some questions about this little matter, sir. You may return to your office, Superintendent Bernal.'

The Subsecretary had a sort of fit and had to be supported by the two guards. Bernal watched them leave, taking the white-faced blonde with them.

'Our colleagues will be along in a moment to make a search of this office, Superintendent,' said the leader of the plainclothesmen. 'President's orders.'

Bernal went back to collect Navarro, and later they sat for an hour in the Cervecería Alemana in the Plaza de Santa Ana, sipping *cañas* of beer and watching the children playing in the sunshine.

'Do you think they'll wrap it up tight, chief?' asked Navarro.

'They've started efficiently enough,' said Bernal. 'It's the next *coup* but one they'll have to watch out for.'

GOOD FRIDAY, 8 APRIL

9 a.m.

His wife shook Bernal awake.

'I let you sleep on, Luis, because you looked tired last night. Here's a letter for you I found in the mail-box on my way back from early Mass. I've left your coffee and *tostadas* on the stove, as I've got to go out again now. I promised the priest I'd help to arrange the extra chairs for the big Mass this morning. Will you be coming?' She looked at him disapprovingly.

'Er, well, yes, if I'm not called out on a case. If I am, I'll leave you a note.'

'Very well. Don't mess up the kitchen, now.' She departed, resplendent in her best bombazine.

Bernal groaned, and turned over the envelope she had left on the bed. It bore the Presidential seal. He sat up, put on his slippers and moved wearily into the dining-room to get a paper-knife. Inside the envelope he found a letter of congratulation, which also informed him of his promotion to Comisario de primera, or Superintendent of the first grade, with immediate effect. They certainly moved fast, thought Bernal; he was impressed.

As he was drinking a little of the awful coffee Eugenia had left him, the phone rang. He went lethargically along the tiled corridor to answer it.

'Yes? Yes, Minister. Yes, I shall be glad to help. The abbot has just rung? Yes, very well. I'll contact Navarro and Martín. You can provide the armed police? Ah, the same men I saw in the Subsecretary's office yesterday afternoon? They seemed to be a capable bunch. Yes, Minister. I'll get cracking on it now. Goodbye, sir.'

Bernal pressed down the receiver rest a number of times, then dialled Navarro's home number.

'Remedios? It's me, Luis Bernal. Is Paco up? Good.
Yes, put him on, please.' He waited, tapping his fingers
impatiently on the window-frame and gazing unseeing
across to the snows which still covered the Guadarrama
peaks. 'Paco! I hope I haven't got you out of bed. The
Minister wants us to take Martín and a team of plainclothesmen and go up to the Valle de los Caídos. The
abbot has rung him to report intruders during the night.
He wants us to investigate and keep a discreet watch over
Franco's tomb. The problem is that they haven't been
able to locate the men on the SDG list who were to be
responsible for digging up the Caudillo's coffin. They may
be hiding out in the sierra, unaware that the **plot** has
collapsed. We'll meet at the office, let's say at nine-forty-
five? Very well. Bring your pistol.'

Bernal consulted the telephone book in vain for Martín's
home number. There were so many people with that
first surname, and he wasn't sure of the second surname.
Nor could he remember the number of Martín's house in
the Barrio de la Estrella, so the telephone directory by
street index was no use. He took a chance and called the
Retiro District Comisaría.

'Has Inspector Martín arrived? He has?' Bernal
breathed a sigh of relief. 'Yes, put him on at once, please.
It's the DGS.' There was a pause. 'Martín? Bernal here.
The Minister has a job for us. Can you be in my office by
nine-forty-five? Good man. Bring your service pistol and
something extra if you have it handy. See you there. Goodbye.'

Bernal hastened to get shaved, and put on a sober suit.
He also chose a dark woollen overcoat; the morning was
chill, and it would be colder still in the sierra.

9.45 a.m.
In his office, Bernal found Navarro and Martín waiting for
him. Martín was carrying a curiously-shaped black leather
attaché case.

'Chief, we've both been promoted a grade,' said Navarro. 'I'm now Inspector de primera.'

'It's congratulations all round, then,' said Bernal. 'I've been made Comisario de primera. Doesn't the new Government move fast? What have you got in that case, Martín?'

'It's one of the new automatic rifles which can be assembled in a few minutes. One of my sergeants has just been instructing me in its use. I've brought my car and my driver, Enrique, Superintendent. I thought he'd be a useful man to have with us.'

'A good idea, Martín,' said Bernal. 'The Minister's sending his team of armed plainclothesmen, and special Presidential warrants for us. He felt he couldn't be sure of the local Civil Guard up there.'

'What exactly do we have to do?' asked Navarro.

'It seems the Abbot of the Valley of the Fallen has reported intruders in the monastery during the night. You'll recall that part of the SDG plan was to exhume Franco's body some time this evening, while the monks were at supper, and bring it by train to Madrid tomorrow. It's difficult to be sure where they intended to transfer it from a vehicle to the special train; presumably at Villalba, or one of the halts further north. The Minister says that the RENFE is investigating. The problem is that the anti-terrorist squads have not been able to locate the SDG team delegated to the task of exhuming the Caudillo. We know their names, of course, from the list we found.'

There was a knock on the door and five grim-faced men entered. Bernal recognized four of them from the previous day, and he introduced Navarro and Martín to their sergeant, whose name was Olmedo.

'It shouldn't take us more than an hour and a half to get to the Valle de los Caídos, Sergeant, if we go on the N VI,' said Bernal.

'Less than that, Superintendent, on the new A6 motorway. Here are the Presidential warrants for you and the

Inspectors. We have pistols and machine-guns.'

'Good, and we have a new automatic rifle,' said Bernal. 'Have you got handcuffs?'

'Enough sets for our prey, I think, sir,' answered Olmedo.

'We'd better get off, then. We three will travel in Inspector Martín's car, but you can lead in yours.'

10.45 a.m.

As they were passing Torrelodones on the A6, Bernal reflected that this could be called the Caudillo's route, running as it did past El Pardo, Torrelodones where the dictator had a private residence, and the Valley of the Fallen, built by political prisoners as a monument to the dead of the Civil War, and ultimately leading to Corunna and El Ferrol, where Franco had his summer palace at El Pazo de Meirás.

Some time after they turned off the motorway on to the side road that led to the Valle de los Caídos, Bernal saw the leading car slow down at the guarded entrance. The plainclothes sergeant spoke to the gatekeepers and showed them his documentation. Both cars were at once waved through, and Bernal noticed that one of the keepers went at once to the telephone in his lodge.

Inside the superb grounds now, they swept up the narrow road which was edged with juniper and eucalyptus; over them towered the high grey crags of the Sierra de Guadarrama, with thick snow on the highest peaks. Just as Philip II had spent more than thirty years building the Escorial to be a monastery and his last resting-place, so Franco had emulated him in this extraordinary construction, fashioned out of the rock. It was curious, thought Bernal; that in his speeches the Caudillo had frequently referred to the reign of Fernando and Isabel, the Catholic monarchs, as the high-water mark of Spanish government, and yet his own reign had much more in common with that of their great-grandson Philip. Both were vain, narrow-minded and oddly inactive men, who ruled for a similar period, had an identical veneration of religious relics, and suffered equally painful deaths, the one for lack of modern medicine and the other through a surfeit of it. Philip lingered for fifty-three days, bloated with dropsy and entirely consumed by suppurating sores, while Franco was cut almost literally to pieces in vain attempts to save his failing frame from a fate which even the cape of Our Lady of the Pillar, specially brought by the Bishop of Saragossa, couldn't ward off.

As the cars stopped at the foot of the rise of wide steps and the esplanade below the enormous granite and concrete cross, they could see a black-habited figure awaiting them, no doubt tipped off by the gatekeeper. Bernal got out and the monk instinctively picked on him as the person bearing most authority.

'Superintendent Bernal? The Father Abbot is expecting you. The Minister has telephoned.'

The others followed the Superintendent and the young monk up the long flight of steps and into the basilica. Bernal thought it probable that it was their first visit, as it was his, to judge by the way they gaped at the long, rocky nave, which had been artificially shortened by the addition of a vestibule, so that it should not exceed in length the nave of St Peter's in Rome. It was a skilful blend of cold modern church architecture and the traditional Francoist style. The canned monkish music emerging from the hidden speakers provided a master-stroke of tastelessness.

The monk showed them into a parlour and requested them to be seated. He slipped through an inner door, soon returning to ask Bernal to accompany him into the abbot's presence. Bernal recalled that this abbot was mitred, and had the rank of bishop.

11.15 a.m.

'Lord Abbot, the Minister has told me that you have had some trouble here.'

'We were troubled this morning, Superintendent, to find the flowers removed from the Caudillo's tomb, though José Antonio's was untouched. The Minister has warned me that some attack might be made today by a group of extremists. Naturally our Order, having accepted the sacred duty of guarding this place, will do everything short of using force to fulfil that trust. We are at your disposal, Superintendent.'

'Can you tell me about today's arrangements, Father? Then we'll take a look at the tomb and the altar, if we may.'

'Of course. We shall be celebrating the Mass prescribed for this Holy Day at noon, after which we strip the cloths from the altar, which remains bare until Easter morning. Tomorrow we have only the Mass of the Presanctified. A number of lay people are sure to arrive shortly to attend Mass, but tomorrow's gathering will be much larger.'

'I don't think there's any risk of disturbance until after Mass, Father. How long will it last?'

'About an hour and a half; much longer than usual. The basilica will then be empty until Vespers at six.'

'We'll keep watch at all times, Father. Could we examine the church now?'

'Of course. Let's fetch the others, shall we?'

The incongruous party of clergy and police made its way into the basilica and approached Franco's tomb. Bernal knelt to observe the edges of it, noticing some disturbance of the cement. He took out a glass to scrutinize the marks more closely.

'It looks as though some tool has been applied to the edges, Father.'

'How dreadful,' exclaimed the abbot, bending close to look. 'No one has ever tampered with it since the interment, so far as we are aware. Has it been opened?'

'No, I don't think so, or there would have been cracking of the cement all round the pediment. But someone has inserted some metal tool on this side. Perhaps they were only probing, or were disturbed.'

'The young monk who was the first to enter this morning saw no one, but on noticing that the flowers had been removed, he came at once to report. The intruder may have slipped out when he was left alone.'

'Was the door unlocked?'

'Brother Alberto opened it when he first came in. The intruder may have hidden in one of the chapels during the night.'

Bernal told Navarro and Martín to organize a search of the whole basilica to look for possible signs of forced entry.

'Parts of the building are *in clausura* and lay people are not normally allowed to enter, Superintendent. But under these circumstances you and your men may go anywhere you wish. I shall explain to the brothers that it is necessary, but I hope you will disturb them as little as possible.'

'Naturally, Father. At present I need only speak to Brother Alberto.'

'I shall arrange it, Superintendent. Is there anything else I can do?'

'Please proceed as usual, Father. It does strike me, however, that my men will be very conspicuous, especially after Mass when the lay people have gone. Would it be possible,' Bernal hesitated, 'would it be too much to ask for a few spare habits for them to put on so that they could blend more into the setting?'

The abbot smiled gently. 'The President has requested our full co-operation. The vestry contains a number of habits and surplices. I cannot prevent your making use of them. I only beg you that no violence be used inside the basilica.'

'Rest assured that we shall do everything in our power

to avoid it, Father.'

'Thank you. We shall provide food and drink for you in the small refectory. We can only offer you Lenten fare until after the *Gloria* tomorrow afternoon, I'm afraid.'

'You are most kind, Father. I think it possible that these extremists will enter with the general public and try to remain behind afterwards. Some of my men will screen the vehicles as they arrive, but I suspect we shall not solve things until later in the afternoon. We shall stay all night if necessary.'

1 p.m.

Mass was still going on as Bernal sat morosely in the small refectory which he had turned into his operations room. Navarro and Martín had watched all the cars that arrived and discreetly screened the people who entered the basilica. The plainclothesmen were distributed about the church, keeping an eye on the worshippers. He had not yet ordered any of them to don monkish habits, reasoning that so long as there were members of the public inside it was unnecessary.

He gazed at the boards of the monastic table, scrubbed white, noting that it was laid for ten. Was the abbot going to join them? Then Bernal remembered the ancient Benedictine tradition of laying an extra place, in case the Christ should come.

He fingered the cigarette packet in his pocket. Not daring to smoke inside the monastery, he had already made numerous visits to the front steps to see Navarro, taking the opportunity of smoking a Kaiser on each occasion. This and the waiting made him jumpier than usual.

Martín now came in. 'Nothing suspicious as yet, *jefe*. I've taken all the car registration numbers and passed them to Madrid to have them checked out. You know we are dealing with the Minister's communications desk direct by telephone, in case the SDG plotters are listening in to the police radio messages.'

'I think they'll move in when everything's gone quiet after two o'clock. Watch for any car that remains behind. We'd better take lunch in turns as soon as Mass is over.'

2.15 p.m.
All the cars had left and the plainclothesmen had watched the congregation carefully to see that none slipped away into a side chapel.

'Nothing, chief,' said Navarro gloomily. 'It looks as though it's going to be a long wait.'

'You'd better get something to eat now, Paco. They've brought bread, and some lentil soup in that tureen. We'll leave the main door of the basilica unlocked and position the sergeant and his men in the chapels. I think they'd best put on a black habit, even if it offends the abbot. I'll place Martín and his driver outside, among the rocks. The abbot tells me they could come back in through a side entrance.'

3 p.m.
The basilica looked eerie in the flickering light from the large waxen candles as Bernal gazed out from the shadow of his vantage point on the pulpit steps. He had nearly dozed off when he heard the creaking of a door from behind him. In the gloom he couldn't make out Navarro hidden beside the high altar.

Two black-robed figures entered and approached the altar steps. Were they monks? He had given the abbot strict instructions that the brothers were to remain in their cells until Vespers.

He saw one of the monkish figures look around and then lift up his soutane and pull out a crowbar. The other did likewise, and they bent silently over the Caudillo's tomb.

Out of the corner of his eye, Bernal saw five more black-habited figures slip quietly out of the side chapels and move quickly along the walls which were in shadow. Navarro still hadn't come into his field of vision.

There was a scraping noise first, then the cracking of cement as the crowbars were inserted. Bernal stood up and signalled with his arms from the pulpit. Navarro appeared and he and the disguised plainclothesmen moved forward with pistols drawn and quickly overpowered the two intruders, slipping the handcuffs on them.

Back in the small refectory, Bernal had the two men stripped of their black soutanes and searched. They were both armed with Star automatics. They surlily refused to answer any questions. The lapels of their jackets bore the now familiar SDG badges, and their identity *carnets* were found in their wallets. Navarro compared their names with those on the Xerox copy of the SDG lists.

'Where are your companions?' Bernal demanded.

'You'll soon find out,' said the older of the two men in an arrogant manner.

'And you'll soon see the inside of Carabanchel gaol,' retorted Bernal. 'Who is the leader of this miserable gang?'

'You'd be surprised,' said the younger man.

They were to be very surprised indeed.

Enrique, Martín's driver, rushed in. 'I spotted a hearse coming up the road, Superintendent, and ran up to tell Inspector Martín. We let it drive right up to the entrance, and waited for the driver and passenger to emerge. It was quite a shock. We've handcuffed the driver to the bumper of his car. The Inspector is bringing the other man in now.'

Martín entered with his rifle pointing at a uniformed figure. As he came into the refectory, the policemen were staggered at the likeness. It was Franco's exact double, even down to the dark glasses and the haughty eagle's beak of a nose and the trim moustache.

'Dear God!' exclaimed Bernal. 'Why did you two try to open the tomb? Here he is in the very flesh!'

Franco *redivivus* now spoke in a high-pitched voice that very nearly resembled that of the deceased dictator. 'I demand to know who is in charge here. These handcuffs are an outrage. Remove them at once.'

'Who exactly are you?' asked Bernal, noting that the impostor was wearing an exact replica of one of the Caudillo's dress uniforms, even with the detail of the red sash of the Laureate Cross of St Ferdinand. Bernal was slowly remembering what he had heard long ago, but had dismissed as an improbable rumour, that at least two men had been used from time to time as doubles for the Caudillo on public occasions when he was too ill to appear in person.

'I have represented the Caudillo on many occasions,' said the impostor, 'and no one ever noticed. Nor will they after tomorrow.'

'But what do you propose to do? Thousands of people filed past the Caudillo's embalmed body in the Royal Palace over a year ago. How can you expect them to believe that he is still alive?'

'They themselves will witness the resurrection on the Palace balcony on Sunday morning, and the King and Queen will be the first to acknowledge it. They'll have no option.'

Bernal remembered the plan to kidnap the royal children, now fortunately foiled by the President's quick counter-action.

'But you are insane. They'll see you and the body together and realize that it's a hoax.'

'How wrong you are. I shall be placed in the casket, they will see my face through the glass lid, and when it's opened I shall emerge and address them. Then they'll believe it all right. If you love your country, do nothing to prevent this action.' His voice rose to a high-pitched screech. 'The Freemasons and reds have returned to besmirch the fatherland. The political parties will bring disaster once more. The treacherous dwarves who have succeeded me will bring chaos and ruin. I call on you as fellow-countrymen, loyal to Spain and to God, to help us bring about this resurrection!'

Bernal cut in. 'Navarro, search his pockets. Let's find out who this madman is. And we'd better strip him of that uniform. We can't take him through the streets of Madrid to Carabanchel dressed like that, or he would be lynched.'

The abbot now came in, and blanched and crossed himself at the sight of the impostor. 'Who is this man?'

'Lord Abbot,' shrieked the impostor, 'don't let them prevent my resurrection! It's the last hope for our country!'

'Sacrilege,' muttered the abbot, 'it's a terrible sacrilege.' Bernal wondered if he was referring to the attempt to break open the tomb or to the double in Franco's uniform.

Navarro produced a *carnet* from the man's jacket. 'He's a retired army sergeant called José Antonio Bermúdez, *jefe*.'

'Ring through to the Minister, Martín,' said Bernal, 'and tell him we are bringing them in.'

9 p.m.
Bernal arrived home rather flushed in the face. He and Consuelo had spent the evening celebrating over a bottle of Cordoníu champagne. He found Eugenia stirring a pot of *sopa de letras* on the butane-gas stove. He slumped in an armchair in front of the television set and mused over the strange events at the Valley of the Fallen. How appropriate the name now sounded.

The plaintive melody that preceded the TV news bulletin came on, with pictures of Gothic churches in various Spanish provinces, as the words *'Conexión con el programa nacional'* appeared on the screen. Eugenia came in with the Cebreros wine, brought in an old brandy bottle which she took twice a week to have refilled in the *economato* where the wives of Ministry employees bought it at a cut rate.

'Supper won't be long, Luisito. Put the cutlery out, will you?'

Bernal laid out two place settings. The TV news was much more delayed than usual. The annoying tune they used to connect the provincial stations with Madrid was now playing, and the architectural interval-film was showing the Monastery of Ripoll. Eugenia came in with the soup and started to ladle it into the cracked white dishes. She was well into her lengthy grace, for which Bernal reluctantly muttered the responses, at the same time pouring himself a good slug of the Cebreros wine, when the *Telediario* newsreel signature-tune suddenly cut in with strident urgency. The announcer looked breathless, and he was anxiously adjusting his tie.

'*We first have some important national news. We understand that at its meeting on Wednesday the Council of Ministers, having considered the findings of the Supreme Court, Sala IV, that the legalization of political parties is not a judicial matter but an administrative one for the Minister to decide, has decreed . . .*' The announcer broke off to clear his throat and to sip some water from a glass.

'*. . . has decided to legalize the following parties with effect from Sunday next, the Day of the Resurrection: one, the PCE – the Communist Party of Spain . . .*'

Eugenia, who had just crossed herself after saying grace, gave a strangled cry and crossed herself rapidly again, twice.

'Oh, Luis! They must be mad! It will be like the thirties all over again! It won't be safe to go out on to the streets! They'll march up and down with red banners and sing the "Internationale"!'

Bernal gazed at the screen and then down into his bowl

of *sopa de letras*, which was full of tiny letters of the alphabet made of pasta; he noticed that s's, d's and g's seemed to figure with surprising frequency, and after them p's, c's and e's.

'We'll all have to get used to a whole new alphabet, Geñita, or, at least, a partial rearrangement of the letters in the old one.'